Knee-high Lies

Knee-high Lies

DAWN FORD

SPL⚡CKETY
PUBLISHING GROUP
Bettendorf, Iowa

Knee-high Lies Published by Splickety Publishing Group,
2306 Southview Drive, Bettendorf, IA 52722

For information about the author visit:
www.dawnfordauthor.com

Book and cover design by Book Marketing Graphics
Cover photo by Photos by JackiO

ISBN: 978-1-942462-15-6

First Edition: July 2017

www.dawnfordauthor.com

Dedication

To my mother who will forever be my biggest fan. I miss you.

Chapter One

(Lie #1: The customer is always right.)

Avery Denton swiped the groceries across the Valley Market's scanner with a practiced hand and smiled politely at Laura Jeffries who unloaded groceries onto the belt. Her two children, five-year-old Tyler and three-year-old Ella, fussed beside her.

She admired the widow, who shouldered the small community of Valley's disdain after her husband's car accident a year and a half ago. He'd been texting and driving. Not only had he died, but a passenger in the other car had been seriously injured. Many people blamed Laura for it.

Laura's face was flushed. "Stop arguing you two!" She shuffled through her messy purse. "Sorry, my card is in here somewhere."

Tyler yanked Ella's doll from her hands. Ella's shriek and subsequent crying drowned out the whirr of the store's freshly oiled conveyor.

Mrs. Herman, who had just walked up to stand behind the family, tsked and planted a fist on her hip. A shopping basket with two small items dangled from her other hand. "Can't you open another line? One that doesn't take *those* cards?"

The sack Avery scanned crinkled as she fisted it a little too tight. There weren't any other checkers. Their newest cashier hadn't shown up, and Tom, who manned the customer service desk, was on one of his dozen breaks. Avery's smile was tense. "Did you remember the milk this time, Mrs. Herman?"

"I don't need milk today." Mrs. Herman shifted the basket from one hand to the other as if the almost empty container held the weight of the world.

"How's Mr. Herman's diet going? Did he find the spinach yesterday?"

Mrs. Herman stopped and pulled out a list from her purse, a frown on her creased face. "Yes. But I forgot the dressing. I'll be right back."

Laura handed Avery her EBT card. "Thanks. I was ready to leave."

"Don't let her get to you. You're just as important a customer as she is." Avery bent down towards little Tyler who stood eying the display with Big Bob cards, his favorite. "You're never going to get your good-boy reward if you make your sister cry. Better say you're sorry." She winked at him.

Tyler, looking properly chastised, hugged his mother. With a quiet, "I'm sorry," he made up with his little sister, who sniffled and was as adorable as could be.

Laura gave Avery a grateful smile. She glanced down at her son. "Okay. But only this time. Next time you make Ella cry you won't get your reward. And get something small for your sister while you're at it."

Face bright, Tyler clapped his hands and found the pack of Big Bob cards he wanted before grabbing a Pretty Princess sucker for Ella. He handed them to his mom.

Avery rang them both up while keeping an eye out for Mrs. Herman. She was as bad as her niece, MaKenzie, who had dumped a bottle of honey over Avery's line yesterday.

"Thank you, Avery. You're the only one who doesn't make me feel like I should apologize when I come through the line."

"I always wanted a big brother who would tease me. Being an only child is pretty boring." Avery smiled down at Tyler, who clasped his cards happily to his chest, a broad smile on his face.

Avery's heart twisted wistfully as she watched them leave. She longed for the times her mother had bought her things like that when she was little. Before. Now if it wasn't in a bottle or eighty-proof, it didn't get either of her parents' attention. Although she'd told the truth that she'd always wanted a brother or sister, it was probably better she didn't have any. It was enough having to take care of herself.

A smear of oil mixed with honey on one side of the line caught her eye. Avery bent down to find the can of disinfectant and paper towels to clean it up before it got on any of the customers and they complained.

Like Mrs. Herman.

Avery's cell phone chimed, signaling ten minutes left of her shift. She bent down beneath the metal check stand to neaten it and dig a handful of plastic bags out of the cardboard case for the next cashier.

Perfume, familiar and expensive, tickled her nose. It flooded her first period biology class for the last semester of her junior year. The perfume, along with its wearer, brought mayhem and misery every morning, and that torture didn't take a summer vacation. This day had been going too well. Avery should've known something would happen to ruin it.

It always did.

She stilled, keeping her head out of sight, one hand clasping the grocery bags tight, the other playing with the frayed strings on the hem of her khaki-colored jeans.

On the conveyor belt above came the *tap, tap, tapping* of a rude shopper.

"Earth to cashier. Earth to cashier. Cashier hiding under lane one." Tom broadcast above her from the customer service desk.

"Jerk," Avery whispered.

Avery stood up, and honey slicked her hand. She wiped it down her cashier's vest, and noticed it was also on her pants. Pursing her lips, she sent Tom a dirty look at the desk a mere fifty feet from her cashier line. Tom answered her with a mocking grin.

MaKenzie Thomas, wearing a form-fitting, scarlet-patterned mini dress which blended well with her sun-fresh tan, stood with one manicured hand flipping a gold credit card onto the check-writing stand. Asia Maloney and Lauren Hughes stood behind her, completing the MaKenzie Thomas fan club.

MaKenzie's green eyes narrowed as she judged Avery with a down-and-back-up glare. A blue, plastic basket, filled with bottles of flavored sparkling water, crab meat, salad greens, and specialty goat cheese crumbles, waited to be rung up on the conveyor belt.

Why her? Why again today? It had only been twenty-two hours since MaKenzie's honey incident.

The alarm on Avery's phone chimed. Five minutes left of her shift.

Avery drug the items across the scanner absently. "Find everything you needed?" The words slipped out from habit, and she bit the inside of her lip.

"No. This Podunk store doesn't have what I need." Lauren and Asia giggled. Scents of coconut and cocoa butter wafted from their sun-baked bodies.

Must be nice to lounge by the pool all day long instead of spending their summers working like she had to.

One of the items didn't scan. Heat pricked Avery's scalp. Something always went wrong when MaKenzie came through her line. She swiped it once more, nothing. Biting back a frustrated sigh, Avery picked the cheese up and input the numbers manually.

MaKenzie kept tapping the gold credit card on the surface beside the card reader. Avery hurried to finish, keeping her eyes down and away from the girl's haughty gaze. The scanner double beeped. She hastened to delete the error.

More giggles. Avery glanced up to see MaKenzie raise her eyebrows at her. Lauren and Asia bent their heads together, whispering behind their hands.

"Will you hurry up?" MaKenzie's voice could have been heard by the people filling gas at the station two blocks away. "I have my senior photo appointment tonight, and I have to eat, then get my hair and makeup done. Not that you'd understand how much work it takes to do a professional photo spread."

Avery's lips trembled and heat washed across her cheeks. She did have her senior photo appointment with MaKenzie's cousin Cindy Herman, whom most seniors in Valley used as their default photographer. Default because there weren't that many studios around Harrison County. So unless she went into Omaha, there were few options. And Avery couldn't afford the bigger studios in Omaha like *some* people she knew.

She bit down a snide reference to MaKenzie needing help to be photogenic. She couldn't lose her job. Not when her parents wouldn't pay for her pictures like most seniors' parents did. And she didn't want to be the only loser in their class to have her photo taken by the brick wall in front of the school for the yearbook.

"Will that be everything?" Avery winced as she said it.

"Fresh crab would be nice. Or maybe some lobster." MaKenzie flashed a perfect, ultra-white smile.

Avery leaned toward MaKenzie, locking gazes with her. "Check Reeser's Bait and Gas Shop. They got in a batch of fresh crawdads last week. The best Iowa has to offer." She smiled as the comment splashed over MaKenzie like acid over paint—all bubbling and hissing beneath the surface. "Your total is thirty-five seventy-two."

The brunette slid her gold card through the reader and punched the screen with the tips of her gleaming, bejeweled nails.

The cash register screen beeped.

Avery cleared the screen and reset the transaction. "Try again."

MaKenzie's loud sigh caught Chantra Berg's attention, and Avery watched as her manager stopped putting the carts back and stared at them.

Another slide of the card and the screen beeped again.

"I'm sorry. It's not accepting the card." A curl twitched at the corner of Avery's mouth. Chantra stepped closer.

"What do you mean it's not accepting the card?"

Was it Avery's imagination, or was MaKenzie losing some of her aloof disdain?

"Maybe there's something wrong with the bank, but it's not going through," Avery grasped the metal counter, bracing herself. "Do you have another card? Check? Cash?"

Lauren's and Asia's eyes were the size of Frisbees. MaKenzie stiffened, confused. A wrinkle marred her perfect forehead and quickly deepened.

"No, I don't have another card. I don't use cash. I don't need to. Just put it on a tab or something." Her brown curls swung with each angry shake of her head.

"I'm not authorized to make tabs for anyone," Avery said as her boss walked up behind MaKenzie.

Lauren leaned over MaKenzie's shoulder and spoke, "If it's a problem with the card, you could call and ask your dad—"

"I don't need to call my dad. The problem is *her*." If possible, MaKenzie's face grew darker, taking on a maniacal twist.

"What seems to be the problem?" Chantra's words dripped like syrup, her forced smile over bright.

"Your employee doesn't know how to run your credit card machine. Put it through again. There's no way it's denied."

MaKenzie's green eyes bulged while spit flew from her glossy lips.

Avery bit her cheek to keep from spewing the ugly remarks that came to mind. She didn't know why MaKenzie had it out for her, but it was obvious she wanted Avery to lose her job. Without a job, Avery couldn't buy her senior pictures or afford necessities, like food and gas. And it wasn't like there was an abundance of jobs she could apply for in this small town.

Not that MaKenzie would understand. Her parents took care of her.

"Let me try," Chantra pulled out her management key and stuck it in the computer.

Once more the cash register screen beeped. "Maybe the reader is malfunctioning. Hand me your card." Chantra's hands shook slightly as she wrapped the card in a plastic sack and ran it through slowly.

Beep.

Chantra entered in the numbers manually.

Beep.

"There's something wrong with the card itself. Let me print this off, have you sign it, and run it by your uncle to approve. I'm sorry for the inconvenience."

MaKenzie burned them both with a glare. "You should be." She signed the slip of paper. "Get those." She told Asia and Lauren before putting her sunglasses on and walking out ahead of them. The girls grabbed the bags and scurried after their leader.

Chime. Avery's alarm went off. Her shift was officially over. "Thanks." Avery said to Chantra.

She dug her key out of the computer. "Why is it every time Little Miss Prissy Pants goes through your line there's trouble? Yesterday was the honey incident, and we had to pay someone to come in and clean out the mechanism under the conveyor belt. Jeff just got over that, and now I have to get him to sign this." She held out the receipt.

Avery frowned, and rubbed the sticky spot on her vest. "The honey was MaKenzie's fault. Even if it had been tampered with, she didn't have to make a scene by pouring honey everywhere." She unbuttoned her vest. "MaKenzie hates me. I don't know why, but since the day I moved here she has gone out of her way to target me."

"You know as well as I do the customer, especially *that* customer, is always right. It would be nice if you could figure your issue with MaKenzie out without having to involve me. I have to keep this job, you know. Three kids and my ex is late with his check. Again."

"Believe me. If I could, I would. Anyway I have to clock out, my shift is over." Avery headed toward the employee break room.

Chantra grasped her arm. "Hey. Can you stay tonight? Alyssa Durand called in, and no one else can come in to cover."

Avery slumped. The only night she had something planned and it figured someone would call in. "I covered yesterday until close. Katie and I are going shopping. Our senior pictures are this Friday."

Chantra took Avery's elbow and headed by Tom at the customer service counter and past the carts. Avery clomped behind her, staring at the bobbling peroxide curls piled on top of her manager's head.

"Look, Avery, you're the only one who ever stays. Just give me another hour. I promise I won't ask again the rest of the week."

Tom's voice crackled above them on the loudspeakers. "Berg line one. Berg line one."

Chantra twisted, facing the customer service desk. "Tom, I'm right here. You don't have to announce it over the intercom."

He grinned.

Turning back to Avery, Chantra muttered, "If he wasn't the boss's son…" She clasped her hands in front of her face. "Pretty please, Avery. I promise you won't regret it."

"Fine," Avery said. "But, only because I need the money. And only for an hour." She reset the alarm on her phone while Chantra left to answer the call.

Back at the checkout line Avery came face to face with Michael Carter—Katie's brother—and his friend, Jaxson Stewart.

"Sneaking candy into the movies again?" She teased them. Jaxson, the taller of the two, wore cowboy boots, dark jeans, a plaid shirt, and a baseball cap. He grinned while placing several items on the conveyor belt.

A blush, red as his hair, crept across Michael's face.

"Do me a favor. Call your sister and let her know I'm going to be late. I'd call her myself but daddy's boy is watching me like a hawk." She nodded toward Tom as she bagged their items.

"Oooo. Going out on a date?" Jaxson handed her a crumpled ten dollar bill. His fingers brushed hers when she took it.

Startled, Avery glanced up at him. Under a swath of blond bangs were sweeping dark blond lashes and gorgeous blue eyes. Her pulse skipped in her veins when she handed him the change. She took a deep breath before answering. "Nope. Just shopping."

Jaxson smiled crookedly, winking at her as they left.

Avery rubbed her hand, eyes trained on the tall farm boy. Somehow he seemed older today than usual. And much cuter.

"I have a coupon for this." Mrs. Smith's words startled Avery.

Mechanically, Avery scanned Mrs. Smith's groceries, but the thrill of touching Jaxson's hand played over and over in her mind.

***

Rock dust chased Avery's car on her way home from work. Thanks to MaKenzie's honey escapade, she needed to change before going shopping with Katie. Her mother's car was parked in the driveway when she pulled in. Avery braced herself; it was never a good thing when her mom or dad was home before six p.m. She had to hurry, though, or they'd never get any shopping done.

Luckily, her mother was nowhere in sight when she entered the two-story farm house, so she headed upstairs to change. However, when Avery went back downstairs, her mother sat at the dining room table. An almost-empty bottle of wine sat in front of her.

"How was school today?"

"School's out, Mom. I was at work." Avery held her car keys in her hand. She hesitated long enough to know her mother was on a bender again. Her bloodshot eyes weren't completely focused when she glanced up at Avery.

"Work? Work shtunk. Thanks for ashking." She took a slug out of the wine bottle and wiped her mouth off with her arm. "Lost a," her mother burped, "dips to Sydney."

The dips, prime land in Harrison County within the Loess Hills, meant a six-figure sale. And her mother had lost out on it to her real estate office's new saleswoman. Her dad was going to go through the roof again.

"Great. I've got to go." Avery slid past the table and headed toward the front door.

"Notsofast." Her mother's words slurred. "Where'n you going?"

Avery pushed her impatience back. Talking to her mother when she'd been drinking was as effective as screaming against the wind, and Avery didn't have time for it today. Besides, only Avery would remember it the next day.

"Bye."

"I said wait, young lady. Who'n you goin' with?" Her mother sat up. She was moving from inquisitive drunk to angry drunk in record time.

"Katie, Mom. I'm shopping with Katie." The less information the better.

She tried to stand but couldn't. "Not with that kind of attitude. You don't just traipse all over willy-nilly."

"I'm NOT, Mom!" She glanced at the clock on the wall before remembering it needed a new battery. She had to get out of here.

Her mom tried to stand again. "Yesh you are. Gimmeyerkeys."

Avery turned to look straight at her mom. It had been a week since she had to do this last, not bad for her life. "Mom, Aunt Penny gave me my car. It's not yours. You can't take the keys because I've done nothing wrong. You're drunk and I have to go."

With a hand swifter than Avery would've guessed, her mother smacked the bottle down on the table. It was a miracle the bottle didn't shatter. "You're a spoiled rotten brat, you know that?"

Irritation and impatience warred inside Avery. Why did everyone choose to be difficult today? "Yes, I know. Goodbye."

"You'll listen to me while you live under my roof, young lady!"

"It's only your roof because Aunt Penny left it to you in her will. I've gotta go. Bye, Mom."

"You h—hate me, don't you?"

And her mother had come full circle. Inquisitive, angry, and then sorry for herself. Avery cursed MaKenzie in her mind, and wished she had never stopped home to get changed, honey or no honey. "Yes, mother. I hate you. If you were to fall off the face of the planet it wouldn't hurt my feelings right now. Are you happy?"

"No!" Her mother wailed. Tears fell down her face in rivers. "My daughter hates me." They looked like real tears, but Avery knew better.

Years ago she would've reassured her mother that she didn't hate her. But that wasn't really the truth now. She did kind of hate her mother for what she'd become. She thought back on Mrs. Jeffries, who single-handedly took care of her kids. It had been years since her mom had taken care of her, and now it was the other way around. Yes, she despised what her mom had become. She wanted her old mother back.

She remembered the mom who taught her how to bake chocolate chip cookies, who took her shopping and tried on funny looking hats, or who put a band-aid on a cut and then kissed it to make it better. But she couldn't muster any empathy toward the pathetic, broken shell of a woman sitting at the table in front of her.

Aunt Penny used to tell her that God didn't give up on anyone. She shook her head. She loved her Aunt, but she had to disagree. God had already given up on her mom. And if God hadn't, she had.

Avery turned around and left.

Chapter Two

(Lie #2: Men in uniform are irresistible.)

Avery propped her feet up on a plastic seat in the food court of Midtown Mall in Omaha. The remains of cheeseburgers, fries, and soft drinks littered the table. Shopping bags lined the floors beside them.

"If you spend the night tonight we can try everything on and see which ones would make the best pictures." Katie wiped her greasy hands on a napkin. "Plus, I got my cheerleader's uniform today. I think maybe I'll wear it and get some pictures by the football field or in the stands." Her strawberry-blond hair was pulled back into a ponytail and freckles dotted her pixie face. Except for the hair, she and Michael looked like twins.

Avery grimaced. "I can't. I have to open tomorrow."

"Glad I don't have a job." Katie stopped, a look of remorse crossing her face. "Sorry, I didn't mean it that way."

"It's all right, Kay. Some of you have it easy, the rest of us schmucks have to work." Avery forced a smile. "Besides, you couldn't pay me enough to babysit like you do. Especially not my manager's brats. I only have to deal with kids a few minutes in line and then they're gone. You have to deal with them for hours."

Katie nodded. "Chantra's are the worst. But it's not so bad. It's better than watching my little brothers and sisters without pay."

"You can't count Michael. He's too old now."

"Old enough to like girls." She leaned over and whispered, "Jaxson drove them to the movies tonight." Her eyebrows bounced up and down. "They were meeting up with a couple of girls."

The hair on Avery's arms rose. She ignored the unease that crept into her stomach. "That's right. Jaxson's supposed to be a junior, isn't he? How old is he?"

"Sixteen. Michael will be fifteen in a couple of months. What is wrong with us? We're dateless seniors. Even my brother has a date." Katie slapped her hand to the table. "We really need to work on that."

"Your mom would die if she knew how much Michael snuck around and didn't tell her," Avery bumped Katie's arm. "You should try it sometime. You could get all kinds of dates if you tried."

Katie wrinkled her nose. "Mom always knows when I'm lying. I'd get caught and then I'd be grounded our whole senior year. I'd have to go through purity classes again. Liz didn't date until she was in college, and only then because she was too far away for mom to know."

Avery snickered. "Is that what she told you? I saw her more than once with someone."

Katie's mouth hung open. "What! You never said anything."

"You never asked. Besides, Liz told me not to say anything so I didn't. I like your sister."

"I can't believe she did that. And that she got away with it." A faraway look crossed Katie's face. "That's so not fair."

Avery shrugged. "You just have to learn how to be sneaky."

Her face crumpled. "I can't. Remember the time my cousin tried to get me to steal something? Oh my gosh. I got hives and threw up. Mom instantly knew something was wrong. I'm incapable of being sneaky without getting caught."

"I know, Kay. But maybe practice makes perfect? Start little. Like don't tell your mom you bought the necklace tonight, and work your way up to sneaking around on a date."

Excitement played in Katie's blue eyes. "Maybe."

The speakers blaring mall music squealed and crackled. *"The mall will be closing in fifteen minutes. Please make your final purchases. Thank you for shopping at Midtown Mall. We value your patronage. Have a pleasant evening."*

Except for a few scattered cars, the parking lot was empty. They walked to their spot in the dark, loaded the back of Avery's car, and drove out of the lot.

While navigating her car down the curving Valley exit toward the back road, Avery heard a loud *pop*. The car pulled hard to the right.

"Shoot! My tire." Avery pulled down the off ramp onto the shoulder. She remembered the morons at the Tire Exchange putting the lug nuts on too tight the last time they had the tires rotated. There was no way she was getting them off on her own.

She flipped the hazard lights on, grabbed her cell phone, and called home. Answering machine. She called her parent's cell phones. Voicemail on both. She dialed Sophie, her other best friend. Voicemail again.

Head on the steering wheel, Avery fumed silently. "This is not what I need right now." Avery ran her hands through her hair. "Kay, call your family and see if someone can come change my tire. I have a spare in the trunk."

Katie dialed. The sweet voice of Mary, Katie's younger sister, rang out from the speaker.

Avery leaned against her car window, her heart panging with envy. Katie didn't know how good she had it with her family. She turned when Katie tapped the screen and ended the call.

"Mary said Mom's in bed with a migraine and dad is over at Liz's apartment fixing something. The movie isn't over yet, and, knowing Michael, he'll have his phone off. Now what do we do?"

"Do you have Jaxson's number?" Avery stifled a strange thrill that flittered in her chest.

"No. Michael always calls him and Mom has his number on the fridge, but I don't remember it."

Avery glanced out at the darkened landscape. "I can't drive any further or it'll ruin the rim. Mom did that once and Dad went ballistic. I'm not going to walk around in the dark, either." Avery shivered. "You never know who might be driving by."

"Someone like Dirkner the Dork?" Katie gagged and laughed.

"Ew. It's summer, imagine his B.O. now. Remember when he asked you to dance last year at the Spring Fling? You couldn't say no because you're too nice, and as soon as you got on the gym floor the song changed to a slow dance." Avery laughed.

Katie shuddered. "Ugh. He always has this little spit ball in the corner of his mouth. It's like a bungee cord when he talks."

"So disgusting! Oh. Geez. I just realized." Avery stopped, her face paling. "We both have to sit next to him at graduation. Gross!" They both fell across the seat in a fit of laughter.

Headlights blazed into the vehicle from behind. Sitting up, they shaded their eyes as they turned to look. A vehicle barreled down the off-ramp, swerving and honking.

"Get down!" Avery pulled Katie back down in the seat, hoping the vehicle would go past them. "No dorks. No dorks. Oh please, no dorks!!" Avery chanted.

Katie pulled out her beaded Rosary, closed her eyes, and whispered prayers.

Avery grasped her friend's hand tightly. "Say a couple for me too."

The vehicle crunched to a stop. Headlights blared like a spotlight inside the car, and a human-shaped shadow moved across their windows. Katie grabbed Avery.

The car shook as the person tried to open the door.

Both girls screamed.

"Hey, you guys need some help?"

Katie's screaming almost drowned out the male voice.

Avery turned to get a look at who was speaking. An army hat sat atop two massive ears. A pair of beady eyes peered out from beneath the olive green cap's bill.

Avery bumped her friend with her shoulder. "Shhh. I think it's the cavalry." She lowered the window an inch.

The man stood, chest stuck out, hands behind his back. He wore camouflage fatigues and tan boots. "You know you have a flat back passenger tire?"

"No duh," she whispered. To the man she said, "Yeah, we know. We were just calling someone to come help us." Avery lifted her cell phone to the window, flashing 911 on the glowing screen.

"We're National Guardsmen. We'll change it for you." Another shadow fell across the window as a second muscled G.I. Joe popped his head by the cracked window. His breath reeked of alcohol.

"Yes. Yes. Yes." Katie's words gushed out like lava.

Avery turned and gave her friend an annoyed look. "Katie, we don't know these guys. They could be worse than Dirkner." She hissed in a whisper.

"Hey, no problem. If you have someone coming, we'll just stay with you until they get here. It's the least we could do."

His over-confident smile prickled Avery's nerves. "We're good—"

"Yes, thank you!" Katie piped up beside her.

Again Avery turned and shot her friend a nasty glare, hoping she would catch the hint.

Katie gave her an innocent look. "What? They're cute."

"Pop your trunk. Really, we can help. It's part of our job to protect the citizens of these United States," The first GI said.

"Especially when they're pretty and stranded on the side of the road on a dark night." The second guy chimed in, winked, and then finished with a wide grin.

Yeah, Avery could imagine what kind of help they'd like to give on a *dark* night. She clenched her hands tighter around the wheel.

Katie giggled. "Oh c'mon Avery. They're soldiers. They can't hurt us. It would be against the law or something. Besides, you said you needed to get home, remember? You have to open tomorrow." Katie smiled brilliantly at the men, her head hovering between the steering wheel and Avery's chest.

She wanted to pinch her best friend in the worst way. Instead she considered their odds. It would take ten, fifteen minutes minimum for any cops to get here, if they were lucky. None of their friends or family could make it. She didn't have any weapons or mace with her.

The GI's started to banter back and forth. They weren't going anywhere. *Might as well get this over with.* Avery reluctantly unlocked the doors and popped the trunk. "Turn your stupid lights off, then. They're blinding me." She pointed to the jacked-up truck, complete with flood lights, roll bar, and spoiler, parked behind her Taurus. "Redneck much?"

The first man chuckled at her remark. "Can't. We have to be able to see to change your tire. Won't take long, I promise." He joined the second GI digging out the spare tire and jack. "You guys need to get out so we can jack the car up."

Katie giggled and hurried out to stand by the GI's.

"Seriously, Kay. Leave them alone so they can change the tire." Avery's cheeks heated. She grabbed her purse and took out the only bill left in her wallet—a ten. She slipped out of her seat, and stuck the bill in her back pocket.

The soldiers changed the tire quickly, despite Katie's overt attempts at flirting with them. Avery walked over as the first one lowered the jack and the other put the flat tire in the trunk. "Don't tell me, your second job is with NASCAR?"

"Nope. We're just that good." Avery's eyes were drawn to the massive teeth in the second GI's face. His grin resembled the fake clacking teeth one of her middle grade science teachers kept on his desk. He'd trapped the hall passes in them, and if anyone tried to steal them they would *clack*, and *clack*, and *clack*.

"It was like karma, you guys coming at just the right time and right place." Katie giggled and flipped her strawberry blond hair.

Avery glanced heavenward and sighed. "They're too old for you, Kay." She held out the ten to the first man. "Here. Take this for your trouble. And thanks."

"No charge, no problem. By the way, my name is Steve. That mongrel is Brody." He held out his hand for her to shake.

Reluctantly she took Steve's hand in her limp one, shaking half-heartedly. Brody held out his hand also. She hesitated, but finally manners took over, and she shook his hand as well.

In an instant, the soldier yanked her against him, her arm bent behind her back. Two moist, rubbery lips pressed against hers in a hard, beer-flavored kiss. Tears stung her eyes as his massive teeth ground against her lips. She stumbled back when he released her and placed a hand on her swollen lips.

Chapter Three

(Truth #1: No News is Good News)

Bile rose in Avery's throat, and she spat on the ground.

Katie giggled and held her hand out. Avery pushed her friend behind her and glared at the men. "What was that?" She bit out.

"Payment in full." Brody winked at her.

Steve chuckled and put his hand on his friend's shoulder. "Time for us to go. You guys have a nice evening."

Throwing the ten dollar bill on the ground, Avery pushed Katie toward the passenger side, almost knocking her over into the ditch. "C'mon Kay." She waited for her friend to get into the car before slamming the passenger door and hurried to the other side. She pushed the automatic lock button as soon as she got in.

The gas pedal touched the mat as she floored it, but with the donut on she had no luck at spinning out. She saw nothing but lights in the rearview mirror.

"That was so romantic. What'd it feel like?" Katie turned to her, a dreamy smile stretched from ear to freckled ear.

"Romantic? There are so many things wrong with that statement, I can't even begin." Avery's hands clenched the steering wheel. "Really, Kay. You need to get out more."

***

The next morning at work, Avery couldn't get the image of the GI jerks out of her mind, and she'd gotten little sleep the night before. Her mother's car had been missing when she got home and still wasn't there when she'd left this morning, and that twisted her gut.

"Avery, why don't you go home? I've got you covered." Chantra's eyes held a strange, guarded look.

"It's only an hour before my shift ends. I can stay and help with the coolers."

Chantra cleared her throat. "You have to go. You have too many hours this week."

"Well, you did ask me to stay yesterday. And my shift before that…" Avery blew off the concern as a non-factor.

Chantra's lips trembled.

"Is everything okay?"

"Yeah. It's good." The bouffant on top of her head bounced as she shrugged. "Jeff's cracking down on overtime, that's all."

"O—kay. I'll go clock out now." Avery took off her vest and folded it as she headed for the break room to check out.

Avery punched her card in the ancient machine and headed toward the glass exit door. She did a double take before the front entrance. Monica Thomas, MaKenzie's mother, stood watching her from the corner near the pull tab ticket machines and video rental kiosks. Chestnut hair pulled back in a tight bun, she gave Avery a pointed look before turning, and pushing through the slow-moving automatic door.

Tom leaned over the customer service desk, watching her. He looked like a fox in a hen house. Although not too different than he usually acted, Avery knew it wasn't a good sign. She waited to leave until Mrs. Thomas got into her BMW and drove off.

Once Avery got in her car and drove through town, she noticed the effects of the storm, which had rocked the town shortly after she arrived at work. Tree branches littered the city streets. In the country, the heavy rains washed ruts in the rock roads, making Avery's car jostle enough to rattle her teeth out. White knuckled, she slowed down to keep from damaging the spare tire, taking twice as long as usual to drive home.

Wet leaves dotted her father's silver car. The last time he'd been home in the middle of the day had been when her Aunt Penny died. But, if there was an emergency, why was her mother's car still missing?

Her heart thrummed in her ears as she walked through the entryway leading into the dining room. There at the far end of the table sat her dad, sober as a judge. His hands were clenched on top of the oak table, his face unmoving and grim. He didn't look up when she came inside.

"Okay, what's wrong? Where's Mom?" Avery studied her father. Her Aunt Penny told her she looked like her mom except that she'd gotten her hair from her father. It was the only thing she'd disagreed with her great aunt about. Although they both had brown hair, Avery's was light brown and wavy where her father's was dark brown and straight. Once when she'd been ten, she suggested she'd been adopted. Her mother scolded her and slapped her mouth. Avery never mentioned it again.

Her father drew in a long breath and let it out loudly. He opened his mouth and nothing came out, so he shut it again. He turned to look up at her, opening his hands like he always did when he talked.

"Okay. Whatever it was, I didn't do it." She'd said it lightly, trying to crack the tension pulsing around her. She'd hoped to make him smile, but he didn't.

"It's your mother." Her dad started then stopped, stuttering to find the words before losing them again.

Her heart hammered like a freight train. "Mom? What about her? Did she lose another sale?" Avery slapped her keys and purse on the table. "Where is she?"

"Dineen left. Packed up. Gone." Anger rimmed his eyes red. "Said she won't be back." His accusing look bore through her.

Stunned, Avery's head swam. Their last conversation had been the worse yet. But her mother wouldn't leave because of what she'd said, would she? "What do you mean she won't be back?"

Her father chuckled once and shook his head. "Don't know why I have to be the one to tell you this. But seeing as I'm left to mop up the mess she's made, I have no choice."

"What? Geez, tell me already."

"You know the banker Phillip Thomas? His daughter's in your grade."

Avery nodded yes. Her ominous radar went from nagging possibility to a full blown alarm bells.

"His lawyer called. Dineen left with him. Said I'd get the specifics later." He swore under his breath. "Most likely when *she* files for divorce."

The bitter sarcasm in her father's tone stung. Avery recalled the way Mrs. Thomas looked at her this afternoon. Goosebumps sped across her skin. "What—what am I supposed to do?" Her knees gave out. She slumped down sideways onto a dining room chair. What about MaKenzie? The possibilities were too crazy to even begin to think about.

"Nothing." He hesitated and a flash of something akin to empathy flickered in his eyes.

It was a look he hadn't given Avery for years, the last time she remembered it was when she fell off her bike and skinned her knee. For a second her chest pinched with longing to be held by her dad again, comforted in a way that made her feel that everything would be all right.

Her dad flung his hands up in the air, stood, and stalked to the front door. When he turned, the softness in his eyes was gone. "Lucky for you, your life doesn't change."

She should be used to it by now, but once in a while she got her hopes up that her dad would become that comforting presence he once was. He was just an angry man who drank too much and became belligerent. There was no going back to the normal dad who soothed her wounds, and made her feel loved and safe.

Avery chided herself. She knew better than to hope. Her lungs closed up, making it hard to breathe. Tears burned her eyes. His words sunk in. Her life didn't change? It had completely changed. It had been turned upside down.

The front door slammed shut, rattling the windows.

Her father's car revved. Shaking her head to clear the fog from her mind, she glanced at the window beside the front door. She watched him narrowly miss her car as he sped out of the driveway. No doubt he was headed for the local bar.

Avery knew she was seventeen, but right now she felt anything but. She wished she had Aunt Penny's lap to crawl up in. Her throat tightened.

Her mother had done some pretty unbelievable things, like all the times she was drunk and forgot to pick her up, leaving her alone for hours after volleyball practice or concert choir rehearsal. It was the reason Avery stopped participating in extracurricular activities.

But this? This took the cake. Because now her mother had left her…correction, abandoned her.

That was unforgivable. "God, why do you hate me?

An hour after her dad's exit, Avery laid out her new clothes for her senior pictures. Snot streamed out her nose. She picked up the stuffed kitten her best friend Sophie won for her at last year's 4-H fair and burrowed her aching eyes into its soft fur. "What was she thinking?"

The kitten didn't respond.

"Your senior year is the best time of your life, Avery. You're never going to forget your high school years, Avery." Using a falsetto voice, she moved the cat's head around like it was talking to her.

She touched a photo of her with her parents. It was taken two summers ago on the Fourth of July, the year Aunt Penny died. Big Jim, a bar owner friend of her mom's, had taken the picture.

They looked like any normal family.

Her mother glowed, like she was having the time of her life. Her father was looking past the photographer, a frown on his face. She just looked bored.

That night her parents had gotten into a monstrous argument, yelling at each other the whole ride back home, and for hours afterwards. A happy family they were not.

"My senior year's going to suck. Big time." She held the cat out and nodded its head up and down in agreement.

Her cell phone rang and she shot up in surprise.

"Hey!" The clear alto voice of her friend Sophie Morris greeted her.

"Hey." Avery wiped a hand across her runny nose.

"So…I heard some story about your mom," Sophie said. "I'm assuming by your plugged up, nasally voice that it's true?"

"Wow, that's a record. Yeah, she's gone. Dad says she'll probably file for divorce." She swiped more tears leaking from corners of her eyes.

"That stinks. You know you can come over any time. Guess I get to pay you back for all that time I spent at your house when my parents divorced."

The line cut out. "Stupid phone…" silence "…in my room." There was a loud shuffling until the line cleared. "There, I'm outside. Do you want to come over now?"

"Maybe some other time. I'm getting ready for senior pictures tomorrow."

"Okay."

Sophie's mom called out from the background. Avery waited while they bickered back and forth, the racket muffling as Sophie put her hand over the mouthpiece.

"Avery, honey," Mrs. Morris's voice broke through the line. "Don't you worry none. Sophie and I will get you set right as rain. We'll do a movie night. Popcorn. Chocolate. Pop. The works."

Avery smiled as another skirmish sounded, and Sophie's voice came back across the phone. "Okay, Muh-therrrrr."

"Whining is not becoming. Tell Avery we'll do a spa night if she prefers. You bought that new bunch of polish. I'm sure there's a decent color in there somewhere." More shuffling.

"Geez. Mothers. Can't live with them, can't get cable without them." Sophie sighed into the phone.

Avery burst out in a half-laugh-half-cry.

"Oh, Avery. I'm sorry. I didn't mean—"

"It's okay." Avery pressed her cold fingers against her swollen eyes.

"So, spa night then? We'll get ice cream with chocolate syrup. No marshmallows though. Remember last time you got sick and hurled everywhere." They both laughed. "And hey, I've got this gorgeous shade of venom polish you have got to see."

Avery wrinkled her nose. "You don't get to touch these little piggies with your punk-puke polish."

"It's venom, and you don't seriously think I would touch those skuzzy, fungus-ridden appendages, do you?"

Avery grabbed the stuffed kitten and sat down on the bed. "Who did you hear it from?" She couldn't keep her voice from cracking. "I can't believe everyone's talking about it already. Dad just told me."

"Don't worry about it. People talk. They always talk. Even when there's nothing to talk about, they find something to talk about. It'll be yesterday's news in two seconds. You'll see. Besides, you always have me."

Avery took a deep breath. "Promise?"

"Pinky swear." Sophie's phone beeped. "Look, I've got to go. Don't do anything stupid, okay? I'll talk to you later. Call me if you need *anything*."

"I'm not going to throw myself on a sword or anything, but thanks for caring."

"Yeah. I don't look good in black. See you soon."

They hung up.

Her phone rang again from a number she didn't recognize.

"Hello?"

"Is this Avery Denton?" The voice asked.

"Yes."

"You tell your mother next time I buy a house it won't be from her. I should've known better than to deal with you people."

Chapter Four

(Truth #2: Some people will disappoint you. Others will amaze you.)

Avery quickly pushed the end button.

You people? She stared at the screen. What was that supposed to mean?

It rang again. Another number she didn't recognize. She didn't answer it. There were four messages. The first was from MaKenzie's friend, Lauren Hughes, calling Avery and her mom names. The next was another person trying to get a message to her mother.

Good grief. She hadn't left town. Why was she getting heat because of her mother?

She deleted the messages and checked her other notifications. One was a ChatterBox blast tagging Avery. She logged on to her computer to see what was said: *"Keep MaKenzie in your prayers, everyone. Her father seems to be going through a midlife crisis."* Comments were already rolling in: *"she and her mom are so devastated," "what a home wrecker,"* and *"how could this happen in Valley,"* and *"guess real estate wasn't the only thing Dineen Denton was selling."*

Her phone beeped again, and again, as more ChatterBox comments came across. Avery turned her phone off. She threw it across the room into the closet where it bounced off the wall and landed in pieces on a pile of clothes.

Of course it was the woman's fault. It didn't help her mother's reputation had taken a hit in the last year. She'd seen her mom and Mr. Thomas talk once in awhile when they went into town, but it never looked romantic, not that her mom had a romantic bone in her body. At least until now. "Stupid MaKenzie and her stupid dad."

Her home phone began ringing. She ran downstairs and picked it up to the same spew she'd had on her cell phone. With a scream, she flung it across the room, and ran back upstairs.

Avery sagged down to a heap on her rumpled bed, clutching the stuffed kitten to her chest as tears soaked her pillow.

***

The next morning, Avery struggled to inhale. One of the doctor shows on television she watched a couple of days ago claimed that people breathed through just one nostril at a time. Right now that was a lie. Her nose and eyes were swollen from crying, resulting in a ninety-nine point nine percent blockage of her nasal passage giving her a high pitched wheeze. "Ugh!" Her scream echoed through the empty house.

Sweat caused her hair to cling to her neck. Checking the thermostat, she found it turned off. "Dang it, Dad. It's over a hundred outside." She flipped the cool switch to on, punching the degree button down to sixty-nine.

Her father always had a cheap streak when it came to bills, but she'd never had to worry about it since her mother always caught the things he did. Like turning off the air on one-hundred and twenty degree days. Her mother would grumble about him and turn it on. It had been like a background noise she never paid too much attention to. Now it was up to Avery to do it. Avery's mouth twisted down, and she fought a fresh wave of tears.

In the living room she spied their home phone strung out behind the couch, the cord stuck out like a pig's tail. She ran a hand across the scratch just above the top of the couch where it had hit when she hurled it the night before. Calls had started flooding the home line her mother used as a secondary work number. "Well, guess I don't have to worry about Mom killing me for putting a mark in the wall now."

She yanked the phone from where it was wedged, and plugged it back into the loosened wall jack. She held the receiver up to her ear. Dial tone. *I didn't break it!* She dialed Katie's number.

"Hey, Avery! I've been trying to reach you, where've you been?" Katie's bouncy voice exploded in Avery's ear.

Avery picked at her shirt. "Oh, you know. Stupid phone company—"

"Well, Cindy Herman called. They had to cancel our pictures today for some family thing that came up."

Avery frowned. The Herman's were related to the Thomases, just like her boss Jeff Price, was. She shouldn't be surprised they canceled. "They didn't say what the 'family thing' was, did they?"

"No. I just figured one of her kids was sick or something. Anyway, I got mine rescheduled, but I didn't do yours because I didn't know when would be good for you. You need to call them. You still have her number, right?"

Katie obviously hadn't heard about her mom, and Avery didn't feel like saying anything. "I have Cindy's number, all right." Did she ever. Who was she going to get to do her senior pictures now?

"I'm sorry, what?"

"I'll worry about it later. You doing anything today?"

"Since I don't have pictures, Mom decided to go do some errands. Wish your phone was working earlier. We could've made plans." Someone yelled in the background. "I have to go now."

Avery slumped into a chair. She dialed Sophie's cell number, but it went straight to voicemail. "Great. A day off and I have no one to do anything with." A ray of sun fell through the picture window, warming her leg. "That's it!"

She ran to her room and changed into her two-piece swimsuit before donning a spaghetti strap shirt and short-shorts. Ice and pop went into a cooler, and she tossed in everything else she would need in a beach bag.

Ten minutes later she backed into an empty, shaded spot at Willow Park beneath one of their trademark weeping willow trees. The grass was green and freshly mowed, filling the air with both cut-lawn and gasoline smells. The scent reminded her of childhood, those simple days when summers were carefree.

Her dad taught her to swim here. Since Valley's swimming pool had been shut down for several years when she was younger, they'd come out to Willow Park's lake many times on summer nights to fish and swim.

The year the pool reopened had been the same year Aunt Penny died, and her mother went back to work. Since Avery couldn't drive until last year, she could count on one hand the number of times she'd used the pool in town. She preferred not to be among a crowd of posers and judgers anyway.

Her memories were bittersweet. Her mom used to bring Graham Goodies cookies to the beach. Avery waited until she was done swimming so the chocolate would be oozing and the graham cracker warm enough to melt in your mouth. They were her dad's favorites.

She recalled the first time she screamed when a fish swam by her feet. It had made both her parents laugh. And one weekend her dad came out and fished off the dock while she sang and picked wildflowers by the water's edge.

Coming to Willow Park was like going back to a happier time.

A group of toddlers screamed as they splashed at the water's edge of the sandy swimming area. A couple of teenage babysitters sat up at the top of the beach next to a picnic table talking and texting. Avery smirked at the groupie girls. A green-and-white football jersey, Valley's school colors, lay across the middle chair. The number ten had been last year's senior quarterback Miles Jones's number. Sadie Baylor—his biggest fan—with her perfect, tanned limbs, sat stretched across the jersey's netted material, laughing at something one of her friends said.

Avery stopped in front of Sadie, blocking the sun. "How's Miles?" She pointed to the shirt.

Sadie raised her sunglasses to look at her. Without saying anything, she put them back in place, shifted in the chair, and turned her head away from Avery.

"I know who you are. Guys, this is the girl whose mom ran off with MaKenzie's dad."

"Can you believe it? We bought our house from her mom." Faith, the girl to Sadie's right, gushed as if Avery were a celebrity.

Sadie lifted her glasses to look at Avery closer. A snide grin crossed her face.

Dani, the girl on the far left, snorted. "Some nerve. If my mom ran away with a married man, I wouldn't go out in public for at least a month."

"Was that supposed to be an insult? My dead grandma could do better than that." Avery turned and left. Sand flipped against her legs as she determinedly strode to the farthest side of the beach area away from the trio.

Avery set up her things, and, knowing how white her legs were, pulled out her lotion. She'd need a generous amount to keep from burning.

A truck rumbled into the park's rocky entrance, drowning out the children and girls, but she didn't look up. The area was surrounded by farmland and a couple of cabins way in the back.

She took off her shirt and and started to put on lotion. A shadow fell over her and she looked up into the dark blue eyes of Jaxson Stewart. He bent down to look at her, hands on his knees. His blond hair swung low over his right eye but she could see the mischievous twinkle. Her heart raced a little faster.

"Need some help with those hard-to-reach places?"

"I think you'd enjoy that way too much." Avery grinned up at him. "Why are you out here? Working on your farmer's tan?" She lifted the sleeve of his T-shirt, revealing white skin beneath it.

He clutched his chest and fell back pretending to be wounded. "Ouch. That hurts." He laughed. "I saw your car and thought I'd come over and say 'hey.'"

Although his stance was relaxed, his eyes held a strange intensity. Avery stiffened as it hit her. "You heard." Avery dug her hands in the sand to keep them from shaking.

"Heard what?" Jaxson leaned down on one knee.

She stared at his scuffed boot and winced at the false innocence inflected in his voice. Her heart stuck in her chest. It was one thing for acquaintances and people she didn't care about to know about her mom leaving on social media. It was another thing for Jaxson to know. However, it was a futile to believe he wouldn't find out. "It's a small town, Jaxson."

His smiling lips straightened to a line as he looked even deeper into her eyes.

"Don't feel sorry for me. I'm tough." Her voice broke, but she pasted on a wide smile.

Jaxson grabbed the lotion and squirted some of the white liquid into his hands. He didn't say a word. The touch of his rough hands on her back sent chills through her body. That surprised her. Jaxson had always been like the boy next door. The intimacy of the moment threw her off guard. She pulled away to face him.

Then she saw them. The trio of babysitters whispering and glancing at them. One held her phone out, taking pictures of Avery and Jaxson.

Chapter Five

(Lie #3: Work hard and you will be rewarded.)

Pic-Wiz? ChatterBox? Who knew? Avery gritted her teeth.

Jaxson rubbed his hands together then wiped them down the front of his dirty jeans. "If anyone knows how tough you are, it's me. I'm the one you saved from getting picked on by Billy Hammer on the school bus. You were this little eighth grader standing up to a senior five times her size. You're one of the bravest people I know."

His eyes flashed for a second before he continued. "I'm still sorry about your mom. Gonna be kind of rough going for a while. I imagine MaKenzie will be all over it." He picked at a sorry-looking blade of grass struggling to grow at the edge of the beach and tore it to pieces as he spoke.

"Ha! Senior year." She raised her hands and shook them like pom-poms. "Yay me." Avery's attempt at lame humor fell flat.

Jaxson swept a stray piece of hair behind her ear. Her eyes fluttered to his face as blood pounded through her veins.

"I love the color of your hair. It reminds me of the honey my aunt gets from her bee hives." He glanced up at Avery, his tan cheeks growing slightly pink. "Anyway. Call me if you need someone to talk to."

She sent a thankful smile at him, unable to form words until her heart stopped beating out of her chest.

"Well, I've gotta go. Dad'll be wondering where I am." Jaxson stood and dusted the sand off his jeans. The gritty dirt clung to his greasy hands.

A surge of sadness pulled at her. She put her sunglasses on to hide her disappointment. "Glad you got a chance to work on that tan."

"Yeah, right. Back at ya." His brilliant smile curved upward. "See ya later."

"Bye," she whispered around the lump in her throat.

Monica, Dani, and Faith all stared as Jaxson strode away. Dani said something to the other girls who agreed and then laughed.

A wave of jealousy struck her. She gulped down a breath of hot summer air. *When did my boy next door turn into a hunk?*

As if hearing her thoughts, the girls turned and sent her withering glares. After Jaxson's truck rumbled down the country road toward his family's fields, Avery gathered up her belongings with all the dignity she could muster, and left. She didn't look back.

***

Three cars already waited in the grocery store parking lot when Avery arrived to open early the next morning. Darkness gave way to a hazy light. An overnight shower's condensation misted into the air as the pavement heated up. Avery groaned as she stepped out of her air-conditioned car into the soupy air.

"Hey." Chantra tossed her cigarette on the ground and blew out smoke.

"Hey." Avery leaned against the brick building. "Three cars already, and it's not even six o'clock."

"Yeah. No rest for the wicked, huh?" Chantra held an envelope out to her. "Look, Avery. I tried to get hold of you yesterday, but you didn't answer your cell phone, and your home phone rang busy all day."

Avery eyed the envelope. "I know…"

"We have to let you go." Chantra's tone was abrupt.

Avery opened her mouth, too stunned to speak.

"It's nothing personal. We have too many employees and not enough income to support all of them. You understand." The older woman fumbled her cigarette pack with one shaking hand, while trying to get another cigarette out with the hand still holding the envelope.

"You have got to be joking. This isn't about MaKenzie and that stupid card the other day, is it?"

Chantra's lighter flared as she lit her cigarette. She took a deep drag, blew out a cloud of smoke, and stared into the parking lot.

"It is, isn't it? I saw her mom when you sent me home the other day. They went to Mr. Price to complain, and you're too chicken to stand up for me." Avery stood with her hands on her hips.

"No, it's nothing like that. We have too many employees, too many overtime hours." Chantra's voice was dull and she wouldn't make eye contact with Avery.

Avery pointed her finger at her now ex-manager. "You're such a liar. I don't care if you have kids. I can't believe you're letting me take the fall for this."

Chantra finally made eye contact with her, the look in her eyes a mixture of sadness and determination. "I need the vest back. I checked your locker yesterday. It was empty. I really wanted to tell you before you got up and came all the way in. Take this. It's your last paycheck."

Avery snatched the envelope from Chantra. "I've covered for you so many times and what do I get back? You suck as a manager, you know it?"

Alyssa Durand, the second morning cashier, got out of her parent's car and walked over to them.

"Is she fired, too?" Avery asked. "Because I was hired before her. You've even written her up for talking on her phone. If anyone gets axed, it should be her."

"That's none of your business. Give me the vest." Chantra held out an impatient hand. "Don't make me call the cops."

"This is lame, Chantra, even for you." One of the buttons snagged Avery's hair as she yanked the vest over her head. She refused to flinch. She stuffed it into Chantra's hands, a hunk of hair still stuck to the button. "Have a nice life."

Avery stomped to the far side of the parking lot where employees were required to park. She got in her car, threw her purse and the envelope on the seat next to her, shoved the gear in reverse, and floored it without a satisfying tire squeal. *Great! How am I supposed to pay for a new tire now?*

Thoughts about how she was going to pay for her photos, how she would get food, and how she would afford gas and extras flew through her mind. She turned without stopping fully at the stop sign, and a green car swerved to miss her. Avery's mouth hung open, and MaKenzie Thomas's hand and mouth matched in obscenities.

"This day just gets better and better."

***

It was too early to do anything else in town, so after slinking past MaKenzie's car, Avery decided to go home. She needed to figure where else she could get a job in town.

The latest Valley News lay folded on the dining room table. Flipping to the advertisements, she saw only half a page listing want ads, the majority of which were for CDL truck drivers or nurses. What was she going to do?

Avery opened the crumpled envelope. Two hundred fifteen dollars and eighty-three cents. No overtime since she hadn't finished her regularly scheduled week.

She set up her computer, and clicked on a site listing jobs for the Omaha/Council Bluffs area. *I'll be lucky to make anything after I pay for gas.*

Her home phone rang.

"Hey!" It was Sophie whose voice was unusually perky. "What's up, buttercup?"

"Looking for a job." Avery crumpled the newspaper and threw it across the room.

"Why?" Sophie's voice faded as she spoke.

"I got fired, all because of that snotty MaKenzie and her Country Club mother."

"Hey, look outside."

"What? Why?"

"Geez. Just do it, I've got something to show you." Sophie's giggle was joined by a deep laugh. The phone went dead.

Avery pulled back the curtains on the front window a fraction. A jacked up, tricked out truck sat behind her Taurus in the driveway. The horn blew. She'd only seen one person with that kind of tricked out truck lately.

You've got to be kidding me. What in the world is that nub doing here?

Sophie's dark head popped up for a second before dropping out of sight as she jumped out of the passenger side of GI Jerk's truck.

"Yo! Avery. Get your tail out here." Sophie yelled from the driveway. Towering heads and shoulders above her was the GI who changed her tire a few nights ago, the same one who kissed her. "Hey Avery! Not leaving until you come out."

Knowing Sophie, she would probably burn Avery's house down if she didn't come out. Taking in a deep breath, she opened the door.

"I've been trying to call you. Why aren't you answering your cell phone?" Sophie's round cheeks were flushed.

Avery glanced over at the GI. He stood behind her friend beaming, his chest puffed out. Her hands itched to slap the look off his face.

"What did you say about looking for a job?" Sophie asked.

"Chantra fired me before I even clocked in this morning" Avery stood back to get a better look at the guy cuddling with her best friend.

"Why would they do that? You're the best employee they have. Especially compared to that other girl." Sophie snapped her fingers.

"Alyssa?"

"That's the one. She is always on the phone and never knows where anything is. She's an idiot. What'd you do when she told you?"

Avery shrugged. "I handed Chantra my vest and left. She said they had too many employees, but I know it was because Chantra let MaKenzie sign off on the receipt since her precious gold card was declined."

Sophie waved her hand. "You hated that job and you know it. Anyway, forget all of that. I want you to meet my new boyfriend, Brody Hunt. Brody, this is my best friend, Avery Denton."

"New boyfriend?" Avery gaped. Not that she hadn't figured it out already. But hearing her friend say the words made it real.

Brody's smile widened as he looked at her. "Nice to meet you. Avery, was it?" Blue eyes swept her from head to toe and back up again.

Avery crossed her arms over her chest. She didn't smile back.

"We've met," she said.

"Really? Where?" Sophie turned to look at the grinning jerk behind her. His arms wrapped around her in a possessive embrace.

"Huh? We know each other?" Brody crouched, his head on Sophie's shoulder as he questioned Avery. His hands moved intimately over Sophie's curves.

Avery inhaled a long breath. "Yeah, we met. The other night. I was the girl with a flat tire." She continued when Brody looked confused. "The girl you kissed. That girl."

"Oh, yeah. Right. Steve and I had just got back from Guard duty and we saw you guys on the side of the road. Remember, babe, I told you at the party when we met about the girls we saved the other night? But, uh, hey." He pointed his thumb and forefinger at her, gun-style. "That was Steve who gave you the peck on the cheek. He thought you were cute."

Avery glared at him. She'd known many jerks in her life, but this one was working his way to the number one spot.

"Hey, you know what? We could double date or something. Steve wouldn't mind, I'm sure. What do you say?" A sparkle lit Brody's beady eyes.

Avery shuddered at the thought.

Chapter Six

(Truth #3: The truth is often ignored for a more convenient lie.)

Avery struggled to keep from physically shivering at the thought of going anywhere with either one of the G-men.

"Hey, yeah. That's a great idea. We're going to a party tonight at the Chute. What do you say, Av?" Sophie's eyes lit up. "Please, please, please?" When Avery didn't answer, a familiar glint of determination lit Sophie's face.

"Two words. Jail bait." Avery ignored the taunting grin on Brody's face. Avery sighed. So, that's how he was playing it, huh? Well, she would be there to show her friend what a jerk he really was. "Where's the party?" Sophie opened her mouth, but Avery raised her hand to stop her from speaking. "But 'no' to the double date."

That afternoon, Avery sat on her bed trying to decide whether or not she would go to the Chute. On one hand, she wanted to see if she could show her best friend what a letch Brody was. On the other, she didn't want to come within a mile of the perv.

Muscles aside, Avery didn't understand what was so great about Brody. He was too tall. His face was long. His toothy smile was way too caricature-ish. The jacked-up, tricked-out truck would be what her mother considered masculine overcompensation.

Avery grinned until she realized she was thinking about her mom. It had been days since Mom had left and there'd been no calls, no texts. Nothing. Pain pinched her heart and she rubbed the spot to ease it.

She glanced at her watch. It was getting late. A car door slammed outside. Dad. She hadn't talked to him since he dropped the bomb about her mother.

She heard the unmistakable sound of her father's clumsy attempts at coming in the house while drunk. He hummed off-tune to a country song. The door slammed shut a little too loudly, and she heard her father clunk up the stairs. He stumbled once, twice, and then the door to his room opened and clicked shut.

Avery waited a couple of minutes before quietly leaving her room. She tiptoed across the landing, past her mom's office area, and halted at the top of the stairs. She put her ear to the door of her father's room. Soft snores indicated that her father had already passed out.

Downstairs in the bathroom, she checked her reflection in the mirror. Hair up or down? Down since she'd probably be going through the woods to find *the spot*. No use putting it up if it would get snagged up anyway. She never used much makeup, so she skipped it and chose her favorite pink lip gloss instead before she left the house.

The party was in full swing when Avery arrived. Night had fallen and she could see the light from the bonfire from a distance. Cars lined both sides of the rutted dirt road leading to the Chute that used to divert excess river water from the Missouri River. When the government changed the flow of the river for flooding issues, it left the chute abandoned and only deep enough on one side to dive in. She parked half a mile down the road. The path was easy to find if you came often enough or arrived in the light of day, neither of which she had done.

From her right side amongst the trees she heard someone throwing up. Avery gagged and hurried away from the sound. She found the walking path that led down to the clearing where an old rusty iron bridge marked the party spot. A bonfire was constructed in the center of an open space beside the Boyer River streaming under the structure. Graffiti colored the beams on each of the rounded sides, much of which had faded from time and weather.

Coolers and kegs circled the fire. Avery scanned the crowd for Sophie with no luck. She did see Steve, the other GI who was with Brody the night they changed the tire on her car. A familiar brunette sat on his lap, playing tonsil-hockey with him.

MaKenzie.

Avery's pulse sped up. She clenched her fists to keep them from reaching out and yanking on her highlighted hair. What could she say? *Thanks, hag, for getting me fired.* MaKenzie would just laugh at her. Avery turned before the other girl saw her, and headed back around the other side of the bonfire, away from MaKenzie and soldier boy.

"Hey, if it isn't Avery Denton. Here, have a drink."

Avery scooted back as a drunken junior slopped a red plastic cup half full of beer in front of her, just missing her clothes.

She glanced back, MaKenzie and Steve were too involved to notice her. "No thanks, Landon." She sidestepped him as he tried to put his arm around her.

"Aw, c'mon. It's a party. Loosen up. Have some fun." He tried to step in front of Avery.

"Your cup is empty, why don't you get me one while you fill it?" Avery smiled at Landon, who wobbled on unsteady legs.

"Nah, I'm good. Let's continue this conversation over there." He pointed to the space beneath the bridge where couples went to make out.

"Hey, is that girl taking her shirt off?"

"Where?" Landon swung around to find the make-believe girl.

"Yeah, over there." She grabbed him by the shoulders and pushed him gently in the opposite direction she intended to go. "I think I heard she has a crush on you, too."

"Thanks, Avery. You're not so bad after all."

"Yep that's me. Ms. Not-so-bad-after-all." She watched as Landon stumbled away toward the water's edge where he found another girl to hit on.

A heavy weight engulfed her from behind. Avery stumbled forward and fell to her knees beneath Sophie's crushing hug. "Avie! You found us. See I told you, Brody. She come. Came." Sophie giggled then snorted. "You *came*. To the party." Sophie slid off Avery with a heavy thud and kept laughing.

"Geez, Sophie! Get a grip." Avery stood and grabbed Sophie's arm to pull her friend up, but ended up being yanked down beside her. A stick in the sand cut into her leg, making her shin sting.

Sophie broke out in a new fit of giggles. A new girl, who Avery didn't know, pointed and laughed at them. Between Sophie and the new girl, neither could quit laughing.

"Well, well. If it isn't my favorite damsel in distress." Brody hauled Sophie up easily. He held his hand out to help Avery, but dropped it when she glared at him. "You aren't having fun yet, there's nothing in your hand. Let me save you from that distress."

Once again Sophie and her friend started laughing, then snorting, then laughing again.

Avery stood and dusted her shorts off and examined her scrape. "You're toad-faced drunk. We used to make fun of people like that."

The new girl spit a mouthful of beer into the air. "Toad-face," she said, making a face. She and Sophie laughed again, this time joined by Brody.

Sophie's face blanched. "Ugh. I'm going to throw up again." She took off running back toward the road, only to end up crawling on her hands and knees at the edge of the trees by the ditch. The second girl crawled after her and held Sophie's hair back as she heaved.

"What do you know? It's just the two of us." Brody's eyes gleamed, the fire turning them a creepy orange.

Avery stiffened. "Is that some kind of pick up line? Besides, I would hardly say we're alone." She waved at the crowd of kids partying around them.

"Aw, come on. Be cool. You're here to have fun, right? Let me see if I can find Steve…"

"Don't bother."

"See?" Brody pointed to Steve and MaKenzie. "Good men are snatched up quick at these parties. Shouldn't have been so late. That could've been you." He shook his head. "Actually, she's a lot cuter than you."

Avery clenched her teeth. "I'm leaving." Avery stepped away from him, sweat dripping down her neck from the heat of the bonfire.

He pointed to the group of kids on the bridge jumping into the water below. Several sported only underwear, one or two were completely naked.

"Skinny dipping!" Brody announced. "That'll cool you off." He reached out to grab her shirt, but Avery twisted out of his grasp.

"I don't need to be cooled off." Avery stepped away from him and searched for the path back up to the road. Or a big stick. She turned in the direction she came in, but Brody grabbed her much the same way he had hauled Sophie from the ground.

"Come on, babe. The party's just starting. Sophie's going to be busy for a while, she'll never know if you don't tell. We can have some fun." His hands strayed upward.

She yanked his arm and pinched it in an effort to get him to quit mauling her, but he was too strong, her efforts too simple to have any effect. "Let me go, Brody."

"Hm?" He breathed right in her ear.

Bile rose in her throat. Her flip-flops were not stable enough for defensive action in the sandy area. She tried to reach behind her to scratch Brody's face, but he was so tall he leaned out of her grasp. His grip suddenly loosened, and she flipped around to slap him, but he caught her arm and pulled her against him.

"Well, isn't this interesting?" MaKenzie grinned at her from behind Brody. Steve stepped up beside her. "Brody, I thought you were here with Sophie?"

Avery caught the glint in her eye, knowing what it looked like. "Let me go, you piece of trash."

Sophie came out of the tree line and stumbled toward them. "What the—"

"This is not what it looks like." Avery stiffened.

Brody stepped back, his hands in the air. "Babe, she came on to me." A fake, innocent look covered his face.

"You liar!" Avery's throat ached from the scream.

"Well. I saw everything." MaKenzie pointed to Avery. "She was feeling him up. Luckily for you I got here in time to stop her."

"What?" Sophie's hair was in disarray with leaves and sticks poking out, but her unfocused eyes cleared.

Avery shot MaKenzie a death stare. "That's not what happened. He was coming on to me." Spit flew out of her tightly clenched lips.

"Really? Cause that's not what it looks like to me."

"I know what it might look like, but you're wrong. Listen to me, Sophie. This guy is bad news." Avery grabbed Sophie's arm. "Let's just leave and we can talk about it."

Sophie pulled out of Avery's grasp. "I can't believe you'd go after my boyfriend like that. And to think—I invited you."

"Clearly, she's jealous because you have a boyfriend and she doesn't." MaKenzie leaned back as though enjoying every second of the scene. "She's always been a little needy, always wanting something that wasn't hers."

"What's that supposed to mean?" Avery stepped toward MaKenzie.

Steve stepped between the two girls. "Hey, beautiful. Let them duke it out. Let's go find someplace more private."

MaKenzie grinned. "Ta-ta Tweedle Dum."

"That's it! You're jealous!" Sophie's voice shook with anger. "I finally find a guy, and you can't stand it."

"Really, Sophie? You believe MaKenzie, of all people? That I'm jealous? Of *him*?" She flung her hand toward Brody. "He's a jerk-faced loser. If you weren't so toad-faced you wouldn't even have to question whether or not to believe that hag."

Sophie's face flushed dark red. "She's a hag? All she was doing was trying to help me. You're the hag." Sophie stumbled past her.

"Hey, babe, drink this." Brody handed Sophie a can of beer.

Avery glared at him. He smiled confidently back at her.

"See Avery. He's nice and polite. You're not." Beer sloshed out of the hole in the can, spilling down Sophie's hand as she motioned toward Brody. More beer poured out of the can as she held pointed it at Avery, causing the dirt to become a frothy muddy mess.

"He lies to you. He lied about the other night when he kissed me. He lied that Steve did it. And now he's lying about coming on to me."

"I'm a Marine. I took an oath. It's impossible for me to lie now."

Avery ran a hand through her hair, wishing she could grab Brody and shake him. "I thought you said National Guardsman. You're such a skeezy liar."

Sophie crushed her empty can. "Geez, Av. It's the Army. You are so pathetic right now. This is like eighth grade with Josh Black."

"I'm not the pathetic one. And this is nothing like what happened with Josh because I'm not jealous." Avery stepped closer to her friend. What happened with Josh had nearly ruined their friendship. Avery wouldn't make that mistake again.

Sophie held her hand up, centimeters in front of Avery's face. "Go home, Avery." She turned and walked away toward the fire and refreshments. "I need another drink."

"Oh, I'll leave all right. And if we're talking about Josh, who was the one who got her heart broken then, Sophie? Who was there to help you pick up the pieces? Me, that's who."

Sophie lurched toward Avery. Brody caught Sophie before she landed face-first on the sand. "I don't need you. As of now you're my FBF."

Avery winced. FBF—former best friend. A term they both coined one day while making fun of MaKenzie and the way no one could put up with being her friend for long. It was the ultimate insult. Fire burned her lungs and tears pricked her eyes.

Sophie disappeared behind the bonfire. Brody winked then wiggled his fingers in a ridiculous, triumphant wave. "Buh-bye, Avery."

Chapter Seven

(Lie #4: Change is good.)

The skies opened up the next morning and poured rain. Avery slumped into a recliner with her laptop. She managed to fill out the online insurance form for her cell phone, using her dad's credit card. She'd memorized the number in case of emergencies.

She logged onto ChatterBox, ignoring the ninety-nine notifications and twenty-three messages. Her wall showed several of her friends' senior pictures, most done by Cindy Herman's studio.

Great, I don't even have an appointment yet. She typed in Sophie's name to look up the name of her photographer cousin. A blank page with a picture of a smiling Brody in sunglasses popped up. Surprise was followed by anger. Avery slammed the mouse down. "She defriended me!"

Raindrops splattered against the big picture window. Their droplets left jagged lines down the glass. Avery closed the laptop and turned the TV on. She turned on the satellite radio station she liked and set about cleaning the house for something to do.

A stain from one of her mother's spilled wine glasses lay under the runner that had been placed strategically to hide it in front of the couch. Two years ago she had promised her mother she wouldn't tell her father about the spill as it would only cause a fight.

Like dad ever notices anything around here, anyway. Avery picked up the rug and shook it out. She waved a hand through a cloud of dust that glittered in the light.

She glanced around the room, her eyes stopping on her mother's bedroom door. Her breath caught for an instant and pain flared like a porcupine in her stomach. It was like that after Aunt Penny died, too. Avery hadn't been able to go into her room to help her mom clean it out. Then her parents had a huge argument, and her mom had moved down to the room. The only times she'd gone in after had been to get her inebriated mother into bed.

She hated the room and all it stood for. Aunt Penny's deathbed and her mother's drunkbed.

Shaking off the feelings like she shook out the rug, she rolled up the rug and took it outside. Rain scented the cool air and water dripped down the roof over the deck onto the petals of the hydrangea bush she and her mother planted shortly after they moved in. Her mom had let Avery pick out her favorite color: a pale violet.

Back inside, Avery picked up the home phone receiver and dialed her mother's cell. It rang, once, twice, and then clicked. Voicemail. Avery hung up.

She breathed through the emotions threatening to bring her to her knees. "I'm not going to cry again. Not when she obviously doesn't care about me. Otherwise she wouldn't have left."

Desperate to vent her feelings, she worked all afternoon on the downstairs, moving, cleaning, and changing, and managed to scrub out most of the stain from in front of the couch. By the time the rain finally disappeared and sunlight streamed through the windows, the house looked completely different. It also smelled better—free of the stale, old shoe smell it had before. She turned and surveyed her work, smiling at how much she accomplished.

Then she took a shower.

The phone rang as Avery finished drying off from taking a shower. She threw on a shirt, wrapped the towel around her hair, and rushed to the living room, almost tripping over the newly moved recliner, to get to the phone.

Katie said, "Hey! I've been trying to call you. Why aren't you answering your cell phone?"

Avery picked at a piece of lint on her shirt. Her friend's voice didn't have its usual upbeat tone. She hadn't talked to Katie since she'd called to tell her Herman's cancelled on them. Now that Sophie hated her, Katie was the only one whose calls she would be missing on her broken phone. "It's not working for some reason. Why? What's up?"

"Oh. Um. Have you been on ChatterBox lately?" Katie asked.

"I was on it a couple of hours ago. Are your pictures up already?" Avery dried her hair while holding the phone between her shoulder and ear.

"Not yet. I just wanted to warn you, some people are saying some stuff on there about you and your mom. Oh, and something about that guy named Brody? Is everything okay?"

Avery sat down in the recliner, towel forgotten in her hand. "I should've called you, but everything happened so fast, and then my cell phone broke."

"What's going on?" Katie's voice was full of concern.

"Where do I start?" She told her friend about her mother, losing her job, and Sophie showing up with that jerk, Brody—everything except that Sophie had been drinking. Katie's mom was the head of Mothers Against Drinking, and Katie couldn't keep secrets from anyone.

"Are you sure it was Brody who kissed you, Avery? Maybe it was Steve. They both look alike, you know. Maybe you got everything wrong. Like maybe he was just goofing off at the party."

"You always want to believe in the best of everyone, Kay. That's going to get you in major trouble someday." Avery curled the cord around her fingers. "Besides, why would Sophie listen to MaKenzie over me? AND she unfriended me!"

"Well, it is Sophie's first real boyfriend. I'm sure she'll cool off and everything will be okay." Katie's voice lilted in a hopeful way as though willing it to be true would make it so.

A car door slammed outside. Her dad was home. "Look, Kay, we'll talk about this later. I'm not wrong. But I've gotta go."

Avery ran her hands through her damp hair, waiting for her dad to come in and see what she'd done. She couldn't help but hope her dad would like the changes.

Keys dropped on the floor. "What the…?"

She had placed the table her dad put his keys on across the room. A vase full of fresh-cut hydrangeas topped it now, the green scent of the cut stems still clung to her fingers. Her hopes crashed in flames around her feet.

After a few more expletives and some slurred comments, her dad came around the corner to the living room. "Who gave you permission to do this? What were you thinking?"

Avery grabbed a throw pillow, and sat up taller. "I was thinking that nothing around here ever changes. I couldn't stand to look at this house any more. Geez, Dad! Since when do I need permission to clean and move a few things around?"

"Nothing's ever good enough for you and your mother, is it? I should never have married your mother. Life would've been so much better without you both in it."

Heat washed over her face. "No wonder Mom left you. She hated living here as much as I do."

"If you don't like it here, there's the door, sweetheart. Don't let it hit you on the way out." Her father's face reddened.

Her stomach ached like she'd been gut-punched. She balled up the pillow and hugged it tighter. "You want me to leave? Just like Mom? That's what you really want, Dad?"

Her father grew still, serious. "Go ahead. Leave. We'll see how far you get." Turning on his unsteady heels, he opened the stairway door, entered, and slammed it. Dust and a bit of the ceiling above the doorway fell on the carpet below. A crack split the corner of the door two feet across the ceiling.

Avery slumped on the couch. Tears streaked hot trails down her face.

The throw pillow she held said, "Home sweet home." She screamed into it.

***

Three days later, her new phone arrived in the mail. She tore up the box, tossing it and all the paperwork it came with in the trash bag before taking it out to the metal trash bin behind the house. She lit a match, and watched as the flames took hold, melting the plastic before sparking the paper afire. Heat from the flames wavered above the pile.

Avery remembered the first time she, her Aunt Penny, and her mother lit a fire in this same spot after they moved in. Newspapers used to wrap china, cardboard from the moving boxes and any extra papers were piled high. Her mother had found broken limbs, and they stuck marshmallows on them to roast to their new home.

Her Aunt Penny brought out the best in her mom. They laughed about everything. Until Penny's cancer had spread. The tumor in her brain was inoperable by the time they found it. Six months later and Aunt Penny was gone, and her mother never laughed again.

Her stomach clenched with the memory. Life had been so simple, so fun back then. The wind shifted, dragging a cloud of smoke in her face. She rubbed her eyes, refusing to admit it was more than the smoke that brought on her tears.

Back inside, Avery frowned when her contacts wouldn't load from her old phone like they should. "Great, I burn the evidence, and now I can't use the manual."

She grabbed her laptop and turned it on. Her mouse's arrow hovered over the ChatterBox's 'CB' logo. Closing her eyes, she clicked it. The page was slow to load. The same ninety-nine notifications came up, but there were more messages than before. She ignored those and scrolled down the home page. Nothing seemed out of the ordinary until she got down to the bottom of the page. Several nasty cartoons had been posted there, each tagged with her name. The original message said, *"can you believe some people think hooking up with someone else's boyfriend is ok. like mother, like daughter I guess. #trailertrash #homewrecker"*

Great, it's all over Pic-Wiz, too. She spent a half an hour unfriending several people, then clearing out her messages and notifications. A new notification popped up. Someone she'd missed unfriending had invited her to like a page in support of MaKenzie Thomas for fair queen.

Curiosity got the best of her and she clicked on the link. At the top of the page was a picture of MaKenzie on a caramel-colored horse jumping over a white, wooden hurdle. The smaller picture was a closer photo of MaKenzie and her horse.

"Poor horse." Avery murmured.

She scrolled down the page. MaKenzie's senior photos, with the Herman studio logo on them, had been uploaded individually. Wasn't she supposed to have had them done at some big studio in Omaha? Every picture had a different, more elaborate outfit. At the bottom was a note stating the picture with the most likes would be used for her 4-H senior photo spread that would be on display during the Harrison County Fair in July.

"I think I'm going to throw up." Avery clicked back and unfriended the idiot that sent her that request. She was ready to log out when her instant message window blipped and opened. Jaxson-Awesomeness-Stewart's name popped up. The message said, *you on?*

She replied, *Nope. I'm picking daisies.*

Jaxson: *sounds like fun. you ok?*

Avery: *Nevr better. How's it going with you?*

Jaxson: *done with chores. too wet to do anythng. im bored.*

Avery didn't know what to say to that.

Jaxson: *you wanna do something?*

Her eyes bugged. Was he actually asking her out?

I don't know. Don't feel like doing much. She typed, but didn't send.

The screen blipped again. *come on. you know you want to*

She ran her hands through her hair. Sighing, she backspaced over the unsent text and retyped. *Sure. Why not?*

Jaxson: *great. ill be there in half hour*

Oh, crud! she thought, *what did I just agree to?*

Chapter Eight

(Truth #4: Should've seen that one coming a mile away.)

Avery sat on a metal patio chair on the front deck of her farmhouse, nervously picking at the flaking paint on the rounded frame. "This is so weird." She bounced her knees up and down. She'd never been on a real date before. Just group things at school.

Her hands trembled as she smoothed down the front of her green blouse. She stood and paced back and forth. The black bird sitting in the silver elm tree crooked a suspicious eye at her.

She pulled out her phone, growling and dropping her arm down when she remembered she didn't have any phone numbers on it. Most numbers she hadn't memorized since it was much easier just relying on her contacts and speed dials to keep track of everything.

Since she'd sat with Jaxson on the school bus years ago, and saw him around school all the time, he'd always been like a younger brother. Someone she could protect and tease. She twisted her hands in her lap.

She looked around trying to envision what the farm looked like to an outsider. The grass needed mowing. The ditch was a jungle of weeds with silver elm saplings growing everywhere. *What was I thinking? I've got to find his number and cancel.*

Rumbling came from down the road. Jaxson's old, blue Chevy truck pulled into her driveway. A wide smile filled his face as he waved through the window and turned the truck off. He opened the door and walked over to meet her.

"Hey! You look great." His gaze never left her face as she walked toward him. He led her to the passenger side of the car, the light touch of his hand on her back tingled on her skin beneath the light peasant blouse she wore.

Warmth flooded her cheeks. He smiled again. Her heart melted and she smiled back before getting in the truck. The bird on the tree flew over her, chirping happily.

The inside of the truck smelled like lemon Pledge. The dash was clear of the layer of dirt that living on dusty roads invariably created. Every inch of the truck was polished to a shine.

"Okay. Ready for some fun?" Jaxson's blond hair was freshly washed and brushed back away from his face, and it curled at the ends. He smelled of body spray and soap with a touch of outdoors. Long lashes framed his twinkling blue eyes. He wore a silver button down shirt over a white undershirt. The wiry arms she remembered from his youth had filled out into muscles visible below the short sleeves.

Her pulse raced and her smile wobbled. "Yep. Sure." She glanced away from his intense gaze, buckled her seatbelt, and stared out the window at her home as he pulled away.

Relief flooded through her when she realized Jaxson was headed north, away from Valley and into neutral territory. They ended up at the Roadside Cafe in California Junction which served ice cream and all types of fried foods. The tables and matching chairs were red with silver edges. Framed vinyl records hung on the walls. A small jukebox sat on each table. For a dollar, you could request songs from a list of country, R&B, Pop, and Hip Hop music.

Avery glanced around and her shoulders loosened when she recognized no one. She smiled at Jaxson as the waitress seated them in a booth and gave them menus. They ordered, and the waitress brought them their pops.

"So, have you gotten your senior photos back yet?" Jaxson asked.

"Um, no. Cindy Herman had to reschedule for some reason, and I haven't gotten ahold of her yet to reschedule." She glanced away from him as she spoke, hoping he didn't see the lie in her eyes.

"Cindy Herman, huh?" Jaxson smirked. "So, when are you gonna call someone not related to the Thomas's to do your pictures?"

She grimaced. "Isn't everyone besides me related to them?"

He laughed. "Well, I'm not related to them, thankfully."

An older, overweight waitress hobbled over to their table. "I'm sorry honey, but I overheard you. I don't know why them Hermans ain't called ya back, but I know someone who does great senior pictures you could call." The woman wiped her hands off on the apron she wore and handed Avery a business card.

She forced a polite smile and took the card. "Thanks."

"Now don't you worry none. What happens at the Roadside stays at the Roadside." The woman winked and hobbled back to the counter where she sat on her swivel barstool. A metal spatula smacked the bell in the serving window, summoning the waitress.

"Well, wasn't that sweet of her?" Jaxson joked.

Avery giggled back, glancing at the card. It was for Precious Moments studios in nearby Harris Grove. She remembered seeing some of their work at the fair before. It wasn't bad. She tucked the card away in her wallet.

***

The food was good for a small café stuck in the middle of the countryside. The old woman left them alone the rest of the time, her nose stuck in a gossip magazine.

Jaxson played with the salt and pepper shakers. "So, I wanted to show you someplace I like to go when I get mad and want to be alone. I wouldn't be offended if you use it." He threw down some bills on the table and stood to leave.

For an instant she hesitated. A date was one thing, going off to places unknown was another. But, looking into his open and honest face, she trusted him. "Okay. Where is this place?" Avery asked.

"You'll see. It's a drive, but it's worth it." Jaxson led her back to his truck, his gentle hand on her back.

He turned down the road they used to drive to California Junction, heading north toward the town of La Grange. Country songs played from an old silver radio in the dash that had dials, which stuck out like the truck's lighter.

They drove past La Grange, around the curving roads, out past several double wide trailers and run down houses. Jaxson turned into a blind driveway and drove up to a cliff overhang on a hill and parked.

From this precipice they could see miles of farmland below. Rows of green corn fields and darker green soybean fields patched the land. It spread out beyond the Missouri River, into Nebraska on the other side.

"You wanted to bring me to Mercer's Hill?" Avery asked.

"Whenever my troubles seem really big, I just drive up here and see how small I really am compared to the whole world. It makes me believe there's got to be something bigger than me out there. Kind of puts things in perspective." A faraway look settled on his face as he stared across the land.

A lump formed in her throat.

Jaxson turned toward her. "Look, I'm really glad you came today. Next week is football camp and then the Fair begins. Summer's almost over already, and I only have a few days of free time before school starts."

Twisting in the seat to face him, she waited for him to go on. Another car drove up the hill and parked behind them. Jaxson put his hands over the steering wheel and played with the rubber wheel cover.

Avery sat back against the vinyl seat. The people from the other car got out and walked around, took some pictures, and then left.

Jaxson laughed, tense and nervous.

Avery couldn't stand it any longer. She put her hand on his arm. The muscles underneath his shirt flexed at her touch.

She pulled her hand back. "Jaxson, what's up? What're you trying to tell me? Is it about my mom?"

He turned sideways to look at her. "Do you like me, Avery?"

The start of realization seeded in her gut. Her hands trembled, and she clasped them. "Of course, I like you, Jaxson. We've known each other forever. Why wouldn't I like you?"

"I mean. Do you really like me?" He sat up, looking directly into her eyes. The sun made his hair shine golden. "I wanted to ask you if you'll go with me. You know, like, be my girlfriend?"

The breath caught in Avery's chest and her eyes opened wide. Did guys actually still do that? Ask a girl to "go steady" with them instead of just hooking up? "Jaxson. I…I don't know what to say."

Jaxson leaned forward, placing a hand on hers. "I know this may have come out of nowhere for you, and you have a lot going on right now. I'm not trying to pressure you or anything." He clasped her hand in his calloused one as his blue gaze bored into hers. "I just really like you, Avery. I have for a long time. I can be a great boyfriend, support you when things get tough."

Avery shook her head. "You don't know what my life is like, Jaxson."

"It doesn't matter. I don't care about what everyone says about your mom. She's not you." He tugged her closer. "I know who *you* are. The rest doesn't matter."

He grazed her cheek with his knuckles. Avery closed her eyes. "I couldn't stand it if something happened and we weren't friends anymore."

"Nothing's going to happen. Nothing can change our friendship. I promise."

Avery gave him a doubtful look.

His smile was replaced by the determined look she remembered from his childhood. "I am your biggest fan, Avery Denton. Say yes. Say you'll be my girlfriend."

Avery studied his face. His blond bangs fell down one side of his face and she lifted a hand to move them so she could see into his eyes. "Okay. Yes."

He swept Avery into his arms and held her tight.

"Seal it with a kiss?" he asked.

She nodded minutely.

He leaned down and pressed his lips to hers.

His lips were soft, the kiss sweet. Avery clung to him, praying she'd made the right choice.

Chapter Nine

(Truth #5 Never turn down an opportunity, it could be a blessing in disguise.)

Avery stared at the business card she'd gotten two days ago at the café, one hand poised above the phone. She mustered her courage, punched in the numbers, and waited for someone to answer.

"Precious Moments Studio, this is Elaine Brooks." The woman's voice was deep and authoritative.

"Hi. I need to make an appointment for senior pictures." Avery rubbed a nervous hand on her shorts.

"What's your name?" the woman asked.

Her stomach tightened "Avery Denton."

"Hi, Avery. Let's see what we have on the schedule." The tip-tapping of computer keys broke through the line. "How soon can you come in?"

"As soon as possible. Oh, first, what are your rates?"

The woman recited the rates, specials and what was included. "Looks like I have a cancelation Thursday around 10 a.m. Now, don't forget that's the day before the 4th of July. You are going to be around, right?"

Avery hesitated. The date had completely slipped her mind. She stuffed down the mixed emotions the holiday brought.

"Avery, you still there?" she asked.

"Yeah, sorry. I'll be here, that time will be fine. Um, I have a budget to stick to." Avery chewed her lip.

"Except for the initial sitting fee, I don't have many extra charges. Some of the other portrait studios throw in fees for this and that. I don't. That way you get more bang for your buck. Now, depending on how many photos and the sizes you need, I'm sure we can figure something out."

"I don't have much family or loads of friends. I won't need much."

Elaine went on to talk a bit more about changes of clothes, inside and outside shots, and what to bring for props if she wanted.

Avery sat up higher in the chair as she called Katie, the heavy weight that been pressing on her gone.

Her friend answered on the second ring. "Hey, Avery. How're you doing?" Sympathy coated her friend's voice like frosting.

Avery pressed her lips together, counting mentally to ten before speaking. "Okay. Hey, are you doing anything Friday for the Fourth?"

"Yeah. My Aunt Katherine is holding a family reunion at her house in Missouri, and we're helping her with it. It is a mandatory family gathering."

"Ah. Mandatory as in you can't get out of it except through death. Sounds like loads of fun. Is your cousin Bart going to be there this year?" she teased.

Katie groaned. "He's at Computer Camp, thank goodness. I got my senior pictures back, you've got to see them."

"Cool. I made my appointment for Thursday, so I should get mine soon." Avery walked from the living room into the kitchen to put her cereal bowl in the sink.

The line was silent for a few seconds. "Oh? With Herman's?"

"No. I rescheduled with Precious Moments out of Harris Grove. She sounded really nice, and I think it will be cheaper, which is now very necessary." Avery sighed.

"Hey, Mom got some stuff to make red-white-and-blue tie dye shirts for the reunion. We have extra. You wanna come over and make some and then you can look at my pictures?" Noises of dogs barking and people talking sounded in the background. Katie's family was always so busy. Avery glanced around her too quiet empty house.

"Sounds good. This afternoon?"

"Okay." The light bubbly tone that had been missing returned to Katie's voice.

***

Katie ran down the deck stairs to greet Avery when she pulled into the Carter's driveway. Inside the house, her two youngest siblings were cleaning up after a snack.

"Where are Mary and Michael?" Avery asked.

"Mary is spending the night at a friend's and Michael has football camp until after suppertime."

"Oh, that's right." Avery murmured.

Jaxson had texted her several times over the weekend, but only after football since practice had started this week. For an instant, she thought about telling Katie about dating her brother's best friend. She'd be ecstatic, Avery knew. But she didn't want to spend the day talking to Kay about kissing him, and how romantic it was that they were going out. She still hadn't gotten used to the idea herself. She'd tell her soon.

"What?" Katie got the dyes out, placing the bottles on the table between them.

"Nothing. Let's get started."

Two hours later, the shirts were dyed and drying outside on the back deck. After they finished the shirts, Katie insisted on painting their nails, using red, blue and silver. It took several tries, but the end result turned out better than Avery imagined.

Rachel and Mark, Katie's two younger siblings, woke from their naps and ran out of their rooms. Katie went in the living room to turn on cartoons for them to watch while she and Avery finished cleaning up the dye mess.

"What're you going to do with the extra shirts we messed up?" Avery studied the first two shirts they tried, the red and blue dye swirled across the white fabric in tiny stars.

Katie frowned. "We've got to hide them from Mom, she'll be so mad I didn't look at the directions until after these were made."

"You know, I saw this last summer and wanted to try it." Avery grabbed some scissors, cut several strips two inches wide from the ruined shirts, and retrieved her flip-flops. She tied the strips to the plastic straps of her shoes.

Katie squealed. "Oh my gosh! That's great." Together they cut enough strips to decorate Avery's and Katie's. After

Rachel started having a melt-down and threatened to tell on them, they tricked out her flip-flops as well.

A half hour later Mrs. Carter came home from work, her arms full of grocery bags. "Hello, Avery. I didn't know you were going to be here. Glad I grabbed that extra hamburger since we have guests." She turned toward her daughter. "Did you get the shirts done?"

"Yes. They turned out great." Katie pointed to the sliding doors where they could see the dried shirts lining the deck rail.

"Looks like they did. Great job, girls. If they're dry, can you fold them up while I make supper?"

Although it was getting close to six o'clock, the sun rested high in the sky, and nightfall was still hours away. The hustle and bustle of the kids running from the family dog gave her a strange sense of nostalgia. She'd never really had this, being an only child, but somehow she missed it.

Scents of taco seasoning filled the air. Avery's stomach growled. Without anyone home but her, she had started to grab whatever she had, and skipping meals became her norm.

By the time she helped Katie fold and carry the piles of shirts into the house, it was time to eat. They hurried to put the shirts back in the plastic bags they took them out of, setting them up away from reach of the younger kids.

Food and plates rose high on the table. Everyone sat down and said grace before eating. Mr. Carter, a quiet man, who had come home while she and Katie were outside, sat at the head of the table.

Avery watched Katie's parents. Mr. Carter talked about how the crops were coming along. Mrs. Carter smiled and nodded at his comments. Mrs. Carter then took her turn replaying the events of her day as a nurse, chuckling about certain patients and their quirks.

Mr. Carter actually laughed at his wife's stories.

It was nothing like the suppers she had experienced growing up. Maybe because one or both of her parents hadn't been home together to sit down to eat for years now. They had—before Aunt Penny died. Avery's heart twisted.

Katie helped her younger brother hold the hard shell taco without splitting it into pieces. Her little sister glanced over and flashed a bulging cheek grin at her big sister. Katie made a face back. Mr. and Mrs. Carter exchanged smiles at Katie and Mary's antics.

Envy lit through her like gasoline on fire. She didn't blame Katie for being unaware of how amazing her normal life was. Avery clenched her fists to ward off the unwanted, ugly jealousy that flamed through her soul. Katie laughed at something her little sister said, her big blue eyes shining with the light Avery adored. Avery smiled back, the delight for her friend easing her pain.

After supper, Avery's stomach ached from the four tacos, rice, and refried beans. She and Katie took charge of washing the dishes, while the younger ones brought in the dirty plates and wiped down the dining room table. Mrs. Carter put leftovers in the stove to stay warm for Michael.

Katie took her younger sisters to get cleaned up for bed, so Avery dried her hands and went to get her purse. She smiled at Mrs. Carter, who sat in a recliner, reading the newspaper.

"Avery, can I have a word with you?"

Avery sat her bag down and walked over to the woman, nervous about what she wanted to talk about.

Mrs. Carter took off her reading glasses, stood, and set them aside on the stand beside her chair. "I heard about your mom leaving. Are you okay? Is everything all right with you at home? It's just you and your father now, correct?" She brushed a strand of hair behind Avery's ear.

"Yeah. It's just the two of us now." Avery bit her lip. "We're good. It's all good."

Mrs. Carter studied her. "If you need anything, all you have to do is let me or Katie know. I'm sure it's hard for a girl your age to be without her mom. I can't imagine what you must be going through." Her concern reached out like an invisible blanket, enveloping Avery in its warmth.

She wished she could tell the woman the truth. However, Mrs. Carter was on the school board, on the city council, and helped with the youth group of Katie's church. Mrs. Carter was the epitome of proactive and social consciousness. An ER nurse in Omaha, she proudly helped children get away from dysfunctional homes and placed in foster care. As much as Avery liked the woman, she didn't want her finding out how bad her dad's drinking problem was.

She'd learned the hard way years ago that the best thing to do with people like Mrs. Carter was to tell them what they wanted to hear. "It is hard. I miss Mom. But, I'm good. I'll call you if I need anything. I promise."

Avery grabbed for her purse when a fight broke out between Katie's siblings and Mrs. Carter left to referee. Michael's red head blazed by the window a second before he entered through the front door. Jaxson walked behind him. Both boys still wore their football pants and sweat-soaked shirts.

Avery froze, her heart skipping a beat. "Jaxson's here?" She whispered in a panic.

"Of course, silly. He comes over every night for supper as payment for driving Michael to football camp." Katie giggled.

"Oh."

Michael walked in sniffing the air. "Awesome! Mexican night."

"Stop! Go clean up first." Mrs. Carter came back around the corner, grabbing the duffel bag from her son.

Jaxson's smile was bright when she managed enough control to look up at him. His hair was mussed and damp with perspiration, his face still flushed from exercise. But her eyes lingered on his lips. The ones that kissed her so sweetly.

He caught her looking and grinned. Mrs. Carter grabbed his shoulder and pushed him toward Michael and the bathroom.

She hadn't expected to see him there. Her heart hammered in her chest with both excitement and nervousness.

"Are you okay, Avery? You look pale." Katie asked.

"No, I've got to go." Why hadn't she told Katie about Jaxson before her parents got home? Because, somehow telling her best friend made it real. And if it was real, invariably something would happen to ruin it.

Chapter Ten

(Truth #6: Just because it rains on your parade doesn't mean there won't be a rainbow.)

Avery hurried to make it to the door before the boys finished washing up, but was sidelined by the family dog running away from Rachel. In her hand she held a Christmas outfit for the dog to wear. The terrier avoided the child, skillfully running circles around Avery's legs in his escape.

Jaxson reappeared first, his hair combed, a fresh shirt on, and smelling like soap and body spray.

Giving up on heading for the door, she stood looking at her shoes in awkward silence.

"Hey. What're you doing here?" His blue eyes sparkled down at her. A swath of damp hair fell across them. Avery's hand itched to sweep it away. Instead she ran her hand through her own hair and then crossed her arms over her chest.

"Helping Katie get the shirts ready for their reunion." Her words sounded stilted even to her own ears. If only the earth would open up and swallow her now.

Jaxson sat down at the table where Mrs. Carter had divided the warm food before she'd left to get the young ones ready for bed. Michael joined him. Avery watched as they inhaled the food. Would she be rude if she just left now? Would it seem weird that she stayed and waited for the two to finish eating? What was the social protocol?

Before she made a decision, Jaxson spoke again, his eye on the red-white-and-blue tie-dye shirts sitting on the counter. "Avery, that reminds me, I was going to call you tonight and see if you wanted to do something Friday. Are you busy?" Michael stopped eating and stared at her.

Katie reentered the room. There was no question that she'd heard Jaxson's question. Her eyebrows were raised so far up her bangs hid them.

"Yes, Avery. Are you busy Friday?" Michael grinned like a feral idiot at her.

She was used to his teasing, but this time it seemed as if she had a spotlight aimed directly at her. Heat flooded her scalp.

Crud! Avery'd waited too long and forgotten to tell Katie about Jaxson. She knew her friend well enough to know Katie would be elated even though she hadn't said anything. This wasn't how Avery wanted Katie to find out about it.

Avery's hesitation must've been longer than she realized. When she looked around all three of them were staring at her. She was sure her face was redder than Michael's hair.

"Yeah, uh, no. I'm not busy."

"Great. I've got to ride in the parade, but after that I'm free. Maybe we can go through the carnival? My parents are having a picnic if it's not too hot. We could watch the fireworks my dad bought later."

Michael fluttered his eyelashes at her, his hands under his chin, smiling like a big idiot.

She ignored the silent razzing. "Yeah. Sounds great. I'll call you later." She grabbed her shirt and purse, and headed for the door. By the time she reached her car, Katie had caught up with her.

"What was that all about?" Katie squeaked in a whisper.

"Kay, you don't have to whisper. The cows aren't going to overhear." Avery dropped the sack with the shirt, flip-flops, and nail polish in the back seat.

"You're not answering my question." She wiggled a finger at Avery.

Taking a deep breath, Avery confessed. "Jaxson and I are dating."

Katie squealed, hugging Avery while jumping up and down in excitement. "Oh my gosh, oh my gosh, oh my gosh! Why didn't you tell me?"

"I'm sorry, Kay. I just didn't know how to bring it up."

Katie held her arm in a death grip. "I want all the gory details. Don't skip anything."

Avery looked up at the house to see if they were being watched. "It hasn't been very long, so there aren't many details. Jaxson asked me out last week. We went out to eat, and then he asked me to go out with him. We haven't seen each other since. There's really nothing to tell."

Katie whispered again. "Did he kiss you?"

"Yes—" Avery didn't get a chance to finish because her friend was screaming and jumping around again. "Kay. Shhhhh."

Katie covered her mouth with her hands, her eyes creased from the smile that filled her face. Michael and Jaxson came out and stood on the deck.

"Seriously, Katie. My ears are ringing." Jaxson teased. His lanky body leaned across the ledge of the deck.

"Yeah, sis. I think you shattered a couple of windows." Michael laughed.

"What's with all the ruckus?" Mrs. Carter came out of the front door. Her yellow hair gleamed under the deck light.

Avery groaned. If Mrs. Carter even thought she and Jaxson were dating, she'd enact her 'friends with benefits clause'. It stated nobody who's dating can come to the house at the same time. Sophie joked that Mrs. Carter didn't understand the concept behind friends with benefits, but Avery wasn't about to be the one to explain it to her.

"Sorry, Mom. Nothing's wrong. Avery just told a really funny joke. You know how Katie is." Michael's cover was so smooth Avery almost believed it.

Although Avery could tell Katie was trying to stand still, she still bounced on the balls of her feet, the smile on her face about to knock the ears off of her head. Avery held her breath.

Mrs. Carter frowned at them. "Time to wind things down. Michael, Katie, you two come in and get ready for bed. Good night, Jaxson, Avery." Holding the door open, Mrs. Carter ushered her children into the house. Katie turned back and waved wildly before her mother shut the door.

Jaxson grabbed his duffel bag and eased down the stairs.

"You look like you're limping. Practice a bit rough?"

"Yeah, first week. We're kind of like punching bags for the upperclassmen." He rested against her Taurus and set his bag on the ground. His blue truck was parked behind her car in the driveway. The crickets chirped in the dark shadows, and a breeze wafted by them.

Out of the corner of her eye, Avery caught the living room curtains move over on the side where Mrs. Carter's recliner sat. "We're being watched."

"Yeah, that's no surprise. So I take it Katie figured out we're dating?"

This close she could smell the soap and body spray he used and the musk of his sweaty body. Butterflies fluttered in Avery's stomach. She should be repelled by the sweaty odor, but it was surprisingly enticing.

"How'd you guess?" Avery smiled down at her feet, a strand of hair fell down over her face. She lifted a hand to brush it out of her eyes, but Jaxson's hand stopped her.

Lightly, he caressed her cheek as he tucked the hair behind her ear. "Well, the ninety-decibel shriek was the first clue."

She laughed, lowering her hand to her side. "Yeah."

Jaxson clasped her hand in his and brought it up to look at her fingers. "Nice paint job."

Stunned that he noticed, Avery smiled. "Thanks."

He turned so his back was toward the house. Drawing her knuckles up with a gentle touch, he kissed them. Fire flew up her arm and settled to a burn in the pit of her stomach. It would be so easy to fall in love with him. She'd known it the day he stopped at Willow Park to check on her. His touch when he put lotion on her back was a memory she couldn't erase. She didn't stand a chance against his charm.

"So, about Friday. I'll meet you after the parade by Honey Creek Park on the east side where the grocery store is. Then we can go through the carnival and hang out at my house later for fireworks. Will that be okay with your dad? He could come, too, you know." His eyebrows rose in question.

Her smile froze on her face. "Yeah, no. He'll probably want to do stuff with some of his friends. You know, commiserate or something." *Friends at bars.* She hoped her voice wasn't as tight as her throat felt.

"Oh, okay. Good." His thumb rubbed circles on the inside of her wrist. Her toes curled.

She turned to open the car door.

"And Avery? Don't forget your swimsuit for our pool."

＊＊＊

A loud rumble woke Avery up the next morning. She opened one eye to peek at her window where sheets of rain battered the glass.

"Seriously?" She yelled at the ceiling. The clock on her desk read 7:00. Four hours until her photo session. "Rain, rain, go away! Far away."

The dark sky matched her mood as she rose to get breakfast. She took her time getting ready, curling her hair, and applying her makeup with great care. She walked up to her room to gather her changes of clothes and noticed it was already ten o'clock.

Beams of light spread across the sky like an invitation to go outside. Moisture left behind sparkled like diamonds on the long blades of grass.

Avery drove between the Farmer's Co-Op office and the C-Store gas station, over the railroad tracks, and turned right onto the two block long main street that was the entirety of Harris Grove. Precious Moments was at the far end of the town. Only two cars were parked along the street, so she pulled in front of the studio. Checking her watch, she saw she was ten minutes early.

A bell chimed when she opened the door to the studio, arms full of her changes of clothing. The woman sitting behind the desk looked up and smiled. "Hi, I'm Elaine. You must be Avery. Come on in. I wasn't sure if you'd show up today, what with the rain and all." She shook Avery's free hand.

"My luck to have it rain on my parade," Avery joked.

"Actually, the light after a rain is great for photography, so it is good luck. Go on back to the dressing room if you need to change and let's get started."

Minutes later Elaine called to her in the dressing room. "Hey, Avery. If you hurry, we might be able to get a picture of you with a rainbow in the background. Come on out here and see."

Avery hurried to finish dressing and walked to the front door where the photographer stood staring across the street.

A perfect rainbow lit the sky behind the train tracks. "That's amazing."

"Just look at this light. Let's get a move on. Are you ready?"

Avery nodded and they both hurried across the street. Elaine quickly fussed over Avery's brown curls before clicking several shots with the rainbow in the background.

"That shirt was perfect for those pictures. It really popped." Elaine stated.

Avery grinned. The outfit, her favorite one, was a white shirt with shimmering beadwork that changed colors when she turned or moved. Her jeans were her favorite pair that had cost her more than she was used to spending on any one item. When she'd found them, she had to have them because they had a butterfly and a flower sewn in different colors on the pockets that matched a dress her Aunt Penny had bought her when she was thirteen. Her cowboy boots finished off the look.

"Yeah." Maybe her luck was changing.

Elaine kept up a conversation the whole time they worked, avoiding anything too personal. Avery relaxed, and before she knew it, the session was over.

"So, what's the budget we've got to work with?" Elaine asked after Avery changed back into her street clothes and sat down behind the desk. The pictures were loading from the camera into her computer.

Avery grimaced. "I have two hundred and fifty dollars max I can spend. I don't need lots, just some wallets and maybe an 8 by 10."

Elaine eyed her. "We should be able to work with that." She pulled up the pictures and scrolled down to show Avery. The best ones were the ones with the rainbow behind it. "Those turned out so well, I can't believe it. Which one's your favorite?"

"Those are amazing. I like the one where I'm standing on the tracks looking back over my shoulder at you. It shows off the butterfly on my jeans." Avery smiled. The pictures had turned out far better than she could have ever dreamed. She hoped Jaxson would like them.

"You like butterflies. Maybe we can get your name put inside a butterfly on the corner. Hey you know what?" A wide smile curved across the woman's face. "I've got a deal for you where your pictures might not cost you a dime."

Chapter Eleven

(Lie #5: What doesn't kill you makes you stronger.)

"Really? I'll take it." Avery jumped at the opportunity.

"Hold on, you haven't heard what I'm asking yet." Elaine stopped, her brows furrowed in thought. "I'd like to take this photo to the fair this year. It's one of the best ones I've gotten so far."

"That's it?" She asked.

"No, no. Hold on. I also need someone to man my table and hand out information at my booth. I have a wedding to do Friday morning and another set of senior pictures Saturday morning. So, it wouldn't be nights, just days that I would need someone to sit in for me. If you do that, and get at least five people signed up for sessions, we'll call it even. Are you free? What do you think?" Elaine took off her glasses and leveled a serious look at her.

She didn't even have to think twice. "Yes!"

Avery called Katie after she got in her car to drive home. She cranked on the air conditioner to ward off the humid heat of the afternoon.

"Hey! You'll never guess what just happened." Avery spoke loudly to be heard above the air blowing gusts out of her vents.

"You won the lottery?" Katie guessed.

Avery laughed. "Try again."

"You were picked by an undercover movie producer to be the star in his next movie?"

"Nope. That's your dream, Kay. Last guess."

"You heard from your mom?"

Pain radiated from a breath which had stuck in Avery's throat. Panic flared for a moment until she found the ability to breathe again. She cleared her throat before speaking again. "No. I haven't heard from Mom. Nothing since she left."

"I'm sorry. I didn't mean to make you sad."

"It's okay." Avery flexed her hands, loosening them from their white-knuckle grip on the steering wheel. "Anyway, I just got the chance to get my senior pictures free. And you'll never believe the ones she took with this gorgeous rainbow behind me." Avery went on to give the details of the session, all mom-related tension slowly dissipating as she continued.

"That's awesome. I can't wait to see them. So, are you going to give one to Jaxson?" Her friend's voice rose in childlike glee.

"Yes. I probably will." Although Avery didn't consider herself a giggly kind of girl, she felt a glee similar to Katie's bloom inside her.

"Will it be the first one you give out?" Katie teased.

"Maybe." Avery smiled and waited to see how long it would take for Katie to break down.

"Oooo. Come on! I want details. You haven't told me any good stuff and you know it. What's the juice?" She demanded.

It felt so good to laugh, so free and light. She hadn't felt this way since before her great aunt died.

"Where did you go? How'd he ask you? What was the kiss like? I want the good dirt." There was a scuffle on Katie's end of the phone. "Hold on." Muffled sound crackled across the line as Katie must've put her hand on the phone. "I gotta go. But you're not off the hook. You will tell me next time we're together."

"All right, all right, all right." Avery promised before she hung up.

Her phone beeped. It was Michael's number. Because of her flat, and the fact Avery didn't have any of her phone book carried over to her new phone, Katie had put all their numbers in Avery's phone the day they tie-dyed the shirts.

"Hello?" she asked, confused to why Michael would be calling.

"Hey, Avery. Jaxson wanted me to call you. There was an accident in football practice, and he's on his way to the E.R." A shrill whistle blew, almost drowning out Michael's words.

"Oh my gosh. Is he okay? What happened?"

"Probably a small concussion, Coach said. I gotta go. If I get caught talking on the phone I have to run laps."

"Okay, thanks for calling." Avery hurried past the slow drivers on the interstate into town.

Even being the middle of the week, the parking lot for Valley's only hospital was nearly full. She ran from her car into the lobby. Having volunteered for the community blood drive before, she knew her way around.

"Hey, Avery. You got an appointment?" Rose, the receptionist, greeted her. She wore scrubs with cartoon pictures on them, her hair pulled back in a knot. Of all the women she had worked with, she'd liked Rose the best.

"No. I came to see a friend. Has Jaxson Stewart been brought in?" The words came out breathy from her hurry.

The woman gave her a knowing look over the top of her glasses. "Sure, he's back in ER room one. I know you're not a relative. Are you his girlfriend?"

Avery glanced around, chewing her lip. Most everyone in the waiting room were elderly people she didn't know or mothers with their young children. "Yeah, I guess you could say that."

"Okay, hon. Let me get the doctor's permission for you to go back and see him." She entered a doorway into the main nurses' station to the ER.

Avery rocked back and forth on her feet. She put her hands into her pockets to keep from wringing them. What was taking Rose so long? She walked over to the partitioned waiting area and sat down just as the nurse returned. She jumped back up.

"Come on in." The door into the emergency room beeped. Avery opened the heavy door and followed the cartoon-clad woman.

"We tried to call his parents, but were only able to leave a message on their home number." Rose grabbed a file on the wall outside of a door labeled ERRM1. "Do you have any cell numbers where we can reach them?"

Warmth from the sun in the car drained out of Avery's face. Her hands grew cold and clammy. "Is it serious? Is he okay?"

"No, nothing like that. Someone just needs to drive him home." She opened the door, but the room was empty. "They took him to the scanner to get some X-rays and make sure it's not a serious concussion. But he was talking and joking when he came in."

Avery stood up taller, the weight on her shoulders dissipating. She blew out a deep breath she realized she'd been holding.

"He'll be back in a second. It'll be a good surprise to have you here when he gets back. He's such a nice boy. You picked a good one." Rose smiled and patted her hand.

Avery blushed. "Thanks." After Rose left, she looked around the sparse room. Machinery and medical tools lined the walls. A small sink sat in the corner with gloves, cotton balls, and tongue depressors in glass decanters on the counter. The floor tiles were the same color as the walls. Goosebumps raced across her arms. It hadn't changed any since Aunt Penny died.

A man with blue scrubs burst through the wide door, navigating a wheelchair with Jaxson in it. Two nurses followed them in, everyone laughing and chatting about football.

"Hey, Avery. You got Michael's call?" Jaxson sounded relieved. His left eye was swollen and red. He was shirtless, a bandage wrapped around his left shoulder. Beside the bandage glowed the scar from the heart surgery Jaxson had as a child.

Avery had forgotten about Jaxson's heart condition. You couldn't tell because he was so energetic. And it had been years since he'd had the procedure to fix it.

She stood back as they helped Jaxson onto the hospital bed. One nurse placed a gray monitor on his middle finger and punched several buttons on the machine. The nurse pointed at him and said, "Don't do anything to set this machine off, Jax." She turned and smiled at Avery. "Keep my cousin in line, will ya? Make sure he stays calm enough so we can release him." The girl winked at her. "I'm going to call Uncle John again."

When everyone left the room, Avery walked over to the bed. "You scared me. What happened?" She tried to avoid staring at his scarred, but handsome chest, focusing instead on his eyes.

"I was on the wrong end of a tackle. Kind of got dog-piled." An adorable sheepish look crossed his face.

She ignored how cute he was for the moment, anger flaring in her stomach. "Dog-piled? Like let's kill the underclassmen kind of dog-pile? It was Shane Pratt, wasn't it? He's team captain now, and I know he likes to be a hotshot. I can't stand bullies, especially ones like Shane! Why do the coaches still let this stupid stuff happen?"

"Hey, I'm okay. It's all good. Besides, with you here to nurse me back to health, the joke's on Shane." He grabbed her hand and pulled her closer to his side.

She brushed her fingers gingerly across his blackening eye. Her lips thinned out, tensing against the fury flowing hot in her veins. How could he think it was okay? "Have you looked in a mirror recently?" Taking a deep breath, she willed back the frustration.

"I only want to look into your gorgeous green eyes." He grabbed her other hand and held her tight, the monitor on his finger pressing into the palm of her hand.

His touch calmed her. "You're going to get me in trouble with your cousin."

They were nose to nose when the door behind them opened.

"Looks like our patient is feeling better." Doctor Kimball entered holding a set of X-rays in his hand, and chuckling. Jaxson's dad followed behind the physician. His jeans had smudges of grease across them, his plaid shirt sweat-stained.

"Hey there, son. Seems like you're on the mend." Mr. Stewart winked at her.

Avery stepped back, arms crossed over her chest, face burning.

"Will I live, Doc?" Jaxson asked, not embarrassed that his father had seen them bent together, almost kissing.

The white-haired physician looked at him over his wire-rimmed glasses, humor sparkling in his faded blue eyes. "No sign of a concussion. Your heart's normal. Vitals look good. The rest are just bruises and strains. Looks like you're going to live after all. I was beginning to wonder how I was going to pay for that new car." He chuckled. "You can take your son home."

"Glad we could keep you living in the manner you've become accustomed to," Mr. Stewart joked.

At Avery's obvious look of confusion, Jaxson explained. "Dr. Hansen delivered me. He's the one who diagnosed my heart condition."

"Your specialists did too good a job. I haven't had to see you much lately. John, I need you to sign some papers, and then Jaxson can leave." Both men walked out of the room, chatting like old friends.

Avery should have realized they would be concerned about his childhood condition. "I knew you were sick when you were a baby. Do you still have problems?"

"Nah. I haven't had anything serious for about seven years now. I have to be tested every year before I go out for sports, but other than that I'm good."

She had stepped close enough for him to take her hand in his again.

He pulled her close to him. "Do you think they'd let me play football if there were any chance I'd have problems?"

She shrugged. "No, I guess not." Her eyes traveled down the muscles on his stomach. The air between them heated. Avery looked up to keep her thoughts out of the danger zone.

"I promise I'll show you how good my shape is at the Street Dance tonight." He wiggled his eyebrows.

Chapter Twelve

(Truth #7: With enemies like you, who needs friends?)

Music blared out of gigantic speakers on either side of the band shell theater in Honey Creek's City Park. A four block square was blocked off for the Fourth of July carnival. Avery drove around twice before finding a spot in the residential area three blocks away.

Corn dogs and cotton candy scented the cool evening air. A chilly breeze carried the electrical charge of a storm predicted for later that night; all mingled in an invigorating rush.

Normally Avery put her hair in a ponytail, but tonight she had made several small braids on the side and twisted them together with the loose hair in the back making a sloppy, but cute bun. She wore another of her favorite outfits: a purple sparkly blouse and bejeweled jeans. But even with the jeans, goose bumps rose on her skin.

Avery clenched her hands against thoughts of who might be here tonight, and of who should be but wasn't. Absent-minded, she walked down the familiar sidewalk, past the neon sign above The Still Bar & Grill, the place her parents always frequented on the Fourth.

A large, leather-clad man stepped in front of her. Thanks to his Irish heritage, Big Jim's white hair stuck out against his ruddy skin. His bulbous nose twitched above a rusty cream mustache. The picture he took of her and her parents flashed in her mind. Where was her dad tonight? Would she see him here? What was her mom doing right now? She fought the twinge of nostalgia the memories brought, determined not to think about her mom or her dad, or let them ruin her night.

Jim's burly arm grabbed her in a side hug, his massive presence swallowing her whole. "Hey, girl. Good to see you. You here alone?"

He set her back down on her feet. Comfort rushed through her. Big Jim knew her, knew her parents, and never wavered from his friendship and support. "I'm meeting a friend."

"Oh? He better treat you right, or he'll have to answer to me." Big Jim pointed to his broad chest, the muscles beneath his grim reaper tattoo flexing in a sinister dance.

She laughed. "He's one of the good guys, Jim. I'm probably the bad influence on him."

"Heh, heh. You keep it that'a way. Say, I heard about your momma. Can't say it surprised me. Your Aunt Penny must be flipping in her grave!" Someone called out Jim's name from inside the bar.

Avery frowned when he turned away. The stab to her heart she'd successfully avoided only moments before took hold. She pressed her hand against her chest.

He turned back to her, oblivious to her inner struggle. "Anyway, I'm real sorry for what you're going through. You just call me if you need anything." Big Jim grabbed her in a bone-crushing squeeze again before he set her down once more, leaving her standing alone in the crowd, a stunned look on her face.

Someone tapped her shoulder from behind, startling her. She spun around.

"Hey, Avery!" It was Davis Stewart, Jaxson's cousin. His dark, curly hair matched that of his sister Trisha, who stood next to him. She stood hand-in-hand with Landon—the junior Avery had seen at the Chute. Landon stared out over Trisha's head, apparently remembering that night and avoiding her.

Avery's eyes watered at the amount of body spray Davis had on. It left her throat burning, and she had to step back from the boy. "Hi, guys. Have you seen Jaxson?" Her words came out choked.

Davis tilted his head. "Last I saw, he was over by the swings waiting for someone."

"Thanks. See ya." She waved goodbye, but Davis caught her arm.

"You going to dance?" he asked.

"Duh, dork. She's at the Street Dance, of course she's going *to* dance." Trisha rolled her eyes. She and Landon laughed while Davis sent them dirty looks and blushed.

Avery had sympathy on him. "Yeah. Why?"

Davis smiled, a grateful look on his face. "Save me a dance, would you?"

She hesitated. "Oh, I don't know. I'm kind of here with someone."

Trisha and Landon both snickered before walking away, hand in hand.

"Oh, okay. Well, if you get a chance, I'll be around." Davis said, eagerness coming off him in waves.

"Sure." Avery wound her way through the crowds toward the outer area of the park and the swings.

Several of MaKenzie's friends stood in a group talking and laughing in the doorway of the flower shop. Avery moved across the street, trying to blend in to avoid their sight.

Jaxson's blond head was easy to spot without his usual baseball cap on. He leaned against a tree. He wore a light blue western shirt with a dark blue t-shirt underneath and jeans. Usually he wore boots, but he had on a pair of blue tennis shoes. Her pulse quickened.

A wide grin lit up his face when he turned and saw her. She walked up to him, her feet barely touching the ground.

"Hey. You changed your hair. I like it." He reached out and ran a finger across the braid pinned beside her ear, sending tingles down her neck.

Although Jaxson was the one with the heart condition, she thought she was going to have heart failure. "Thanks, I wanted to look special for tonight." She bumped him with her shoulder. "You look pretty amazing with that black eye."

He put his arm around her waist. "Just call me Rocky."

The smell of his body spray set off fireworks inside her. It wasn't too strong, like Davis's. She was sure he could hear her heartbeat as it raced through her body.

They made their way toward the music. Dozens of couples and young children danced on top of the concrete square in front of a rounded stage. Huge speakers vibrated to the beat as a country band belted out a love song.

Next to the stage, an area had been roped off, separating the beer garden from the small white building that served food and non-alcoholic drinks. Benches and chairs were set in rows on both sides—the beer garden side full while the other side had several spots empty—filled mostly with older people.

The heady scent of loose-meat sandwiches, the best in the county, made Avery groan. "Hungry?" Jaxson asked as they stood in line to buy something to drink.

She hadn't had time to get something to eat before she came, not that there was much in her cupboards or fridge at home. "Yeah, a little."

Jaxson paid for two pops and a loose-meat sandwich basket that included chips and pickles. They headed to an empty spot beneath an older covered building. The wooden benches had seen better days, several coats of bright-colored paint chipped off in varying places, but they were clean. There they were sheltered from the cool breeze, now thick enough for them to sense the rain it promised. Jaxson sat with his back to the wall, facing the stage, and straddling the bench. Avery sat down in front of him. She finished the sandwich quickly, giving Jaxson the pickles, knowing she could easily eat another one before she was completely full.

Davis walked up to them. "Nice shiner! I thought they were going to have to shock you back to life after they laid you out like that." His glance took in Avery from head to toes.

Avery frowned at him. "That's not funny, Davis."

Jaxson took it in stride, laughing at his injuries. "I've been through worse. Gets the girl, though." He hugged Avery to his chest.

Davis gave an awkward, half-hearted laugh. "Yeah, right. See you guys later."

A familiar voice cut through the noise. Avery glanced toward the beer garden. Sophie sat amongst a group of ten people right and next to a man dressed in a military uniform. Brody. Her friend's face was flushed. Raucous laughter drowned out the normal din of voices.

A knot formed in Avery's throat. She looked away toward the band stage and watched the dancers.

"What's up between you and Sophie?" Jaxson took a drink of his pop.

She cringed. "Why?"

"I haven't heard you talk about her, and I saw the way she glanced at us when we walked by." He put his chin on her shoulder. "Is this about that Brody guy?"

She fidgeted. Avery didn't want to tell him about Brody, but it was all over ChatterBox. "She's mad at me because the other night at the Chute, MaKenzie made it seem like I made a move on her boyfriend."

"Did you?" Jaxson's breath tickled some loose hair on the side of her head.

She turned to look at him straight in the eye. "No, I didn't. He's a perv, a liar, and a nub."

"Okay," Jaxson said before looking away.

She stiffened. "Okay, what?"

"Okay. I believe you." His blue eyes were somber and trusting as he stared down at her.

"Thank you." Tears prickled her eyes. She hadn't realized how much it would mean for him to believe her.

Lights flickered to life over the dance area as the sun set. Sophie and her group made their way onto the concrete floor. The dancers moved in haphazard sync in a group dance as the band played a popular song. Avery would have thought the effort amusing had Sophie not been among the dancers. Between her pigeon-toes and the too-high heels, she was not graceful at all. But Brody made the most of it, holding on to her and bumping into her on purpose.

Jaxson leaned in and whispered, "Let's go out on the next slow dance."

His chest was up against her back, arms hung loose at her sides. Avery savored being this close to Jaxson. A calm sense of security she so seldom felt settled over her. She allowed herself to relax against him, careful to avoid his injured shoulder. "I'd love to."

She lost sight of Sophie in the throng of dancers. Several songs played before the music shifted to a slow one. Jaxson took her hand and led her to the dance floor.

Her heart raced. It wasn't the first time she had ever danced with anyone. But it was the first time it had ever mattered.

She was glad she chose her comfortable, heeled sandals. Her arms would have been stretched to reach his shoulders had she been wearing flip-flops. They moved well together. Jaxson kept a comfortable distance between them, not too close and yet not too far. The song ended too soon, and they headed back to their bench.

She had her hand in his when someone bumped into her on the side of the dance floor.

It was a muscled guy wearing a Honey Creek football jersey. His dark hair was a mess of curls. He caught Avery's arm as she jerked back. "Sorry," he said. He smiled at Avery.

Jaxson moved closer to Avery and put his arm around her waist. Someone bumped her from behind.

"S'cuse me," came the slurred voice. Sophie's voice.

Avery hadn't noticed her and Brody dancing as they had made their path around the dance floor, she'd been too wrapped up in Jaxson.

Sophie wrinkled her nose at Avery. "Oh. It's you. My FBF. Tired of spreading lies about my boyfriend, yet?" She looked at Jaxson and laughed. "Babysitting?"

The football guy and his friends laughed.

Avery stood up straighter and ignored the Honey Creek group. "Better than statutory charges." She didn't hear the next comment out of Sophie's mouth because Jaxson pulled her toward their seats. The football players were laughing and pointing at her and Sophie.

"What did you do that for? I was just getting started." A breeze cooled her anger-heated skin.

Jaxson spun her away from the sight of her FBF. "I know." He laced her hand in his. "I was saving you from something you might regret later."

"Well, if it isn't Avery 'my mother is a home-wrecking whore and so am I' Denton. Isn't that the guy I saw you all over the other night?"

Avery dropped her head at MaKenzie's words. She knew this night was too good to be true. Something was bound to spoil it.

"Does that make you MaKenzie 'my father's a dirty rotten fornicator' Thomas?" Sophie's voice rang clear, though still slurred.

Chapter Thirteen

(Lie #6: The opinion others have of you is their problem.)

"Maybe you should spend a few nights thinking about your own dad's behavior instead of doing whatever it is you do…like suck the joy out of others' lives." Sophie held MaKenzie's skinnier cheerleader's arm in a tight clasp.

MaKenzie tore her arm out from Sophie's grasp. "Tweedle Dee standing up for Tweedle Dumb. How precious, you're still friends. You must like swapping dates."

"MaKenzie, just walk away. Don't make yourself look like a fool." Jaxson scowled at her.

"And leave you with your precious new girlfriend alone? I don't think so. You know what her mother did, right? It's not the first time, either. Next time you talk to your mom, Avery, you should ask her how it feels to finally weasel her way into my dad's life."

"You little…" Sophie stepped toward MaKenzie.

The football players and GI men formed a circle around them, drawing everybody's attention.

Jaxson held out his hand, stopping Sophie from continuing her tirade. "This isn't about Avery's mother, MaKenzie, and you know it. So quit attacking her."

Avery twisted, giving him a questioning glance. Jaxson stared at MaKenzie, anger making his nostrils flare.

Brody walked up behind Sophie and handed her a red plastic cup, breaking the terse silence.

"A red cup, really? Did you at least get a mixed drink? Beer is so Hicksville." MaKenzie flipped her perfectly curled hair over her shoulder.

Lauren and Asia walked up to MaKenzie, laughing at her dig. They were all dressed in skin-tight outfits that dipped in the front, revealing their bikini tan lines.

"No. I'll just throw up like some people I know." Sophie pointed her cup at the other girls, sloshing the amber colored liquid around. She chugged half the drink, crinkled the cup, and then threw it at them.

The girls jumped back, shrieking. MaKenzie swiped at the beer running down her short dress.

Brody chuckled. The Honey Creek's football players all laughed.

Avery silently applauded her friend. *No, make that former best friend.*

"Let's go before this gets any uglier," Jaxson said as he turned her around and led her back toward the street.

Tears stung her eyes as they walked. When had everything gotten so complicated?

Jaxson stopped at the opposite end of the park where they had entered. "Don't listen to MaKenzie. Her opinion doesn't matter."

"What were you talking about with her, anyway? Why was she really doing this?" Avery crossed her arms.

A corner of Jaxson's mouth curled downward. "Just that she's not mad at you. She's mad at other stuff, and she doesn't need to take it out on you. That's all." He grazed her cheeks with the backs of his fingers.

A pebble of doubt twisted in her gut.

"Let's not think about anybody else." He leaned down, his breath warm against her chilled skin. "Let's just concentrate on us."

"That I can do." Avery grinned before kissing him.

***

The next morning Avery arrived in Honey Creek an hour earlier than the parade start time to get a decent parking spot. People sitting on blankets and lawn chairs covered the sidewalks and grassy banks along the parade route. Children ran back and forth toting plastic shopping bags or ice cream buckets ready for the promise of candy.

The oak tree on the courthouse lawn was one of the best spots to sit as it stretched out half way across the grass and held the most shade of any place in town. Since Avery had outgrown chasing for candy, a spot up next to the tree was the perfect place to set her chair up.

She bought an ice cold bottle of water from a clown pulling around a cart of balloon animals, stuffed toys, and a cooler full of drinks. The July humidity already made her sticky with perspiration, although it was only eight thirty in the morning. It was going to be one scorcher of a day.

A loud speaker across the street at the sheriff's office played tinny patriotic music. The emcee spoke over it to make announcements about the sponsors of the parade, expounding the highlights of floats and displays from years past. Avery was bored out of her skull. What was she doing here? Parades were not her thing.

Her thoughts drifted back to the street dance. And to Jaxson. She was touched by his sweet attention, but wary. Her dad used to tell her if it seems too good to be true, it probably is. Not that she believed everything her parents told her, but this one had been true in the past.

Jaxson was quickly becoming the brightest part of her life, and if she was honest about it, it scared her. Good things never lasted. The past few months had proven that. Her parents' marriage was over, her best friend hated her, and she lost her job all in the matter of a couple of weeks. Could life get any worse?

Avery chided herself. Asking if it could get any worse was like inviting trouble. Her phone buzzed, breaking her out of her thoughts. It was a text from Jaxson.

Jaxson: *where are you?*

Avery: *Courthouse lawn. why?*

Jaxson: *wanted to be sure i saw you when i go by.*

She smiled to herself. *I'll wave at you.*

Jaxson: *cant wait to see you later.☺ meet me at the park after parade?*

Avery: *OK.☺*

A familiar-looking woman setting up an umbrella chair to Avery's left caught her eye. When she turned, she knew why. It was MaKenzie's mother, Monica Thomas. Several other people sat up chairs and blankets around her. Their umbrellas were as large as the ones for patio tables, and hinged so they could be adjusted. A guy Avery recognized as a Valley city council member secured the umbrellas behind the women's chairs, allowing an ample amount of shade. The women eyed him like dogs watching a bone, but he didn't seem to mind.

Avery slid down in her seat. She put her sunglasses on and turned to face the other way. Their voices carried, however. At first they discussed the council member and what they wouldn't do to be twenty years younger. The conversation quickly moved to Monica and Phillip Thomas's marriage status. Her fingers clutched the metal armrest of her chair when they started talking about her mother.

"Do you think it's a mid-life crisis?" The woman who spoke wore an outfit fit for a magazine, matching in every detail from her hat to her sandals. Her mocha-tanned legs shone as if oiled. On her arm clinked several bracelets, and glittering rings adorned most of her fingers. "I mean, what was Phil thinking? Leaving you for *her*?"

"Now, now, Claudia. We aren't going to ruin the day with talk of my soon to be ex-husband. Dineen may think she's won, but I will get the best of him when the divorce goes through."

Claudia Griffin worked at the Courthouse as County Treasurer and her husband owned a large real estate agency in Honey Creek. Even if Avery did not know who they were by name, she'd recognize them from the newspaper ads and political flyers that often accompanied their mail.

"You're giving up so easily? I thought you had more fight in you than that, Monica," another floppy-hat-wearing woman stated. She swung a colorful Chinese fan in front of her face, sweat glimmering on her brow.

Mrs. Thomas's shadowed outline in the umbrella spun to face the woman. "The first time I was determined, and I fought for him and won. Bad news like her never changes faces. I've worked eighteen long years. I'll get what I deserve. It's only a matter of time now. Besides, if they are together, I don't have to keep his guilty little secrets any longer." Her words held an acidic tone.

The floppy-hat woman spoke. "I heard you got the upper hand on the competition the other day. Did Jeff put up much of a fight firing that girl?"

"My brother would not have the grocery store if it weren't for me. He doesn't have room to complain after all I've done to keep him out of trouble. And as for that girl," Mrs. Thomas waved her hand as if "that girl" was of no consequence, "girls like her are a dime a dozen. She'll be on welfare with a kid on her hip before you know it. Jeff can hire someone else in a heartbeat."

"What about the bank fiasco? Did your attorneys manage to get your account from being frozen?" Claudia asked.

Mrs. Thomas's laughter was bitter. "My attorney has spoken with the bank and with Phillip. Just because he quit his job does not mean they were allowed to close our accounts. They've opened them back up. What happened to MaKenzie in the store the other day won't happen again."

"Hold your ground. It's your town, after all. I'm glad Lucky Realty finally got the hint and fired Dineen Denton. Out with the trash." The floppy-hat woman spoke as if she were discussing the weather.

Welfare. Trash. *That's all they see.* Enough was enough. Avery stood and folded up her red lawn chair. Gathering her purse, she turned and walked back across the courthouse lawn.

It took all of her strength not to break down. She concentrated on her feet, the uneven ground blurred from tears, but two hands on her arms caught her. The chair she had been carrying dropped to the ground at her feet.

"Hey, hey. Slow down there. Aren't you headed in the wrong direction?"

Avery jumped as if she'd been shocked. Mr. Stewart's kind eyes, so like his son Jaxson's, gazed down at her. Behind him gathered the whole Stewart family, except for Jaxson and his younger brother Riley who were both in the parade. A traitorous tear slid down her cheek which she quickly swiped away.

"Whew! Sure is hot, huh?" She mumbled, rubbing her hand across her forehead for effect.

Mrs. Stewart stepped out from behind her husband, a blanket and basket full of food in her arms. "Hi, Avery. I was hoping to run into you. Would you like to come sit with us? I brought snacks." Mrs. Stewart raised the basket to entice her. Emily, her five-year-old daughter, stared at Avery from behind her mother's legs.

"Thank you. But I'm not feeling so well after all. You know, the heat. I think I'm just going to go home. Will you tell Jaxson I'm sorry I missed the parade?" She didn't feel well, but it was deeper than the physical. Her soul was bruised too. Still, she felt awful for lying to the Stewarts.

Jaxson's three-year-old little sister Delilah grabbed Avery's hand in her chubby little one. Avery looked down at the curly-headed cherub face. Delilah's eyes were darker blue than Jaxson's, but held the same twinkle. "You can sit by me. Perty pease?"

Her heart flipped in her chest. What was it about this family that got under her skin so easily?

"Now Delilah. Avery's not feeling well. What do we do when you're not feeling well?" Mrs. Stewart, asked her daughter.

The little girl clapped her hands together. "Tuck me in my bed, bring me hot chocolate, and read me stories?"

Mrs. Stewart smiled. "That's right. Avery needs to go home and go to bed if she's not feeling well."

The little girl's smile filled her face. "Oh, goodie. I make the bestest hot chocowate, Avie."

Avery picked up her chair, hiding a grin at the enthusiasm Jaxson's sister inherited from him. It was tempting to stay just to talk with her.

"No, cupcake. You have to stay with us and watch Jaxson and Riley in the parade. Don't you want some candy?" Mr. Stewart spoke, an indulgent look on his face.

"Yes, yes, yes!" Golden curls bopped up and down on her head.

Mrs. Stewart put her hand on Avery's shoulder. "Are you sure you don't want to stay, even for a little while? We've got great seats over at my sister's house under her trees. Far away from the central lawn and gossip fest that I'm sure is going on. Plenty of shade."

Avery glanced back at the umbrella group. She relented. "Okay." She followed the Stewarts and prayed that it would be a Thomas-free zone.

Jaxson's 4-H float rode by half way through the parade. The theme of the parade was "Growing American Spirit." They'd won first place in their division, and it was easy to see why. Mr. Stewart had loaned the group his long hay trailer which they painted red, white, and blue. Adorning every corner were dozens of corn stalks, soybean plants, flowers and all kinds of vegetables. It looked like a mobile piece of farmland.

The 4-Hers wore tie-dyed red-white-and-blue shirts suspiciously like those Katie and she had made for the Carter's family reunion. Just like the tie dye shirt she was currently wearing.

"Look, Avie! You and Jaxson match." Delilah hugged Avery before running toward the street to grab a handful of candy her brother had tossed out at them.

She waved, hoping her face didn't show how completely thrilled she was to see him. The rest of the parade went by in a blur as she tried to sort out her feelings for this boy who had once been a younger, boy-next-door kind of friend.

"Avie, I wike your shoes. Whewh did you get them?" Delilah and Emily were both playing with the strips of denim and tie-dyed shirt on the straps of her shoes.

She laughed. "I can help you make them. Do you have any extra pieces of jeans lying around?"

"Do we Mom? Do we have extra wying awound?" Delilah begged her mother.

"I'm sure between Jaxon and Riley we have lots of scraps you can use. You need to ask Avery first if she's coming over to our house before worrying about pieces of fabric for your sandals. Ask her if she's feeling better."

The curly mop of a girl bounded into Avery's arms and whispered in her ear what her mother had told her to ask. The shyer, older Emily came over and put her hand on Avery's arm, her eyebrows raised in question.

"Okay, okay. How can I say no to both of you?" Avery laughed when the girls shrieked and ran around like two puppies chasing each other.

"Hope you're feeling better, cuz it looks like you're going to be busy entertaining two little girls all afternoon." Mr. Stewart chuckled.

They all packed up their blankets and chairs and made their way back to their cars.

Avery admitted to herself that it was better than being alone. By a long shot.

Voices caught Avery's attention as she walked back to her car. No sidewalk graced the vacant property she crossed, and behind a lilac bush she spied MaKenzie and her mother arguing.

"When am I going to get my card back?" MaKenzie's fists were on her hips.

Mrs. Thomas looked down her button nose at her daughter. "I already told you to be patient. If I work this right, you won't have to worry about your father's oversight or spending limits. We'll be right where we want to be."

"We? You mean you. You had to push and push. My summer and senior year are ruined because you couldn't wait." MaKenzie stomped her booted foot, and her plum suede-fringed skirt swung back and forth. The cream button-down shirt complimented her golden-tan skin.

"You'd better watch that smart mouth of yours. You might be able to wrap your dad around your finger, but I'm not him. You and I both know you're a spoiled rotten brat. Besides, only one of us has her whole life ahead of her. That certainly isn't me. I'm getting what is mine once and for all. You'll be fine." Mrs. Thomas lifted her arm and flung her manicured fingers in a dismissive wave.

And for a moment, Avery felt bad for MaKenzie.

Chapter Fourteen

(Truth #8: Once you get a taste of something good, nothing else will ever be the same.)

Avery had waited until both MaKenzie and her mother walked away in opposite directions before she went to find her car and pick up Jaxson. She didn't need MaKenzie finding out she'd heard the argument, especially since she'd started to feel bad for her. Avery shook off those thoughts. Tonight was about her and Jaxson.

Jaxson rode with Avery to his house since his parents towed the flatbed they'd used as a float. She glanced at him as she drove.

"So, what's up with the shirts?" she asked.

He chuckled. "We were doing the tie-dye shirts for the float first." He shrugged. "I told Mrs. Carter about them since she was looking to do something for the reunion."

"Uh, huh. Right." Wearing matching shirts with her boyfriend should have annoyed her, but it was sweet in a weird way.

His smile widened. "You're not implying I did that on purpose, are you?"

"Yes, actually. I am." She punched him.

He grasped his arm. "You wound me, fair maiden. You think that I, a knight in tie-dye armor, would do such a heinous thing?" He laughed. "If I'd have thought of it, I would've. It just happens to be a happy coincidence."

She pulled into his driveway. "I don't believe in coincidences, happy or otherwise. You, my friend, are sneaky." She motioned from her eyes to his. "I've got my eyes on you."

His parents and siblings were piling out of the truck ahead of them, everybody carrying something from the float or the truck into the tan two-story farmhouse.

Jaxson unbuckled his seatbelt. He turned toward her in the car and took her hand in his. "I'll have to live up to the dastardly fiend you think I am, then."

Avery narrowed her eyes at him. "Bring it, Stewart. Now that I know what you're truly like, I'll be harder to catch in your sly traps."

Delilah pounded on Avery's window, making her jump and blush. "Avie, c'mon."

She grabbed the chips she bought at the supermarket and followed Jaxson into the farmhouse. The family buzzed around, busy putting things away and setting up for the party.

"Jaxson, I need you in the kitchen," Mrs. Stewart called out.

"In here, Avie." Delilah tugged at Avery's arm, dragging her to the couch in the family room.

Avery was in the middle of showing Jaxson's sisters how to put the cloth strips on their flip-flops when Davis and his sister, Trisha, entered with their family. Trisha wore a two-piece swimsuit topped with an intricate crocheted beach cover and sleek, heeled sandals. In her arm she carried a beach bag with several items, including a blow-up pool lounger.

Trisha glanced at the shoes they were decorating, and with a mumbled "cute" walked out to the pool to sunbathe. Davis leaned over them, untying one of the knots. Delilah and Emily chased after him screaming and crying.

The farmhouse filled with relatives, many Avery knew from around the county, and some she didn't. When Jaxson's sisters finished working on their flip-flops, they ran off to their rooms, wearing their "new" shoes, to play with two of their cousins. Jaxson was outside showing some relatives the fireworks his father bought, leaving Avery alone.

It was like being a third wheel to a crowd. What was left of her family rarely ever got together. The Stewarts all joked and talked like old friends. Avery wasn't sure how to act.

She walked around the first floor of the house, studying the photos of everyone that lined walls and shelves everywhere. There were pictures of the kids by the pool in the summer, jumping into leaves in the fall, building a snowman in the winter, and splashing in the rain in the spring.

A lump formed in her throat. The only photograph they had in their house was an old photo of her mother's family her Aunt Penny had had up forever. There weren't any school photos of her or family shots besides the one in her room with her and her parents.

Her mother claimed it was because she wasn't an interior designer. She didn't hang pictures or knickknacks, and her dad couldn't care less. Still, hurt pricked her heart that her family couldn't bring themselves to get a frame to put a picture of her up somewhere.

The difference in their homes was obvious. Her home was a dysfunctional, disorderly mess. His home was a pinnacle of a loving family. What was she doing here? She wasn't trash like the women from the parade said she was, but here…here she didn't belong.

Avery crossed her arms to fight the wave of insecurity that threatened to make her run far, far away. A composite of Jaxson's school photos hung in a frame above the stairway which led to the second floor. She moved up the stairs to get a better look. The pictures started in Kindergarten and ended with his freshman picture. She remembered when she was in fifth grade, the year she moved to Valley. Jaxson would've been in third grade. He had been such a little pipsqueak with enormous blue eyes and Dumbo-like ears, scrambling to make his way up the steps into the big, yellow bus. *Wow, how things changed.*

She smiled and put her hand on the glass, as if by touching it she could feel him beneath her fingertips. He had matured in the past year. More than she realized.

"See anything you like?" Jaxson stood on the step below her, his head level with hers.

"You were cute. What happened to you?" She ruffled his hair.

"Ay, not the hair." He put his arms around her waist. "What'd you mean, I WAS cute?"

She looked him straight in the eye and smoothed down the hair she'd mussed. "Well, you're still kinda cute. Just not as cute—"

He pulled her in for a quick kiss. "Oh really? How cute am I now?" He gave her another pecking kiss. "How about now?" He tilted her head down and pressed his lips against her forehead.

"Get a room, man." Davis smacked Jaxson on the arm. "You guys gonna come out to the pool sometime this century?"

***

Avery changed in the main bathroom. Her suit was two years old but even though it still fit, she hated that she couldn't afford a new one right now. She wished she owned something like Trisha's crocheted cover-up to dress it up a bit.

Someone knocked at the door. "Avery, are you in there?" It was Jaxson's mom.

She rushed to pack her clothes into her beach bag. "Yes. I'm sorry. I'll be out in a minute."

"Oh, no hurry. Jaxson wanted to know if you were changed yet. We're all out by the pool."

"Okay, thank you." Avery looked down at herself. Jaxson had seen her in the swimsuit before. She shouldn't be this nervous. But that was before he asked her out, when she thought of him like a brother. Well, almost. A wave of heat washed over her remembering how he had rubbed lotion on her back.

Air conditioning chilled her as she walked through the house toward the patio doors that led to the back deck. The backyard lay hidden from view of the road. It was the first time she'd seen it.

Pulling back the blinds, she studied the backyard and pool. Rectangular tables filled with bowls and platters of food stood next to the house. Round tables with chairs surrounded the pool area. Steps led to the pool that rose above the sitting area.

A canvas roll-out roof hung over the majority of the deck. However, due to the direction of the sun there were only small spots of shade. The green and white fabric flapped from the breeze of two large fans set at each end of the wooden floor. Adults sat talking at the tables while Jaxson and his cousins played a game in the pool.

Something tugged on the towel tucked under her arm. "Avie, you coming?"

Avery scrutinized Delilah's sunburned face. "I think you need something on that." She tapped the girl's nose.

"I gots some." Her pudgy hand came out from behind her back. She held a spray bottle of sunscreen. "We can't spway it in the house though, 'cause Mommy says it'll get on stuff."

Avery grinned at her seriousness. "Okay. Let's go outside and get you taken care of."

The scent of chlorine permeated the humid air as they walked hand in hand toward the table near the pool where Jaxson's mom reclined on a wooden patio chair. "There you are. I wouldn't go in the pool yet, Avery. The guys have a water football death match going. It isn't safe." Water sprayed over the pool above them, drenching her towel.

Davis's head appeared over the side. "Sorry. Hey, Avery. You coming in?"

She wrung out the corner of the towel. "Nope."

"Have a seat." Mrs. Stewart patted the damp chair next to her. She sprayed down Delilah, and then sent her off to play in a tree house not far from the deck. Screams and squeals leaked out of the windows of the painted wooden structure built into the tree. Delilah managed the steps that led up to a door in the bottom of the house like a pro.

Avery laid the towel on the cushion of the seat before sitting down.

"What's your dad doing today?" Mrs. Stewart asked.

Avery stared out at the backyard afraid if she turned to face Jaxson's mom, the truth would show in her face. "He's hanging out with some friends of his."

The ice tinkled in Mrs. Stewart's glass of lemonade as she took a drink. "Have you heard from your mom lately?"

Avery contemplated what to tell her. What would Mrs. Stewart think if she told the truth?

Glass shattered against the deck. A red-faced woman stood pointing a finger at the man sitting next to her. "You're a stinking liar and a drunk." She flung her arms wide. "See what you did."

"I should have had Jaxson warn you about the family. We have a couple of embarrassing drunks. Don't pay any attention to them." Mrs. Stewart's words would've been light had they not been spoken through pinched lips.

The man at the table rose, getting nose-to-nose with the woman. Jaxson's uncle—Trisha and Davis's dad—moved in, jerking the man's shoulder. "Danged if you two don't ruin every holiday. Drunks aren't welcome here. You need to leave."

A stiff Mrs. Stewart got up, and steered the duo into the house.

Water dripped on her arm. "Hey!" Jaxson knelt by her side. "Sorry about that scene. It's my uncle and his fourth wife. Ever since they married, he's been frequenting the bar she owns. They're never sober." He shrugged. "It's so embarrassing, being related to them. Even their kids are wastes of space. Must be in the genes."

The smile on Avery's face froze. What was he saying? That if your parents were loser drunks, that made you a waste of space? Avery thought of her mom and dad's drinking. She refused to be like them. Even when she had the chance, like at the bonfire, she never indulged because she hated the way people acted when they drank.

Jaxson was busy drying himself off with a towel to notice her staring at him. The scars on his chest were reddish-purple against his skin. Would he know that her parent's alcoholism created similar scars on her? Only hers were beneath the surface? What would he think if he really knew what her parents were like?

She'd never tell him. Ever.

Chapter Fifteen

(Lie #7: You can't start a fire without a spark.)

Yells sounded in the pool above her. The game was over. Jaxson's cousins exited the water, leaving a watery trail everywhere they went.

Davis dumped a glass of ice pellets on Jaxson's head, spraying her with water. "You guys need to cool off." Davis took off running, Jaxson close on his heels.

On the landing by the pool, Jaxson caught up to Davis and shoved him sideways. Davis's arms flailed in the air seconds before he hit the water. All of the cousins sprang into action, racing back to the pool. Water flew everywhere as they wrestled one another, each one trying to out-dunk the other.

Avery's smile was a bit wooden as Jaxson's words echoed over and over in her mind. Would she be able to hide her life from him? How many lies would she have to tell to keep him from knowing the truth? Was having a relationship with Jaxson worth all the lies?

She glanced around at the Stewarts, all of them talking and laughing like a real family. She wanted that. No, she needed that. It would be worth whatever lie she had to tell, as long as they didn't find out the truth.

When Jaxson returned to Avery's side, he shook his hair out, drenching her in chlorine-scented water. She squealed, putting her arms up and kicking her legs out to shield herself.

"How's it feel to be dating a winner?" His hands clasped her wrists, and he leaned in for a kiss.

She pushed on his chest, giggling. "I wouldn't know."

His face was only centimeters from hers. Water dripped off his long lashes. "So that's how you're going to play it?" His breath was minty, as if he had just brushed his teeth.

Avery's pulse quickened. "That's how it is."

Jaxson slid his arms under her knees and behind her shoulders and hefted her into his arms.

Horrified, she screamed, "Jaxson, put me down!" He carried her up the stairs, to the pool, and tossed her in. She could hear applause erupt even before she slipped fully into the water. When she rose to get out of the pool, several people held up signs with numbers on them.

Jaxson jumped in. With three long strokes he was beside her. "Those scores were a little low. We'll have to practice some more." The gleam in his eye assured her he would keep tossing her in until he got a ten.

"No do-overs." She jumped up behind him and dunked his head in the water. The scores were much better that round.

Later that evening, as the sun burned low in the horizon, Jaxson's family set up chairs and blankets along a hill behind the Stewart's back yard. The adults kept their distance farther up, away from the bug-ridden slope Jaxon and Avery walked to. Parents kept the younger children who hadn't fallen asleep near the lighted area of the pool.

His father and uncle went down to a plowed area where they placed the fireworks for the night's show. There were no trees or buildings around to obscure the view, and for the first time in years, Avery found herself excited to watch the display.

An evening breeze cooled the summer air. Crickets chirped in the grass around them while the younger kids chased lightening bugs. It was about as corny as a Norman Rockwell print, but Avery didn't mind. It had been amazing spending time with the Stewart family. She didn't want it to end.

Jaxson spread a thick sleeping bag out for them to lie upon along with two cushions from an outdoor wicker chair to rest their heads. She snuggled in one of Jaxson's hoodies he'd grabbed for her while getting the sleeping bag.

She turned her head toward Jaxson. "I really like your family."

He grinned back at her. "Yeah, except for my uncle and his wife. Talk about a crazy family, huh?"

Avery stiffened, remembering his comments about his uncle and cousins.

"Hey. I didn't mean to upset you."

"Jaxson, you do not want to compare crazy families with me. I would win, hands down." She joked, but her stomach churned. For a second, she longed to confide in him about what her life was really like. But, that couldn't happen. He'd judge her just like everyone else. What started as a spark of possibility for the barest millisecond sputtered and died. All this domestic normality must have been getting to her.

He narrowed his eyes at her before changing the subject. "Tell me about your senior pictures. We got side tracked by my ER visit the other day." He chewed on a long piece of grass as he spoke.

She was glad for the switch in topics. She told him about the rainbow, and shared details about the photo shoot. "Elaine, the photographer, said if I could work the booth at the County Fair she would cover the cost of the pictures. It would only be during the day when she had photo sessions."

He pointed the chewed up blade at her. "I'll come by and bug you then. There will be free time between my showings when I have nothing to do. Did she say when the pictures will be done?" He took her hand, threading his fingers through hers, and lay down on his side facing her.

She put her other hand against his chest, feeling his strong heartbeat. "That's good since I'll probably be bored out of my mind. But I'm stoked to get any kind of discount on my pictures, which will be done soon. I'm going to have to find a job soon, though. I have to get a tire for my car before I wear the donut completely off."

He brushed a loose strand of hair behind her ear. "I'm sure your dad is glad for the discount, but isn't he willing to help pay for your tire?"

She grabbed at the grass in his mouth, missing it when he pulled away. "You know how parents are."

A rush of air blew over Avery. Someone flipped a blanket out, and then flopped down on it behind her. Relieved at having escaped talking more about her dad, she turned to find

Davis next to her, lying down on the crease between their blanket and his.

"Ready for the fireworks?" Davis breathed hard, the walk down to the area having winded him. He lay on his side, propped up on one arm mirroring Jaxson.

"Davis, you really need to exercise more if that walk did you in," Jaxson joked.

"Nah, I was running around before I came down here." Davis rolled to his back and looked up at the dark expanse above them. Avery glanced up. Stars glinted from their heavenly home. "Anyone know the constellations?" Davis asked.

Avery and Jaxson both shook their heads. She scooted closer to Jaxson, trying to insert more personal space between her and Davis. He reminded her of Katie's cousin who had developed that huge crush on her. Her stomach pinched at the thought. She hoped Davis didn't have a crush on her.

"Thanks for making me look everywhere for you, dork." Trisha stood above them. "Move over." She kicked at her brother, wanting the spot he currently occupied.

"Get your own blanket. This one's mine." He grasped the blanket, possibly fearing Trisha would jerk it out from underneath him.

Trisha dug her heel into Davis's shoulder. "Move it or lose it, loser."

"Ow! You're such a brat." Davis sulked, rubbing his arm. He glared at his sister as he moved over.

"Want some?" Trisha sprayed her arms and legs with bug spray, handing it over to Avery.

"Thanks." She sprayed some on, careful to avoid getting any in their faces. It was weird having Trisha be nice to her since she used to be MaKenzie's best friend. Not that Trisha ever openly made fun of her like MaKenzie, but Trisha did not travel in the same social circles Avery did. She wasn't sure if she trusted her or not.

"So, your mom. How're you doing with all of that?" It was getting so dark that Avery couldn't see Trisha's face well enough to tell if she were really interested or waiting to pounce upon the answer.

"Fine, I guess," Avery hedged.

Trisha ran her hands through her damp black hair, using her fingers as a brush. Avery marveled at how it always seemed to be in perfect order. Trisha leaned down on her elbows, her face turned upwards as if she were sunbathing in the moonlight. "I'm really sorry about your mom leaving. That would suck. I'm sure MaKenzie and her stuck-up posse don't make it any easier."

Avery frowned. She recalled the conversation MaKenzie's mother had with her cronies before the parade. "No. It's been fun. Kind of like a walk in the park. Not a fan of MaKenzie's anymore, I take it?"

Jaxson snorted. "Sorry." He took her hand in his again, twining his fingers with hers. Davis laughed at his cousin's outburst.

Trisha smiled ruefully. "Not so much. Did you hear some drunk chick spilled beer all down the front of that expensive outfit she wore to the street dance? Too bad Daddy's not here to buy her a new one. Hilarious."

Had it been anyone but Sophie, she would be laughing with them also. She didn't understand why Sophie stuck up for her to MaKenzie, except that she hated her more than she hated Avery. "Yeah, I saw it. Firsthand."

"Seriously? Oh my gosh! I would've loved to have seen that. Priceless." Davis pulled on his side of the blanket. "Knock it off, freak!" Trisha yelled. They wrestled around, each one holding a separate side of the quilt.

"I'm on the ground. You're hogging the entire blanket I brought out for ME to use."

"There's more in the house. Geez, ya spaz!" They continued their tug of war.

Avery almost felt sorry for Davis, until he yanked the blanket hard enough to knock his sister over and into her. Trisha's head smacked against Avery's mouth.

"Ow!" both girls cried at the same time.

Jaxson's arm was around her immediately, rolling her back against him. "Knock it off, Davis."

Avery had never heard Jaxson get upset or yell at anyone. She was more than annoyed with Davis herself. However, she didn't want them to get into a fight. "I'm okay, Jaxson. Trisha, are you all right?" She put her hand over the swelling lip, tasting blood that came from the split on the inside of her mouth.

"I will be as soon as I get my hands on him." Trisha got up, slipped out of her heeled sandals, and took off at a run after her brother. She caught him in a few easy strides and tackled him like a football player, pummeling her squealing brother with her fists.

"Let me see." Jaxson tilted her head back to get a look at her. He touched it gingerly with his finger. "You sure you're okay?"

His concern warmed her and she smiled. The cut hurt and she rubbed the spot. "Yes, Dr. Stewart. I've had worse, I'll live."

His crooked grin spread across his face. "Too bad it wasn't the eye. We would match."

Avery laughed and playfully punched him. "Yeah, like you I'd rock that look. Just call me Rocky two." Jaxson tickled her until tears ran down her face. "You're going to make me a slobbering mess."

Jaxson caressed her lip with his thumb. "Yeah, but you rock the slobbering mess look." Laughing, he kissed her.

It was sweet, like the first time he kissed her on Mercer's Hill. Her toes curled and she put her arms around him.

Just then the first of the fireworks went off, lighting up the night sky.

Chapter Sixteen

(Lie #8: Time is only an illusion)

The rest of Avery's weekend crawled by. Jaxson and his siblings got their animals and displays ready to present at the Harrison County Fair. Trash would be the only thing left of the carnival and Fourth of July celebrations in Honey Creek. With Sophie not talking to her and Katie out of town for her family reunion, there was nowhere for her to go.

She tackled the mounds of dirty clothes in the laundry room, discovering two fifty-dollar bills and a skeleton key left behind in the wash bin. The bills were laid out on her dresser in her room to dry flat. They'd buy gas and groceries, and hopefully were her mom's so her dad wouldn't have reason to talk to her.

The key she remembered her Aunt Penny wearing around her neck. Why? Where was the lock it opened? Avery walked around the house, but the key didn't match any of the doors. She found an old necklace chain and after threading it through the end, put it around her neck.

On Sunday morning it was too quiet in the house. Her father's car was not in the driveway. A mixture of fear and disgust swept over her. Either he was sleeping it off in the parking lot of some bar, or he had found someone to go home with. Whatever the reason, she wanted to be gone when he finally came home. If he came home.

Dew dampened her pant legs as she shuffled across her yard. The lawn needed to be mowed. By the time she got to the car, her jeans were soaked a third of the way up to her knees. Except for her car parked in the driveway, it looked like the farmhouse was abandoned, not unlike so many others that dotted the countryside. There was no way she could start the ancient mower. The dumb thing always took her dad several good yanks to get going.

Avery recalled her Aunt Penny telling her "love them or leave them, you can't choose your family." Aunt Penny was right, but she just couldn't help wishing her family were more like the Norman Rockwell Stewart family.

Then she remembered the scene with his aunt and uncle. She took some solace knowing even the Stewarts weren't perfect.

Windows down and radio blaring, Avery took off into town to pick up some groceries. The convenience store was packed with motorcycles lining the parking spots and gas pumps. She circled Main Street and headed east to the Dollar Store, but a sign on the door stated it was closed due to renovations. That left only one store opened on a Sunday: The Valley Market.

Traffic back to the other side of town thickened and slowed. Old people and families clogged Main Street. *Great, church must've just got out.* She turned down a narrow alley leading to the grocery store.

She fought the old habit of parking in the back spaces, farthest away in the employee spots. Instead, she parked in the front. Just because she didn't work here anymore didn't mean she couldn't shop here. She'd successfully avoided it since Chantra fired her.

Even so, she hurried into the store, willing herself invisible. Heat tingled her scalp as she slipped past Tom in Customer Service to grab the first cart she saw. The wheel rattled and she stiffened. Tom's stare burned holes in her back as she left the cart there and grabbed another one—just like so many other customers she'd labeled rude before. Now she understood why they left the carts in different places.

Luckily, she knew the store inside and out, and it wouldn't take long to get some food and leave. She rolled past the first three aisles and made it to the shelves of convenience foods. She tossed several items in, and swung around to head toward the meat counter when her cart collided with another one.

"Geez, tard-o. Watch where you're going." MaKenzie, dressed in a conservative suit, stood behind the other cart.

Avery moved to go around the other girl, but MaKenzie yanked her cart sideways, making a screeching sound and leaving black marks on the white, speckled linoleum. Avery tried to maneuver to the other side, but MaKenzie whipped her cart backwards.

Avery's fingernails dug into the soft flesh of her palms. She remembered the conversation she overheard between

MaKenzie and her mother. But she still didn't completely understand why MaKenzie had always had it out for her. "What is your deal? Why do you hate me so much?"

MaKenzie's snide demeanor changed to a look of pure loathing. "Because you exist." In a flash MaKenzie turned and strode back down the aisle.

Stunned, Avery stared at the microwave containers of ravioli and macaroni and cheese.

"Excuse me."

Avery automatically pulled her cart over, but she realized MaKenzie's empty cart was still in the middle of the aisle. "I'm sorry." She pushed the other cart behind a display of soup that touted noodle shapes from a hot new children's movie.

"Not a problem, darlin'. Some people just ain't got any manners." The elderly woman looked at Avery over her bifocals and patted her shoulder as she passed by. She turned back and looked Avery straight in the eye. "Don't you mind her. There's always been mean girls around. Even in my day."

Avery smiled, but her down in her gut she knew it was more than MaKenzie being mean for no reason.

⁂

Avery's dad's car was in the driveway when she got home. Unsure whether he would be sober and angry or drunk and belligerent, she tried to be as quiet as possible as she hurried to put away the meager amount of groceries she'd bought.

She couldn't stop thinking about MaKenzie's comment. It struck deep, although she knew how mean-spirited the girl could be.

"What're you doing?" Her father's voice surprised her and she jumped, dropping a can of soup on the floor. It left a small gouge in the dingy linoleum kitchen flooring.

She bent down to pick up the can and catch her breath. "I'm putting groceries away."

"How'd you get money to buy groceries?" His stance was accusatory.

She thought about the money in the laundry and kicked herself. It was probably his and he was missing it. She should've left his clothes and made him do his own laundry.

She figured she could hedge enough to get him off her back. "I had a job, you know."

He crossed his arms. "One you lost after your mother left. Try again. Where'd you get the money?"

Was he really standing there accusing her of buying groceries? "What is the problem, Dad? Last I checked it was the parents' job to take care of their kids. And thanks for rubbing in the fact I lost my job." She went to walk around him and go to her room, but he held his arm across the area between the kitchen bar and counter on the other side.

"You got a roof over your head. You're taken care of. And the next time you decide to sneak into your mom's room and steal money from your Aunt Penny's bank account, remember I can have you arrested for it." He grabbed the bag of chips she'd just bought, turned, and slammed the hallway door as he stomped up the stairs to his bedroom. Dust trickled from the crack in the ceiling.

"Wha—?" She spoke to empty air. What did he mean by Aunt Penny's bank account? Her estate had been closed, or at least she thought it had. Her mother always complained there hadn't been any money left behind, and that Penny had left Avery her car. Her mom had really gone through the roof over the car.

Avery was forever thankful that her great Aunt Penny had the foresight enough to leave her the car. There was no way she'd have ever had any freedom if she hadn't had the Taurus. Her parents certainly wouldn't have bought her one when she'd gotten her license. They hadn't even paid for her license.

He'd said she snuck into her mother's room. She hadn't been in there since before her mom left. Maybe she should sneak in there and try to figure out what he was talking about. Noise from the television in her dad's room slipped through the closed hallway door. He had it on full blast. He probably had whiskey up there, too. She remembered finding bottles hidden around the farm several times before.

She wasn't taking any chances of getting caught in her mom's room since her dad was home. Better to wait 'till he was at work. Right now she needed to get out of this house.

Avery headed down the road without really taking in the scenery. A horn blared and Jaxson waved to her from his blue truck. He was driving the opposite way. She slowed down and pulled over into a field access road as he made a U-turn and pulled up behind her. They both got out.

"Hey, I was just headed over to your house." Jaxson strode over. Tiny gnats flew around their heads.

The thought of him coming over to her house with her dad in his mood made her twitch. She shifted from one foot to the other, hoping Jaxson wouldn't notice. "Oh? Why?"

"I talked Dad into letting me have the afternoon off so I could spend it with you." He stood in front of her, his hair damp and smelling like soap.

"Oh really? What were you thinking about doing?" She took his hand in hers and smiled up at him.

"Well, I was going to try to talk you into spending the afternoon at your house. Where were you headed when I honked?" He leaned into her, sandwiching her between his long body and her car.

She had to think fast. There was no way she would let him come over to her house. Especially not today. "Dad's watching some baseball game. He can get really loud. You don't want to go to your house?"

He shook his head and kissed her. "Mom's helping Delilah with our 4-H club to get their stuff together for the display."

"There's a baseball game at the park." She giggled as he nuzzled her cheek.

"That's where Dad is. Riley's playing."

"You should be there to support your brother!"

"It's the first game I haven't been to." Jaxson put his arms around her and pressed her closer. "There's a matinee in the theater. We could sit in the back."

"Race you there."

Chapter Seventeen

(Lie #9: What you see is what you get.)

Fair Week arrived and Jaxson was busy getting his calves ready to show. He was President of his club and was running for Fair King, which kept him busy.

She'd almost forgotten what her dad had said about her Aunt Penny's money. When she'd returned home and found two empty whiskey bottles on the bathroom floor, she chalked it up to her dad being drunk.

Monday afternoon she'd sat staring at the door into her mother's room. Avery remembered when they moved in with Aunt Penny after she had been diagnosed with breast cancer. At the time when her mother said she owed her aunt, Avery thought it was money she owed.

No one would tell her exactly why her mother owed their aunt. But her mother never paid rent. She'd been there to care for their aunt during her chemotherapy and illness afterwards. It hadn't been fun, but her Aunt Penny always made everything seem like an adventure. Until the adventure was over.

The house was clean to sparkling. And she had even tried to start the lawn mower, with no success. Tuesday came and went, but Avery only managed to touch the doorknob. She couldn't turn it. By Wednesday afternoon, she was going stir crazy. The Fair's talent show and tractor pull were both scheduled for seven p.m., so she got ready early and left for Valley City Park. She texted Jaxson to let him know she'd be there.

The tang of fresh manure and hay swirled around Avery as she walked through the different barns housing the livestock. She searched for Jaxson's name on any of the plaques above the animals and found it above a sleek black heifer. The Stewart's wooden 4-H chest, where they kept their tools, sat on the outside of the heifer's pen, but there was no sign of Jaxson.

She made her way out of the barn area, careful to sidestep small piles of manure that the club members hadn't cleaned up yet, and walked over to the Grooms Exhibit Hall. The exhibits were already set up, and since the building was air conditioned, she took her time exploring. When she exhausted her interest there, she moved over to the Commercial Exhibit Building.

The first person she saw was Elaine, her photographer. Precious Moments booth was in the back corner of the building across from the Arts display.

"Hey, Avery. Coming to see where you'll be working for me?" The woman's smile warmed her.

"Yeah. The bathroom is just a few steps away. Always a good spot." Avery laughed.

Elaine showed her a few things she would need to know in order to work the booth before telling Avery to close her eyes.

She hoped Elaine wouldn't surprise her with a dorky outfit or costume she would have to wear, but she closed her eyes as instructed. When she opened them, Elaine unveiled a large portrait of her on the railroad tracks in front of the full rainbow. Set in an elaborate carved frame, the picture was done in the most expensive format the photographer offered.

"I wanted to show off what I could do with my new software, and I used an oil canvas technique. Looks just like a painting, doesn't it? It costs extra, but I put a rush on it so it would be here in time to showcase it. What do you think?"

Tears filled Avery's eyes.

A squeal pierced the air behind her. "Oh my GOSH! Avery, is that your picture?" Katie's knack for stating the obvious had both Avery and Elaine laughing.

"I entered it into the Pro Pho contest for local photographers. Wouldn't it be great if it won?" Elaine motioned to another booth half way down to the other side of the building. "Aren't you glad the Hermans cancelled on you now?"

Cindy Herman looked straight at them. If looks could kill, she and Elaine would be toast.

Avery turned back to look closer at her portrait. She couldn't speak. It was far better than anything she could've hoped for.

Avery and Katie walked around the exhibits once more, even stopping to admire Katie's pictures at Herman's. Her friend's enthusiasm made everything seem brighter than it was when she went through on her own. They sauntered over to the carnival to see if anyone was there that they knew. So far she had not come across Jaxson or any of his family.

"So, tell me. How'd your Fourth go?" Katie bumped her shoulder into Avery's.

"Actually, really well."

"What about Jaxson? And this time I want details." They sat on a bench set out for the VFW bingo stand. It was an open-walled covered building with benches placed around it in a square. Katie handed two veterans wearing blue-and-yellow vests a dollar bill. The vets handed them a stack of bingo cards.

Avery glanced around. They sat at the far end, away from the more serious hopefuls, their backs to the animal barns and the Soldier Memorial behind them.

The caller announced the numbers over a microphone. The speakers screeched with feedback. Avery waited for the noise to die down.

Avery told Katie everything from the parade, to the bar-b-que and pool, to the fireworks. She kept the theater a secret, holding it close and untouched, safe from any kind of fate turning on her.

"C'mon. That's the tame stuff you tell your parents. Give me the real dirt." Katie reached over and pushed a plastic cover across a number on Avery's card.

Someone yelled bingo and everyone else groaned. Avery fished out a couple more quarters for the next game. Katie's look never wavered from Avery's face. She was not about to give up asking.

"Okay, fine. It was fabulous, all right. Jaxson is…" She tried to find the right word.

A heavy weight plopped down next to her on the bench. Avery gasped as she swung around to see who it was.

"Jaxson who?" Sophie picked up the quarters, pretending to study them.

"Oh my gosh! Avery, didn't you tell Sophie about Jaxson?" Katie started to go on but Avery held up her hand.

"Whoa, Kay. Wait." She looked at her FBF. "First of all, why do you care? And, second of all, you saw me with Jaxson at the Street Dance. Don't say 'Jaxson who' like you don't know, when you insulted him right in front of me."

Katie's eyes were wide open, but at least her mouth was shut.

Sophie slapped the quarters down on the wooden slab used as a table. "Okay, okay. I'm sorry. I got MaKenzie real good though. You have to admit that was funny." Her friend grinned.

"It was a good one," Avery said, trying not to smile. "So why are you, my FBF, now talking to me? You called me a liar, remember? Wouldn't believe that I didn't hit on your skeezy boyfriend." She wasn't going to let Sophie get off easy, not when she'd been such a snot.

"What's an FBF?" Katie leaned over Avery to ask.

Sophie laughed and then snorted. Avery put her hand over her mouth to keep from laughing.

Katie giggled. "What are we laughing about?"

Sophie laughed harder at the look of bewilderment on Katie's face. The snort that followed caught everyone's attention around the table. Several people laughed at them.

Katie looked more confused than before. "I don't get it."

Avery couldn't help it. She started laughing. The vet who gave them their cards asked them to leave. They'd become a distraction.

They all got up, still in hysterics, and left.

"Oh, my gosh. Sophie, you have to see Avery's portrait in the Commercial Building. Then you can tell me what an FBF is." Katie skipped ahead of them toward the Exhibit Hall.

"You didn't tell me why you're talking to me." Avery sent a sidelong glance at her friend.

Sophie crossed her arms. "Brody and I got into a fight. We broke up."

Avery narrowed her eyes. "Did he hurt you?"

"No. I just got tired of the attention he gave to any and every girl around. And my mom figured out I'd been drinking. I got grounded, and he called me an infant. It's over." Pain shone from her green eyes.

Avery spun on Sophie. "Ha! Well, you deserved that after acting like a hag to me about that jerk-face at the Chute and at the Street Dance."

Katie's green eyes were huge. "You guys were fighting? I hate going to family things in the summer. I miss all of the good stuff."

Avery glared at Sophie. Although her friend looked repentant, she wasn't ready to forgive and forget. "There was no 'good stuff' to it."

Sophie flounced her arms down to her sides. "I'm sorry. Really I am. I should've known you wouldn't be like that, okay? It's just he was so nice. And he's a great kisser—"

Katie leaned into Avery's arm to get closer to hear the details of Sophie's love life.

"Ugh! La, la, la." Avery put her fingers in her ears. They walked into the shade from a large oak tree in the center of the park.

Sophie yanked Avery's hands down. "Geez! I'm sorry. You don't have to be a jerk about it."

"I'm not trying to be a jerk. I think Brody is disgusting and have since I first met him when he kissed me. It wasn't Steve, either." She pointed a finger between Sophie and Katie, daring them to contradict her.

"Okay, fine. You're the most loyal, golden retriever friend someone could ever have. If I promise never to take you for granted again, will you forgive me?" Sophie's lip trembled and she looked at Avery with puppy-dog eyes.

"You don't deserve it." Avery crossed her arms, but her heart was melting.

Sophie nodded. "You're right. I don't. I'll be a better friend." She held out her pinky.

Avery studied her. She hooked her pinky in Sophie's. "Fine. I forgive you."

Katie pulled them together for a group hug. Sophie pulled out first.

"C'mon, Sophie. You have to see Avery's picture." Katie steered them back toward the Commercial Building.

"Who'da thunk it?" Sophie growled at the people lined up in the building making slow progress toward the Precious Moments booth.

"It's the tractor pull and talent show. Guess it's popular this year." They made it half way down the right hand path, but an elderly couple with canes and a chatty woman who stopped and talked to everyone slowed them. There was no getting around them.

Closer to the Precious Moments booth, Avery saw a familiar blond head. He stood talking with Elaine. A girl she did not recognize walked up beside Jaxson. She wore a white sash. The only word Avery could make out was "Princess."

"There's your loverboy, cougar-girl." Sophie poked her in the side.

Just as Avery slapped her friend's hand away, she watched as the girl leaned up and placed a kiss on Jaxson's cheek. Jaxson put his arm around the girl when she fell into him and their lips connected.

Sophie crossed her arms, crooking her hip in full-on attack stance.

Avery knew that look well. Between that and the heat prickling behind her eyes, she needed air, and fast. She steered Sophie past the lurkers, past Herman's Hotshots where Katie was bent over trying to find her own senior pictures among dozens on poster boards.

They made it out of back door before Avery gave in to her confusion and screamed.

"What was that about? Don't tell me he just let another girl kiss him!" Sophie pointed toward the building.

"I don't know." Avery paced back and forth, agitated. She was breathing so fast her head began to tingle.

"Okay. Let's sit so you can calm down." Sophie grabbed Avery's hand, pulling her next to her on a bench. "Now breathe slowly. You're going to hyperventilate."

"I can't help it." Avery settled against the wooden back of the bench, her hands over her eyes to keep from crying. "What am I going to do?"

"I'll tell you what I'm going to do. I'm going to go kick some Princess hide." Sophie started to stand, but Avery held her back.

"Don't, Sophie."

"What do you mean, don't?" Sophie raged, her face turning bright red. "I don't know who that girl thinks she is, but she's going to regret ever touching your boyfriend."

A tear trickled out the side of Avery's eye, making a slow path down her cheek. "How did I think this was ever going to work? I can't believe I allowed those big blue eyes to suck me in. What am I doing?"

MaKenzie walked around the corner, her head bent down, not looking at where she was going. A pink, "Harrison County Fair Queen," sash rested over her red-and-white checkered shirt. She wore daisy duke shorts and sleek pink cowgirl boots. Put two pigtails in her hair and she would've come straight out of a cartoon.

Avery swiped at her cheeks, trying to remove any sign of distress. Sophie's hand tightened around her arm. Avery shook her head. She couldn't handle both the kiss and MaKenzie right now.

MaKenzie looked up. She stumbled when she saw the two friends on the bench. In a flash she disappeared into the building.

"Did that sash read Swine Queen or Heifer Queen?" Sophie asked, giggling.

"No. I believe it said Drama Queen," Avery stated.

Both of them broke out in laughter. Katie poked her head out of the door. "Hey, guys! Did you see? Jaxson's Harrison County Fair King!"

Chapter Eighteen

(Truth #9: A throne is only a bench covered with velvet.)

"What did you just say?" Avery asked.

"Jaxson is the King! Isn't that awesome?" Sophie slapped her hands over her ears when Katie squealed.

Avery frowned. She took a brochure from the bench and fanned herself. Her head spun as she hyperventilated again.

"Aren't you excited?" Katie came over to them, her eager expression falling.

A mother with her three children walked in between them, the child in her arms screaming about wanting to go to the carnival.

Sophie whispered. "Guess who the Queen is?"

"Who?" Katie whispered back.

"MaKenzie Thomas." Acid dripped off of Avery's words. She folded her legs and hugged them against her chest.

Katie's mouth fell open in a gasp big enough to swallow a bee hive. "Shut your mouth!"

"Watch the language," Sophie teased.

"What're you going to do?" Katie asked.

Avery put her head on her knees. She rocked back and forth. "Why does God hate me?" Her vision became blotchy. She had to get a grip. "Oh my gosh. I'm losing it."

Katie bent down. She wrapped her arms around Avery while Sophie rubbed her back.

"Why docs MaKenzie being queen stress you out so much, Avery? I mean, I know you hate her and all, but all they do is take pictures together. It's not like she's going to kiss him or anything."

"No. The only person kissing Jaxson is that other princess."

Katie must've been confused because Sophie continued. "Right before we came out here some girl kissed him. Right on the mouth. Looked kind of like he was hugging her and enjoying it. I can hunt her down for you, Avery. I'm ready to beat some cheating haggish hide."

"No. That can't be right. Jaxson wouldn't cheat on you, Avery." Katie's incredulous tone grated on Avery's frayed nerves.

If this is how Sophie felt when she thought Avery had been after Brody, she almost understood how she had acted. The urge to rip things to shreds pulsed inside her. "I've got to get out of here. I can't do this." Avery shot up, knocking Katie down in the process.

Avery hurried past the Grooms Hall toward the carnival area. She dug in her purse to find her keys.

Davis stepped in front of them. "Hey guys. You going to the tractor pull?"

"Out of our way, nub." Sophie put her arm out and, without breaking stride, flung him to the side.

Davis grumbled under his breath as Avery followed her friend's footsteps.

Katie brought up the rear. "Hi, Davis."

Avery rolled her eyes at Katie's sunniness toward everyone, even in the middle of a crisis.

They made it to a picnic table on the other side of the playground. Sophie sat on the top of the table, her legs dangling over the side. "Man, I could use a drink."

"Seriously?" Avery demanded. She found her keys, but not her phone. *Dang it.* She'd left it in the center console of her car. Sophie bounced on the worn wooden table as Avery flopped down next to her.

"Yes, seriously." Sophie pulled a cigarette out of her purse and lit it.

Katie's eyes widened. "When did you start smoking?"

"A few weeks ago. It's no big deal." She blew out a stream of smoke.

Avery wrinkled her nose. "No big deal? It's gross. And could kill you. But no. No big deal."

"Uh, oh. Don't look now, Avery." Sophie hopped from the table. She flicked the cigarette to the ground and stepped on it.

Avery turned to look, waving her hand in the air to clear the smoke.

"Hey, Avery. I thought I saw you come this way. Didn't you hear me calling your name?" Jaxson grinned.

"Don't you talk to her." Katie shook her finger at him. Jaxson stopped. "What?"

Katie was not done yet. "You don't get to talk to her. You…you…you need to leave." She poked her finger into Jaxson's chest.

Avery sat in silence as her friend stood up for her. Jaxson raised his eyebrows in question when he glanced over at her. His white button down shirt was tucked into his dark jeans. The boots he wore made him taller than before. A red rose boutonniere was pinned to his shirt, indicating he was on the Fair Court.

"Looks likc sweet little Katie told you, your majesty." Sophie mock bowed at Jaxson.

Jaxson crooked his thumbs through his belt loops. He bent his head sideways at them, narrowing his eyes. "What am I missing?"

Avery's pulse pounded in her ears. She didn't want to argue with him in front of her friends. She doubted she had enough strength to hold Sophie back if her friend got too angry. "Give us a minute, please."

Sophie put her hands up in surrender. "I'll be over there if you need me." She pointed to the swing set.

Katie stood in front of Jaxson and glared at him.

"Down, girl. Let's let them talk." Sophie grabbed Katie's arm and pulled her along.

Jaxson watched the two girls walk away. He turned to Avery. His eyes were wide, his mouth hung open before snapping shut. "I've been looking all over for you. I sent you texts." He walked toward her. "Are you mad at me or something?"

Avery closed her eyes. She couldn't look into those blue depths and think clearly.

"Avery, what's wrong? What'd I do?" Desperation filled his voice.

She shook her head, the words refusing to come out of her mouth.

"Avery, please. Tell me what's wrong." His shaking hand was cool against her cheek.

She pulled away, digging the keys into her palm in an effort to control her emotions. "I saw that girl kiss you earlier in the Commercial Building." She opened her eyes then, tears trickling down her face.

He put his hand on his head. "Geez. That was Maggie. She was congratulating me on making Fair King. We're in the same 4-H club."

Avery took a deep breath. "It looked like you two were kissing."

He stepped back, running his fingers through his hair. "She tripped or something. I was only trying to make sure she didn't fall. You know those stupid high heels you girls wear." She didn't smile at his attempt at humor. "Honest, Avery. It wasn't what it looked like." His lips twisted down, his gaze begged her to believe him.

She wiped her face with her hands, the salt of her tears melted on her tongue. "Congratulations on being King, Jaxson." She walked around the end of the picnic table, desperate to get away.

He moved to the other side of the table by her. "Avery, please." Tears glistened on his long eyelashes. "Don't leave. Please. There's never been anyone else. It's only ever been you."

Pain ripped her heart into small pieces.

He shifted, digging his hands in his back pockets. "It started that day on the bus when you yelled at Billy Hammer for making fun of me. He was such a jerk, but you stood up to him, almost made him cry. Remember? Then you sat down next to me and held my hand. I think I've loved you ever since that day. Please, you gotta believe me." He whispered the last sentence, his head bowed down.

Avery's heart pounded at Jaxson's declaration. Sweat slicked her shaking hands. Had Jaxson actually said he loved her? Emotions swelled inside of her as memories of the day he mentioned flooded her mind.

Billy Hammer was the biggest bully she'd ever met and a son to friends of Aunt Penny. She'd spent the afternoon at his house after they moved in with her aunt, and his mom talked about his bed-wetting problem.

Years later, he chose to make fun of Jaxson because his heart condition made him smaller than the other kids. Nobody would stand up to him, not even the bus driver. She stood up and told everyone how Billy wet the bed until he was in junior high like a big fat baby. Jaxson had been in sixth grade, and she in eighth.

She folded her arms in front of her, both to steady her racing pulse, and to warm her chilled arms. She grinned. "You're not that small anymore."

He looked up at her, hope shining from his face. "I didn't kiss her, Avery. I wouldn't. I didn't know that was going to happen, I swear."

Avery did believe him. She scuffed dirt with the toe of her tennis shoe. "I…It caught me off guard." She shrugged. "I had to keep Sophie from decapitating her." She gave him a tentative smile.

"I'm so sorry."

She sniffed back more tears. "Don't let it happen again."

In two long strides his arms were around her. He held her tight, his face buried in her long hair. "I promise."

Her arms went around him automatically. The churning in her stomach died down, and a bubble of warmth exploded in her heart, melding the broken pieces back together. She breathed in the now-familiar smell of his body spray and closed her eyes. The flower boutonniere poked at her, but she ignored it. He drew back to look at her, brushing the tears off her face with his thumbs.

"So, you and Sophie are best friends again?" He played with a strand of her hair.

Avery smacked him on the arm. "Jerk-face."

He laughed and pulled her close again.

But she couldn't ignore the pain at seeing the girl kiss him. It was the first time she'd ever given her heart away. And her heart was in way over its head. And if she were honest with herself, it terrified her.

The sight behind Jaxson only reignited Avery's anger. MaKenzie stood, watching her and Jaxson, her face smug. She caressed the pink sash, grinned, and walked away.

Chapter Nineteen

(Truth #10: Actions speak louder than words.)

Friday morning the sky opened and dumped rain. Avery's shirt and nice slacks were soaked by the time she reached the Commercial Building at the Fair.

"Did you bring something to change into?" Elaine laughed at her.

"No. It wasn't raining when I left home." Avery frowned as she shook wetness off her arms. She had wanted to make a good impression, dressing up for the mock-job.

"Well at least my shoot today is inside. Otherwise I would be in a worse mood than you right now." Elaine went over everything Avery needed to know before leaving.

On the table, a decorative jar held slips of paper for the Precious Moments contest for the most popular picture. There were pictures of chubby-cheeked babies, families, weddings, and singles like her senior portrait. Below the table, Elaine stored extra pamphlets listing the fees for her sessions, and sheets of paper with nine squares of voting slips. There were none left on the table, so Avery got out the scissors and began cutting more out.

She ignored the pointed looks the girls at Herman's Hotshots gave her. Avery wished the display booths hadn't been placed so close to each other.

The trickle of people slowed down after the initial run for dry cover. People stopped and talked to her about her portrait, and most delighted in the captured moment. Avery basked in the attention. It wasn't long before the morning was over.

Soon, though, Avery had to use the bathroom. She glanced around, not knowing what to do since Elaine hadn't gone over that part with her. The stalls weren't far—just on the other side of the door—so it wouldn't take long. Avery decided to take a chance and go as quickly as she could.

She straightened out the table, making sure the boxes beneath weren't showing, and then dashed out the door to the restroom.

When she returned, she placed her purse back under the table and sat down. The jar on the table was empty. It had been three-quarters full before she left. Avery looked around suspiciously. Her eyes widened and her mouth dropped open when she saw that her portrait had been spray painted with three letters: *W, H,* and *O.* Whoever did it was in a hurry, since the *O* was unfinished at the top. The paint jagged up and over the beautiful frame and ruined both the picture and the frame.

A cold sweat broke across her scalp. Her hand shook as she reached out to the picture, the new paint wetting her fingertips. A lump formed in her throat. What was she going to do? Should she call the police? She couldn't call Elaine. The photographer was probably still in the middle of taking pictures. And besides, what would Elaine think when she came back to find something happened on Avery's watch? She could kiss her senior picture deal goodbye.

"What in the world?"

Avery turned to see Mrs. Stewart. Her eyes were wide open, as was her mouth. She moved behind the table and gathered her in a hug. "Oh, Avery. You poor thing. Who could've done that?"

She shook her head. "I don't know. I just went to the bathroom and came back. The paint's still wet." Avery held out her stained fingers.

"Don't you worry, sweetie. Let me go get someone. You stay right here." Jaxson's mother left through the back exit.

Avery plunked down on the metal chair. How much did the portrait cost? Would she have to pay for it now that it was completely ruined? She sat, stunned, as people walked by, stopping and staring at her and the picture.

A crowd formed. Several women whispered to each other behind their hands as they stared at her and the picture. Then some kids came by, pointing and laughing at her. Avery had loved the attention before. She hated it now.

Mrs. Stewart and a man walked up to the booth. "Avery, this is Frank Whitman. He's in charge of security at the fair. Go ahead and tell him what happened." She placed her hand on Avery's shoulder.

Avery took the next few minutes to explain what happened. A uniformed officer stepped through the gawking people, and shooed the onlookers away. She went through the same questions again for him. Time seemed to slow down, the people walking by blurred together.

Mrs. Stewart stayed with her until the men investigating left. She had another woman bring a sheet to cover the portrait. "Sweetie, I have to go get the girls. It's Jaxson's big day of showing, and John wants to be there when he does, so I have to go with them. We'll be busy with everything until suppertime. Are you going to be okay?"

Avery braved a smile. "Thank you, Mrs. Stewart. I don't know what I would've done if you hadn't come when you did."

"Call me Janelle. I'm glad I was here to help. I'll be back when I can."

Avery shrugged. "It's okay. Elaine will be back soon."

"Everything will be all right. I promise." Mrs. Stewart touched Avery's arm.

Avery watched as she walked away. Her throat tightened. Moments such as these brought back thoughts of her mother. She forced the thought deep inside her and locked it away. As she settled in the metal chair, her gaze rested on Herman's photo booth. Several women bent close to each other, whispering. One pointed a discreet finger in Avery's direction as she talked.

Heat crept up Avery's neck. Her stomach rolled over.

"That's a look." Elaine walked in front of her, breaking her view of the other booth. "Why did you cover your portrait?"

Avery braced herself, but she couldn't find the words to say anything.

Elaine was silent for a moment before tugging the cover off of the portrait. "Who did this?"

Avery hung her head, unable to look Elaine in the eye. Her stomach tightened and she thought she might throw up. Taking a deep breath, she pulled the paper the officer had given her containing his report off the table.

Elaine plucked the paper from her hand. "Well, isn't that convenient?"

Avery rushed to explain. "I'm so sorry. I don't know how it happened—"

"Hey, hey. Darlin', I don't blame you for this."

Avery looked up then. Elaine had her hands on her hips, staring down at her. She sure looked like she was mad. "You don't? But, I had to use the bathroom and left the table unwatched. It's my fault. I'll pay for it, whatever it cost."

"You have a right to use the restroom, Avery. I'd expect you to. And if it weren't for you, the booth would've been unattended anyway. Whoever it was did NOT have the right to deface your portrait and insult you like this." Elaine smacked the paper down on the table. "That's not okay. And no, you're not going to pay for it. That's what insurance is for."

She put her hand on Avery's arm. "Darlin', I'm so sorry this happened. In this old world things happen that just don't make sense. Wrong, hurtful things. It's just a fact. Some people make themselves feel big by making others feel small. Their day will come. But don't you ever let them win by feeling less than what you are or changing who you are. Ever."

The vehemence in her voice startled Avery. She stared at Elaine wide-eyed.

"Okay. Now, I'm going to the administrative shed to see what I can find out." Elaine's steps were lively as she walked back across the building, pushing her way through the women standing in front of the other photography booth.

When she returned she brought two cheeseburgers, chips and cold bottles of water. "I was starving, so I stopped by the food shed on my way back. Hope you're hungry."

Avery smiled, surprised at the woman's generosity. "I am. Thanks."

"It's the least I can do for someone who had a worse morning than I did." Setting the pamphlets aside, she spread the food across the table. "All right, girl, eat up."

Word must've spread. People came up to them and expressed their sympathies over what happened. The sincere outpouring of support touched Avery. She hoped Jaxson would stop by, but he texted that he had to help his younger brother in his showing.

"I didn't expect so many people to come by and tell you they're sorry about the picture," Avery said during a lull in the action.

Elaine turned toward her. "You know, it's not just me they're saying those nice things to. A lot of people really liked your picture. And it wasn't just my amazing skills as a photographer. I had a wonderful subject, and, wow, did we ever have good timing on that rainbow or what? I pray for those moments every time I go out on a session. Man, when it happens, you're glad to be a part of it."

"Thank you. For everything." Avery crinkled up the greasy papers from her food.

"You're planning on coming back tomorrow, right? You won't let this scare you off, will you?"

Avery grinned. "I'm stubborn. I'll be back."

"Good. I'll see you then." Elaine waved as Avery walked out the back door. It had been a long day. Her clothes were wrinkled from the rain, and her hair was a mess. She didn't relish the thought of going home to change. The Dollar Store's renovation was finished. She would start there.

Deep in thought, she walked into someone.

"Hey, Avery. Not looking where you're going?" Davis put his arms around her.

She shoved him away. "Seriously, Davis. Personal space." She started to walk around him, but he stepped in front of her.

"I heard about your picture. Man, who would've done something like that?" His smile belied his tone.

She frowned at him. "Stupid idiots, that's who."

"You've got yourself some serious haters. If you ever want to talk about it, I'm here to listen." Davis leaned closer.

Closer than she was comfortable with. "Yeah. Right. Bye." She walked away, turning after a few feet to look back at him. He was still watching her and smiled bigger when he caught her glance.

Goosebumps prickled her arms. *Creeper.*

Chapter Twenty

(Truth #11: Be careful what you wish for. It just may come true.)

A very left the Dollar Store dejected. They hadn't restocked everything so pickings had been slim, and she refused to use the last of her cash on something she wouldn't wear again. She headed home to change. It was probably for the best anyway since Jaxson had texted earlier, empathizing with her about the portrait and apologizing that he was stuck doing Fair King business. He was going to the derby with Michael and some other friends later and would be busy until then.

She frowned. Would he be taking pictures with MaKenzie as Fair Queen and all of the purple-ribbon winners? She remembered the look on MaKenzie's face last night when she was hugging Jaxson. Her cell phone buzzed, jolting her from her thoughts.

"Hey, Avery. I heard about your picture. Was it really awful?" Katie's concerned voice calmed her.

"It kind of was. It was the topping on a crummy day." Avery pulled into her driveway. It had turned humid after the downpour, and now sweat made her wrinkled clothes stick to her. She looked forward to getting in the air conditioning and taking a shower.

"Sorry I couldn't be there. I'm babysitting until seven. You want to go get something to eat after?"

"How about pizza at eight?" Avery asked.

"Deal."

An hour later, she had showered and walked up to her room dressed in a towel. Her dirty clothes outnumbered her clean ones. No one was left to get after her about her laundry, and as much as she hated to admit it, she missed it. She changed into sweats, gathered everything off her floor, and took it downstairs in the laundry basket.

The bathroom was as bad as her bedroom. A musty smell hit her as she emptied the wooden hamper into the basket. The clock in the kitchen read 2:15.

Avery stuffed the washer with the first load of her clothes and went to the living room to find something to do for the next half hour. There were three messages on the machine. A couple of bill collectors, which was a bit unusual. Even though her mom missed commissions lately, they'd always been able to pay the bills. She hit the delete button after all of them—writing down anything important—and left the note in the spot where her dad put his keys every night.

A loud rumbling coming from the back of the house surprised her. She grabbed her heart.

It was coming from the laundry room. *The washing machine!* It thudded across the floor as she ran into the room.

The load was lopsided, probably because she had crammed it with as many clothes as she could so it wouldn't take all day to wash and dry them all. Water dripped down her arm and onto the floor as she adjusted the load. Avery slugged through the jumble, digging out the most non-essential pieces and dropping them into the emptied clothes basket from her room. Water leaked out the holes in the plastic and ran across the floor.

Geez! How many things can go wrong in one day? It took longer than she liked for the dried, old mop to soak up the mess, but she finally managed to get things under control just in time to put a second load in and dry the first. Now, however, she was soaked for the second time that day. And this time she had nothing to change into.

A rush of realization sparked in her. *Mom wears the same size I do.* Her footsteps faltered. She still hadn't found the courage to enter that room.

It was either do it or walk around naked since there weren't any clean towels. Avery walked through her living room to the door that led to her mother's room. Her heart raced, her breathing became shallow. She stepped back to the recliner, and waited until her breathing steadied.

Stupid. This is stupid. Scared of opening a door. It's just a door. Avery walked straight to the door and swung it open. It looked like the aftermath of a tornado. Not that her mother had been a great housekeeper the last couple of years. But the normal chaos was nothing compared to this. Clutter fell out of the closet as if someone had flown through the contents, flinging aside the unwanted items as they went. Shoes and clothes littered the unmade bed.

Avery walked over to the dresser first. A thin layer of dust covered it. Her mother kept her personal items there. The top drawer, where she saved her handmade birthday cards and pictures, remained intact and full to the brim. Curious, she leafed through the contents, not finding anything other than what she knew was there. Socks and underwear cluttered the larger drawer underneath the smaller top drawers. Shorts and t-shirts filled the next drawer. The bottom drawer had books, notebooks and miscellaneous papers.

She took a t-shirt and sweats from the second drawer. She dropped her wet clothes on the bed and walked over to the closet. The bi-fold door hung off the track, propped by boxes and clothes. The metal bar was empty except for a few clothes hangers and a couple of old sweaters in the back.

Avery looked down at the jumbled chaos. *Why did you leave me, Mom? Is there something here that will tell me why?*

She piled the errant clothes against the wall behind her, adjusting the bi-fold door so it didn't fall on her head. There were several shoe boxes, old purses, and brown boxes full of her mother's possessions. Photos from when Avery was a baby filled one shoebox.

She dug through everything, sifting through old makeup, jewelry, finally hitting pay dirt with a box on the shelf stuffed with old letters and photos she didn't remember seeing before.

Rubber bands held bundles of letters together. There were folded notes from her mother's friends in school—none of whom she had ever heard of—some correspondence from her deceased grandparents, and letters with her aunt's handwriting.

She ran her fingers over the last bunch. Curiosity got the best of her. The rubber band crumbled as she worked it off, leaving a red strip where it had dried against the paper. They were letters from her dad to her mom. Nothing too romantic. Things like where they'd meet and when. She wondered how her father ever won her mother's heart.

No dying words of endearments, no hearts or "I love you's." Her father ended the letters with *Yours, Greg.* Not the stuff of romance movies, and definitely not what she was looking for. She loaded the letters back into the box. The bottom of the box held four school yearbooks, each one engraved with her mother's maiden name, Dineen Rae Morgan.

She opened the first one, surprised to see paragraphs of cordial comments, signed by classmates. The first few pages had no pictures, so messages filled them. Black-and-white photographs captured students and staff alike in a smiling tribute to a time long gone. Avery scanned each picture, catching her mother in various school activities and clubs. Her teenage face smiled at her from the center of the freshman class.

Blinking back tears, Avery opened the next one, and the next. Glee club. Volleyball. Speech class. *A Midsummer Night's Dream.* They all held her mother and father— suspended in time. The second book showed her father's senior year which was only her mother's sophomore year of high school.

Just like her and Jaxson. Hair rose on her arms.

Oddly, there were no pictures of them together. The only pictures were of her father in his clubs with his friends and her mother in hers.

She read through all of the messages to see if there was one from her dad. There wasn't one.

The last yearbook was her mother's senior year, only it was from Valley, Iowa, and not Grand Island, Nebraska like the others. The inside cover had paragraphs written by different people, all similar in sentiment, each describing how wonderful or sweet her mother was. Many concluded Dineen Morgan would go far in life. Bitterness settled in Avery's stomach.

She knew her mother spent a summer in Valley, but she didn't realize she'd spent her senior year with Aunt Penny. Why?

The pages were all the same until she reached the prom photos. Stars and streamers were the backdrop as her mother stood smiling as if she didn't have a care in the world. She was surrounded by several well-dressed girls and guys, but there wasn't an indication of who would've been her date. Below the photo was a paragraph of choppily written script, smudged as if it had gotten wet and was wiped dry.

"Dineen, I'm so glad you came here this past year. You're amazing! I love you.

An ocean roared in Avery's ears as the blood rushed to her head. She searched the paragraph under the photo to find the names: Phillip Thomas, Monica Price, Dineen Morgan, and several others she didn't recognize.

I can't believe it. Mom went to school here? And stood next to MaKenzie's mom and dad, Monica and Phillip! No one ever told Avery any of this. In fact, her mother rarely talked about high school, only saying she and her dad went together. The one time Avery pressed her for answers, her mom made her go to her room, so she'd decided to quit asking.

How in the world had her mom and Monica ever been friendly enough to stand next to each other, especially with Phillip in the group?

She had asked for answers and all she'd gotten were more questions.

A key in the door caught her breath. "I don't care how many lawyers you have. You've already taken everything away from me. Why should I do anything else for you or for her?" His curse-laden yells echoed across the living room into the bedroom where she stood, frozen to the spot.

"You should've thought of that years ago. This wasn't my choice. She's not my problem. You wanted her so bad. Come and get her."

Come and get whom? Her mother was gone. Wasn't she? Avery stood as silent as she could until the upstairs bedroom door slammed shut, rattling the windows.

Avery pulled out her cell phone. With a deep breath she dialed her mother's number. She was going to get answers one way or another. It went to voice mail.

"Yes, Mother. This is your daughter. If you ever want me to talk with you again, you need to call me back. Like, now."

Chapter Twenty-One

(Lie #10: Life is not about rainbows and butterflies.)

Avery stared unseeing at the Pizzeria's menu. Thoughts stormed through her mind. If only there was someone she could ask about her mom or her dad. The only person she knew to ask or who would know anything besides her dad would have been her Aunt Penny. And if tonight was any indication, talking to her dad wouldn't go anywhere.

Why couldn't she have a nice, normal family instead?

Katie walked in, her face alight. Avery couldn't help but grin despite her swirling emotions. She silently thanked God for her friend's shining personality.

"Oh my gosh! What a day." Katie whirled into the booth across from Avery. "Oh, shoot. I'm sorry. Your day was kind of messed up, too."

If you only knew. She shook off the thoughts of her dad's irate phone call. Instead, Avery waved her hand at her friend. "Let's forget all about it and have some fun."

Katie squealed in agreement.

Heavy scents of baking bread, spicy tomato sauce, and browning cheese filled the restaurant. Half a pizza filled Avery's stomach, but she kept nibbling on the crusts and picking off meat and pieces of cheese. Katie chatted about the kids she had babysat that afternoon, but Avery's mind kept going back to her mother's yearbooks and the secrets they held.

Katie would think her mother's past love life terribly romantic, but Avery didn't want to confess she hadn't known her mother went to high school in Valley. Katie would ask questions she couldn't answer.

Why had her mom kept that information from her? What was the big secret?

Katie kept talking, oblivious to Avery's distractions. A half-hour later, several cars pulled into the parking lot, and people filled the empty tables and booths. A table full of teenage guys chatted enthusiastically about the demolition derby.

"Looks like I gotta go pick up Michael from the fair." Katie wiped her hands with a red-and-white checked napkin. She nudged Avery with her foot. "You want to come with and see your boyfriend?"

"I—" Five guys step into the Pizzeria. The sight of Jaxson took her breath away. A black cowboy hat, the sides of which curled up instead of lying flat, sat perched on his head. He had ditched his normal t-shirts for a designer gray shirt, and the boot cut jeans made him look slimmer than he already was.

The group walked toward their booth. Michael, Davis, and two others she didn't know teased Jaxson and punched him in the shoulder. A blush graced his face.

"Hi." Avery scooted over to allow Jaxson room to sit next to her. Michael sat next to his sister, and the other three grabbed empty chairs from the tables around the booth. Davis sat closest to Michael, his chair backwards so he draped his arms across the back of the seat. Avery sat in the corner of the booth, turned toward Jaxson, and had no way to avoid looking at Davis without getting a crick in her neck.

"I thought I had to pick you up?" Katie asked.

Michael shrugged. "Jaxson gave me a ride."

"Yeah, and Grant brought us." Davis nodded at one of the guys Avery didn't know.

Michael grabbed a slice of pizza.

"Hey!" Katie protested.

"What? I'm hungry." Pieces of chewed up pizza flew out as he talked. All the guys laughed.

Chantra Berg walked in, dressed in a tight-fitting t-shirt and shorts. She resembled the picture of a mushroom that was framed on the wall by the front door. Avery would have laughed had Chantra not been the person who fired Avery to save her own job. Chantra and two of her divorced friends stood in line waiting to be seated.

Jaxson put his hand over hers and squeezed. Avery smiled up at him and leaned against his shoulder. She was relieved when Chantra and her friends took a booth out of view.

"You guys finished with your pizza?" Davis's hand hovered above the pie.

"I was going to take it home," Avery allowed her irritation to show.

"Oh. Okay." The dejected tone of his voice almost made her change her mind. "Don't like pepperoni anyway. It's for girls."

Michael stopped mid-bite. "You're the girl, Davis." He crumpled up a greasy napkin and threw it at him. A heated conversation followed.

Jaxson whispered in her ear, "Bet you wish you would have come to the derby with us, huh? Forget about the pizza. Wanna get out of here?"

The bickering back and forth grew in intensity. One of the other guys grabbed a piece of pizza and smashed it into Davis's face. Sauce splattered everywhere.

Avery rested her head against Jaxson's shoulder, and away from watching Davis. "Yeah. Let's go."

Jaxson swung his long legs to the side of the booth and rose. He held his out hand.

"Have fun you guys." Katie wiggled her eyebrows up and down.

"We will. Oh, and Davis, the pizza's all yours." Jaxson laughed.

His cousin's grumbling followed them as they left the restaurant.

"Your truck or my car?" She asked as they walked out.

"My truck. I have a surprise for you." He led her to the blue pickup, clutching her hand tight in his.

"I don't think I'm up for any more surprises today." Avery pulled on his arm.

He stopped and turned. "Even if it's a good one?"

She gave him a doubtful look.

"C'mon. Trust me." He tugged on her hand, a mischievous grin on his face.

"Ugh. Why can I not say "no" to you?" Avery relented, hoping she wouldn't regret it.

***

The Chevy truck wound its way up a stretch of Loess Hills along the Lincoln Highway and rumbled up a private dirt road. Avery bumped up and down beside Jaxson, unable to get him to spill any details of the surprise.

"Ask any of my family. I can keep a secret." A greenish glow from the dashboard lights lit his face.

"Everyone has an Achilles heel. I just have to find yours." Bugs flashed in front of the headlights, the unlucky ones splattering on the windshield.

Jaxson pulled the truck to a stop on a summit and turned the headlights off. Avery gazed over the dark landscape. Stars glittered across the clear night sky.

Leaning across her, Jaxson opened the glove compartment and pulled out a box. The light from the yawning compartment shimmered off its metallic wrapping. "The gold ribbon was Delilah's idea." He ran a hand through his hair as he handed the package to her. "Consider it a belated birthday present."

She fingered the bow, unable to look him in the eye. "I can't believe you got me a present."

"I remember back a couple of months ago when you spent the night with Katie for your birthday." He grinned. "I couldn't come over because you were there."

She laughed. "Right! The Carter's one-friend-over-at–a-time rule. I'm surprised Katie's mom let you in the night we did the tie-dye shirts."

"Yeah." He chuckled. "Open it."

Avery unwrapped it, careful not to tear the pretty wrapping. Inside the box was a necklace. A butterfly hung from a gold chain. The wings of the butterfly had pastel-colored gems that matched the pattern from her jeans in her senior picture.

"Oh." Avery's voice came out breathy, "Jaxson, it's beautiful."

"After what happened today, I wanted you to have this to remember to always have hope and never give up. Butterflies don't live a long life. Life is too short to be miserable about things you can't control."

He took her hand and placed it over his heart. "Do you feel that?"

She did. His strong heartbeat made her pulse race.

He hooked her chin with his other hand, forcing her to look straight into his eyes. "The doctors all said I wouldn't live past a year. But mom and dad both said I was a fighter. That I had some amazing will to live or something." He shook his head. "I've had almost a dozen surgeries so far, and I'll probably have a few more before I die. But the pain? All the difficulties? They didn't last. I don't even think about it most days."

She touched his cheek where his black eye had turned a mustard color. He closed his eyes as she brushed the bruised spot with her thumb.

"My Grandma Stewart says nothing lasts forever, and life won't always be so hard." His hand slid across her palm and his long, slim fingers twined through hers.

She glanced up at him. "Do you think she's right?"

"She's never been wrong. Says you just have to have faith and believe."

Her heart twisted. She wished it could be as easy as believing something and having it come true.

"You know I believe in you." Jaxson's grin was contagious.

Looking into Jaxson's eyes, Avery could almost believe anything he said. "Do you know how amazing you are?"

"Yeah?"

"Yeah," she said, handing him the necklace so he could put it on for her. Goosebumps shivered down her arms at the touch of his hand on the back of her neck.

"Avery, look." Jaxson pointed to a falling star streaking across the evening sky. "Make a wish."

Closing her eyes tight, she made the biggest wish of her life. She wished that despite nothing good ever seeming to stick around, the happiness of this moment would last forever.

Chapter Twenty-Two

(Truth #12: Never sneak up on people.)

E laine was waiting at the table when Avery arrived Saturday afternoon to cover the fair booth. She was emptying the votes for favorite photo out of the glass jar from the day before.

"Good turn out last night?" Avery asked.

"You betcha." Elaine rose to leave and grabbed her purse and camera case. "It may be busier today, but don't worry about leaving the booth." She pointed to a guy standing by the back door. "They've added security."

Avery's eyes widened. She had never seen security at the fair. *Oh, they probably weren't obvious before.* The beefy guy guarding the back door looked more like a bouncer. Any trepidation she may have had from yesterday melted away.

Elaine glanced at her watch. "I should be back in three hours. See ya later, kiddo."

The crowds came in waves with the heaviest before and after noon. Avery smiled and made small talk with everyone who stopped by and added votes to the jar. A clipboard held a sheet for people to sign up for future photography sessions, and by the start of the third hour Avery had fifteen solid sessions and four people who had questions for Elaine to call back later.

"You did a great job," Elaine said, motioning to the sessions sheet when she returned.

Warmth flooded Avery. "It was nothing."

Elaine stopped. "It's not 'nothing,' darlin'. You signed up more people in one afternoon than I usually do during the whole fair." She smiled and clapped her hands. "I do believe you're hired."

"Hired? For what?"

"For the job. You're going to be my assistant. My kids have been after me to find someone who can do some work so I'm not bogged down like I have been lately. You've just proven to be quite the asset. You told me you needed a job." Elaine slapped the table, laughing. "Voilà! Perfect solution. Just say 'yes' and it's a go."

The woman's eager energy amazed Avery. And she had been so cool about the portrait. About everything really. "Okay. Yes."

"Great! You'll start on Monday morning at nine. And Avery, I want you here at six tonight to help me announce the winner of the favorite portrait." Elaine gave her a serious look. "Now, you go have some fun." She shooed Avery out of the booth.

Visions of new tires, senior photos, and cupboards full of food danced in Avery's mind.

Excited, Avery headed over to the RV area where the 4-H families kept their campers during the fair. Jaxson mentioned he would be sleeping in today since he had nothing left to show, and no mandatory 4-H chores. She wanted to share her big news about finding a job with him.

The RV area was a scaled-down version of a trailer park. Clothes and towels hung up to dry on makeshift clotheslines. Each RV had grills and coolers. It was all so homey.

The picture of families chatting and laughing around open fires that came to mind cut like a double-edged sword in her heart, both stinging and wistful. She shook her head.

"Avie. You want to color wiff me?"

Avery looked down into Delilah's angelic face. "Hi, Delilah. Actually, I'm looking for Jaxson. Is he around?" She walked over to the picnic table where the little girl sat, crayon in hand. She'd scribbled over a princess picture with purple, her favorite color.

The three-year-old continued to color as she spoke. "Daddy made him check on Sunny."

"Who's Sunny?" Avery waved at Mrs. Stewart through a window in the RV.

Delilah giggled. "She's his cow, siwwy."

Avery couldn't help but laugh with her. "I see. Maybe I'll go check up on Sunny, too." Avery walked across the park toward the cattle barn. Inside she found Jaxson sweeping the walkway clean of debris, his back toward her. There were fans blowing on the animals to keep them cool, so he didn't hear her approach.

Avery poked him in his sides. Jaxson swung the broom around and smacked her in the face with the handle. Stars exploded behind her eyes and cheek, warmth trickling down her nose.

"Avery," Jaxson dropped the broom handle, startling the cattle. "Oh my gosh, I'm so sorry." He grabbed her by the shoulders and walked her away from the bawling animals to the other side of the barn to sit on his wooden 4-H chest.

Avery tried to reassure him, hand clutching her nose. "Id was by fault. I shouldn't hab dried do subrise you."

Jaxson sat in front of her, leaning over to look at her face. "Let me see." He studied her nose, running his fingers lightly over the bridge and across her right cheek.

Avery swallowed and inhaled gently. "I'm such an idiot. Remind me never to sneak up on you again." The pain made her eyes water. "Is my nose bleeding?" She put her fingers up to her nose to check. Her cheek throbbed.

"No, it probably feels like it since I smacked it pretty good." He chuckled.

"What's so funny?"

"You're going to look like me, just not quite as heroic, Rocky two. Or is it three now?" He teased.

She sent him a sarcastic grin. "Nice."

"You're going to need some ice." He took out his cell phone and called his mom. "Your dad isn't going to, like, kill me or anything, is he?"

"What?" she asked, confused.

"When he sees your shiner. He's not going to put a hit out on me, call the cops, or anything, right?" His teasing held a serious note.

Avery wished her dad would be so concerned. "Oh, no. He's been busy. Probably won't even see it before it disappears."

Jaxson tilted his head. "Tomorrow's Sunday. It'll be kind of hard to hide that for a whole day."

Unease gnawed at her. She was ashamed to tell him that she never saw her dad these days. She avoided him as much as possible. And when she had a chance to see her dad he was always drunk just added icing to the forbidden-topic cake.

"Nah. He sleeps in and then does stuff around the farm. You know, there's always something that needs to be done." Her voice squeaked.

Avery looked away from Jaxson's piercing blue eyes. She felt horrible lying to him, but the alternative was too embarrassing to admit.

She cleared her throat. "Do you have something to drink?"

Jaxson left to get her a bottle of water. Avery stared at her sneakers. A hand on her shoulder brought her out of her thoughts.

The icepack Jaxson's mother handed her already dripped from the heat.

"Thank you."

"What in the world happened?" Concern lined Janelle's face.

Avery rolled her eyes, smiling. "I snuck up behind Jaxson thinking I'd surprise him. He swung around, and I walked into his broom handle."

Janelle covered her mouth with her hand to stifle a laugh.

She shrugged. The pack was cold against her skin. "It's okay. You can laugh. It is funny. If you aren't me, anyway."

"Good thing you got your senior pictures taken already, huh?" Janelle sat on the chest next to her.

The ice numbed the area between Avery's cheek and nose. "That's the truth."

"Look, why don't you come lay down in the camper for a bit with the icepack. It would be much more comfortable than trying to keep your head tilted back the whole time." Janelle stood.

"You're probably right."

Jaxson ran to them, a bottle of water in his hand. "Hey, where are you guys going?"

"I'm taking Avery over to the camper. It'll be easier for her with the icepack." Janelle's hand guided Avery through the RV camp.

"But…" Jaxson was clearly flustered.

Avery stopped walking and looked at him. "What's the matter? You have underwear hanging around or something?" She giggled at the thought.

"Well, Jaxson, why don't you run ahead if you're so worried about your mess, and clean it up, like it was already supposed to be. We promise to go slow so you have time, right Avery?" Mischief danced in Jaxson's mother's eyes, and her lips quivered with humor.

"I'd love to see how messy you really are."

Something between a groan and a grunt rolled out of Jaxson's chest as he took off ahead of them.

They laughed at how quickly Jaxson flew into action.

"So, is he like a slob? Does he have a teddy bear he sleeps with that he doesn't want me to see?"

Janelle's wide smile made her eyes crinkle at the edges. "The camper was a mess this morning when I walked in with the girls. I told him to pick it up, but he didn't get a chance to before he left to clean the cattle barn." She hugged Avery with one arm. "He's not used to having a girl drop by. Maybe this'll inspire him to keep it picked up."

The camper had a little air conditioner in one of the side windows, so it was cool inside. However, when Mrs. Stewart opened the door, a dusty smell mixed with dirty socks and boy body odor whirled around them. It was worse than any locker room she'd ever smelled.

"Emily, Delilah, and I go back home at night. You might say this is a bachelor pad. It could probably use some air freshener." Emily and Delilah sat on the couch watching a movie on a DVD player. Both girls nodded.

Jaxson ran his hand through his hair, his tan face flushing.

His mother began tidying the dishes in the kitchen area. "Avery, go ahead and lie down on the bed and relax. Son, you need to finish cleaning out the stalls. Avery will be fine with us."

The door to the camper creaked as he opened it. "I'll be back shortly."

Avery shifted the ice pack so she could see him. "Okay." She picked up a wrinkled sock with the tips of her fingernails. With a scowl, she tossed it at Jaxson's sisters.

The girls screamed and squealed while she and Janelle laughed. Jaxson's mouth was a thin line as he bolted back to the cattle barn, leaving the RV door ajar.

"I wonder what's gotten into that boy?" Janelle murmured.

Avery shifted on the unmade bed, trying to find a comfortable spot. When that became impossible, she got up and made the bed, bumping her shin twice due to the tight area she had to work in.

"Bonsai!" A streak of blond curls and purple sundress flashed by Avery. Blankets and pillows flew everywhere as Delilah flounced on the bed, followed by Emily's smaller pounce. The bed was their trampoline.

"Girls! Avery just made the bed. Besides, do we jump on beds?" Mrs. Stewart scolded them.

Delilah and Emily sat on the bed, eyes wide with remorse. They shook their heads no at their mother's question.

"And why don't we jump on beds?"

"'Cause the monkeys fall off and bump their heads." Delilah smiled up at her mother.

"That's right. Now help Avery straighten it out, and then it's time for us to go to the pie auction."

The girls squiggled their bodies over the blankets, smoothing out some of the wrinkles they created. When the giggling girls left, Avery remade the bed. Nose throbbing from bending over, she put the last pillow back in place. A folded up piece of paper fell to the floor.

Avery picked up the paper, an envelope. Loopy letters formed Jaxson's name. The *N* of his name had a heart drawn above it. She turned it over. Curious. On the back it read: *We make a cute couple.* A winking smiley face completed the message. She pulled the contents out. It was a photograph of Jaxson, MaKenzie by his side, and the others on the fair court lined up in front of the show barns. The handwriting looked familiar, but she knew exactly who owned the expensive perfume wafting off of the paper.

Jumping as the front door creaked open, Avery dropped the icepack.

Jaxson strode in, his shirt damp with sweat. "Got back as quick as I could." He stopped abruptly, eyeing the envelope in her hand.

Chapter Twenty-Three

(Lie #11: Everything in life can be attributed to luck, whether good or bad.)

Face flushed, Avery's pulse raced. She handed it to him. "I was making the bed when this fell out."

Caught between anger and hurt, Avery wavered on whether or not to confront him. She'd already jumped to conclusions about the kiss and that princess. Jaxson didn't seem like someone who would hide anything.

The musk of sweat and manure swirled around her as the air conditioner blew over Jaxson's body. He grabbed the note and opened his mouth.

Someone knocked at the door the instant before they flung it open. Heady, expensive perfume wafted in, mixing with the sweat and manure. Avery's stomach clenched.

MaKenzie flounced in. "Sorry I'm late, Jaxson—" Her green eyes widened as they fell on Avery, her flushed cheeks paling for an instant before brightening with a spiteful smirk.

Avery stared at her, hands itching to smack the wicked grin off her painted face.

"What are you doing here, MaKenzie?" Jaxson's face was beet red. Avery couldn't tell if it was from embarrassment or anger. He shoved the envelope with the photo in his back pocket absentmindedly.

MaKenzie stuck a manicured fingernail between her two sparkly pink lips. "We always meet here first. I just assumed—"

The screen door squealed open. Jaxson's dad stepped inside the camper and stopped before he bumped into MaKenzie. "Hey, Jaxson, you need to clean up and get down to the show barn. They're all waiting for you."

"I was just trying to hurry him along, Mr. Stewart." MaKenzie's fake laugh grated on Avery's nerves.

"I've got to shower first." Jaxson shifted from one foot to the other, staring at the blue carpet.

"MaKenzie, why don't you go tell them Jaxson's on his way." Mr. Stewart looked over at Avery and winked. "Let's let the boy get all pretty."

Avery's smile was stiff.

Jaxson leaned back against the kitchen counters to let her pass. "I'll call you later, okay?"

She pressed her lips together, but didn't answer him.

MaKenzie's curly brunette head bobbed down the two steps before she skipped away. Avery imagined a laser shooting out of her eyes—aimed dead center in the back of MaKenzie's head—and envisioned the millions of pieces of fluff that would explode into rhinestone pieces.

Mr. Stewart held the door open for her. Avery hoped he couldn't see or sense the violence she felt against the other girl at that moment.

Avery navigated on autopilot through the RV area in the opposite direction of MaKenzie. She drew a deep breath, the action stinging her swollen nose. Between the picture and MaKenzie's appearance, she'd forgotten about her injury. *And I forgot the ice.* There was no going back to get it now. Zigging around the final RV's, she exited the camping maze.

Trisha Stewart's feet crunched against the loose rock of the access road that curved around the park. She pointed to Avery's face. "Geez. What happened to you?"

"Ah, that's nothing. You should see the other guy," Avery joked.

"I heard about your senior picture. Did they ever figure out who did it?" Trisha's slick black hair was braided and coiled around her head. On anyone else it would look old fashioned, but on Trisha it looked sleek and trendy. Just like the bohemian top and shorts she wore.

Avery glanced down at her jeans and t-shirt. "Nobody ever said. I guess Elaine's still going to do the photo contest tonight."

Trisha eyed her watch. "Well, see you around."

"Hey, before you go, can I ask you a question?" Avery put her hands in her jeans pockets to keep them from shaking.

Trisha narrowed her eyes. "Yeah, sure."

Avery kicked a rock with her sneaker before continuing. "Has Jaxson ever had a girlfriend before?"

Trisha wrinkled her nose, as if the thought of her cousin having a girlfriend was repulsive. "I don't think so. Why?"

"I just wondered. Never mind." Avery waved her hands.

"Jaxson's had a crush on you for a long time. I don't know how you never figured it out." Trisha stopped, a slender finger tapping thoughtfully at her chin. "Don't let that viper get to you."

"Which viper? There seem to be a few crawling around lately."

"MaKenzie. She asked Jaxson out last summer during fair, and he turned her down flat." Trisha splayed her hands out in front of her, studying her scarlet nails. "Whatever trouble she's up to, I'm sure he couldn't care less. Really."

Avery remembered the unexpected look that crossed MaKenzie's face when she entered the camper. "I wish it were that easy."

"It is. The only thing she likes better than her reflection in a mirror is making other people miserable. I should know. Besides, Jaxson never liked her." Music blared from Trisha's phone. "Hey, I've got to go. Remember, don't let her get to you."

Avery waved as Trisha departed. She leaned against the wooden fence lining the road around the park. Checking her cell phone, she realized she had forgotten to turn it back on after she left Precious Moments booth this morning. Her phone flashed, showing that she had missed four calls and had three messages.

The first three calls were from her dad's cell phone, with one message garbled and indecipherable, but clearly not her father's voice. The fourth call was from Rose, the receptionist at the hospital telling her that her dad was in the hospital and she needed to come down as soon as she got the message.

Chapter Twenty-Four

(Lie #12: The only thing to fear is fear itself.)

Blood rushed to Avery's head. The nurse didn't say what his injuries were. What if something really bad happened to him? She'd be completely alone with no way to call or contact her mom. A headache bloomed behind her eyes.

Avery hurried to her car, stomach in knots. The drive to the hospital took forever as the traffic in and out of the park was bumper to bumper. Rose greeted her when she entered the ER, her friendly face a beacon to Avery's eyes.

"I had to call you since we were unable to reach your mother." Rose sent her a knowing look, her swift steps leading down the ER hallway.

Avery groaned, imagining what her father was brought in for. They stopped outside ERRM3. "What happened?"

Rose put her hand on Avery's arm. "I heard it from a cousin of a friend of mine. Your father had a run in with another man inside The Still Bar & Grill. Had to do with your mother and that banker." She waved her hand as if it were unimportant. "It continued outside where your dad got the worse of it. But you didn't hear it from me." She pointed toward the doorway.

"Who else was involved?" Avery turned fearful eyes toward the woman.

Rose shook her head. "Can't tell you that. I could get in enough trouble just by telling you what I already have."

The nurse opened the door. Her father was hooked up to an IV. Mechanized noises filled the air. Scratches and bruises covered his face and arms. A cut along his hairline was stitched.

"Thanks, Rose," Avery whispered, walking across the sterile room. He lay asleep on the hospital bed, snoring. What she could see of his shirt was stained with blood and something else equally disgusting. The smell of stale cigarettes, puke, and alcohol gagged her.

The doctor came in the room. "You're Avery, the daughter?"

Avery wiped her sweaty hands down the fronts of her jeans. "Yes."

"He looks worse than he is. No broken bones. Just some bumps and bruises from the fall and a cut that needed stitches. Nothing major. We're rehydrating him so he doesn't end up back in the ER again tonight. But, as soon as the IV runs out, we'll release him and you can take him home."

Avery braced herself for the truth now that she knew her father would be okay. "Was he charged with anything? Public intox? Assault? Drunk driving?"

The doctor's lips turned down. He eyed her over his glasses. "Not that I'm aware of. He was brought in by a friend, a big guy with a motorcycle tattoo on his arm. Said your father fell outside his place. No charges since it's a private residence." The doctor handed her a note that was clipped to the inside of the chart. "He left you a note, though. Said you knew him. Your dad's a lucky guy. Not everybody has someone watch over them like that."

"Big Jim," Avery murmured when she opened the note.

Avery, I tried to call you, but I couldn't hold on to your dad and talk at the same time. I'm sorry I had to leave him at the ER, didn't want to get him in any trouble. I told the Dr. he fell. His car is at The Still when you can retrieve it. Take care, Jim.

"Thank you, God," Avery whispered. Big Jim was like a guardian angel who wore leather and chains. At least there would be minimal gossip, even if Rose's friend's third cousin twice removed knew about it.

The doctor's gaze rested on her. "Like father like daughter?" He pointed to her face.

Her hand flew up to cover her bruise. "Sweeping accident. You should see the broom." Her humor sounded lame even to her own ears.

He walked over and examined her injuries. "Might need to get an X-ray."

Avery pulled away from the doctor's prying fingers. "It's all good. Really."

The doctor stared at her for an uncomfortable moment before relenting. "Better watch out for those pesky brooms from now on."

She nodded. "I will."

"You know you can tell me anything if you need to. Everything you say here is held in the strictest of confidence." His demeanor was stern, but concerned.

"It really was an accident." She shrugged it off. "This just hasn't been my lucky day."

An hour and a half later, Avery helped her groggy father into the house. Knowing there was no way to lug her dad's dead weight up the stairs to his room, she steered him to the couch. There she covered him with a blanket.

She held her half-dead phone in her hand. Before she could talk herself out of it, she dialed her mother's cell. Someone besides her needed to know what happened to her dad. It instantly went to voicemail. With a shaking voice, Avery left a short message.

Jaxson had texted her before she left the hospital, wondering where she was, no doubt. She ignored the messages, wishing the past day hadn't happened at all. Tomorrow, after she managed to buy a new charger, she'd handle him. Not tonight.

When Katie's texts came in next, she turned the phone off. Her stomach growled and she realized she hadn't eaten since ten that morning. The small amount of groceries she bought from the grocery store was gone. She found an old bag of popcorn in the back of the spice cupboard that even the mice that always showed up in cold weather hadn't touched.

Their chest freezer was in the laundry room. The contents stuck together in a big freezer-burned Popsicle, *probably from the electricity going off and the contents thawing and then refreezing when it came back on last winter.* "Ugh!"

The meat and veggies had to be a couple years old at least, probably from the days when her mom made supper for the family before Aunt Penny died. They'd been a real family back then.

Stuffing the sadness away, she poked at the Popsicle with her finger and accepted the fact there was no way to get anything useful from it. *Should've insisted on bringing that pizza home from last night.*

She grabbed her purse and headed back into town to get groceries. Now that she had a job, she could actually afford food again. Her conscience pricked her. She had skipped out on Elaine to pick up her dad. Hopefully her new boss would understand.

Her arms were full of bags when she returned, and ran into her father in the kitchen. The cupboards were all open like he'd been searching for something. *Why did the alcohol have to wear off now?*

"Where you been?" He shot her a bloodshot glare.

Avery stared at his twitching hands, anger flaring in her gut. Her dad hadn't spoken to her the whole ride home. Now he had the nerve to ask her where she'd been? She glanced into his face. "Before or after I brought your sorry hide home from the ER?"

"Don't use that tone with me." Words slurring, he ran an unsteady hand through his disheveled, graying hair. It stuck up in greasy spikes.

Avery's blood burned in her veins. Was he serious? "You want to know where I've been? I've been here, Dad. Cleaning the house, working to pay for my own groceries, doing your laundry. Where have YOU been? You ask where I've been when you can't be bothered to come home sober in what? Two, or is it three years now?"

She slammed the peanut butter on the counter. "Oh excuse me. I'm sorry. You *did* make an appearance to tell me my mother left you. You accuse me of stealing money, which I have no idea what account you're talking about. And I get static for 'using that tone' with you?" Avery was screaming by the time she finished.

"I'm the parent here. I'm in charge." Her father thrust a finger at her. The finger managed to stay still, but his legs wobbled as he stood glowering at her. "You don't get to parade around and do whatever you want, whenever you want, young lady."

"Oh, right." Avery slapped her head with her hands in mock surprise. "I forgot. You're the parent." She dropped her hands and glared at him. "Have you noticed, Mr. Parent, that there are no groceries in the house? Have you noticed, Mr. Parent, the lawn needed mowing a month ago? Did you realize, Mr. Parent, that I've been the one doing it all? Taking messages from bill collectors. Doing your laundry. Cleaning the house." She pointed a loaf of bread at her father, the contents squished where she clasped it. "Making sure your CHILD has food to eat, with money from HER job. Real parental, DAD."

She glowered at him, knowing full well it had partly been the money she had taken from his clothes while doing laundry that paid for the food she just bought. But still, she resembled a parent more than he did, and they both knew it.

Her dad's nostrils flared and his eyes bugged out like she'd never seen before.

She wasn't done though. "Oh, and, Mr. Parent. I'm the one who got the call to go get her drunken, idiot father from the ER and bring him home safely. I'm not the one out there getting soused and picking the losing side of a fight. I'll use whatever tone I want." She smacked her hand on the counter.

He moved before she knew it, his body towered over hers. Gone was his sloppy, inept drunken demeanor. A shot of adrenaline pumping through him must've momentarily sobered him, clearing the glaze from his eyes.

If Avery hadn't been quite as mad, she would've known to be afraid. But she was more than mad. She was furious. At him. At Jaxson. At MaKenzie.

The slap to her cheek blinded her seconds before pain burst behind her uninjured eye.

"You are *not* my daughter. I was generous enough to raise you as mine, and this is how I'm repaid?" He spat at her, his breath still acrid from cigarettes and alcohol. "Then again, I shouldn't be surprised. Rotten apples don't fall far from the tree. Probably end up pregnant before you even graduate. You know, follow in your mother's footsteps."

Avery's hands shook as she cradled her throbbing cheek. Her lungs seized in her chest.

He laughed at the stunned expression on her face. "Your innocent act doesn't fool me. Don't think I haven't heard about you and your little boyfriend. I won't be supporting any more illegitimate babies, though, so I better not ever catch you with him, or any other boy for that matter. You'll think that smack was a walk in the park." He stared at her, his lips turned down in an ugly grimace. "Worthless. Just like your mom."

Avery used every ounce of energy she had not to flinch at his words. She refused to show him that what he said was cutting into her soul like pieces of broken glass, leaving behind thousands of miniscule, unseen nicks—damage worse than the slap to her face.

He swung around and stomped up the stairway to his bedroom, slamming the stair door hard enough to loosen the plaster from the dining room ceiling. Dust and chunks rained over the table.

She grasped counter's edge, her lungs finally working, and inhaled great gulps of air to keep from screaming.

***

Sophie's phone went to voicemail three times, so Avery called her home phone. Mrs. Morris answered it.

"Hey, Mrs. Morris, is Sophie around?" Avery unsuccessfully tried to keep the waver out of her voice. She held a quaking, icy hand to her newly bruised cheek, while trying not to drop the cell phone with the other trembling hand.

"No. She told me she was with you." The line crackled.

Great.

Avery closed her eyes, working hard to keep her breathing normal. She had to think fast. "We got separated. I thought she got mad at me and went home. So…she's not there yet?" She rushed on without waiting for an answer. "Okay. I'll keep looking for her." She hung up.

Terrific. Now she got her best friend in trouble. Why didn't Sophie warn her she was using Avery for her cover?

Now what? She couldn't stay home, even with her dad passed out. Going back to the Fair was not an option, not with marks on both sides of her face. Anyone seeing her right now would know something was very wrong.

Avery quickly stuck the perishable groceries in the fridge; it was too hot outside to keep them. Then she gathered the rest back in the bags. Upstairs she grabbed a pillow, blanket, iPod, and some clothes she had folded. She tiptoed past her dad's bedroom, keeping her ears trained on the snoring behind the door in case it stopped. In the bathroom she stuffed her toothbrush and paste, brush and makeup into her beach bag. She refused to look in the mirror. Arms full, she headed to her car and took off.

She drove in circles for an hour thinking about what her dad said, wondering what it meant. Questioning why her mother left and hadn't come back—or even called her yet. Her life seemed to be going around in the same circles. Just when she thought she saw a horizon—a light at the end of her proverbial tunnel—she'd hit a curve, and around she would go again. She wanted off this un-merry-go-round.

The digital clock on the dash read 11:00 when she turned into the sharp incline to Mercer's Hill. Her donut spun on the rock, but she punched the gas and made it up the steep incline. She parked in the farthest corner next to the peak and turned off the car.

The night sky was cloudy and dark, lit only by the glow of a fingernail moon. Cool evening air rushed over her face as she exited the car. Her tears had dried up long before, leaving her frozen, numb.

A metal cable fence set up along the hill's edge was easy for her to scale. She stepped through thigh-high weeds to reach the drop-off overlooking the road a hundred feet below. Heart racing, she glanced over the side of the hill.

Avery started laughing. The ledge had crumbled and fallen. The hill bubbled out below her. Somehow she imagined an ocean cliff where she could stand on the precipice of danger above the jagged rocks below, the wind blowing a billowy dress around her legs, before she plunged to a martyr's death.

"So much for scoffing in the face of mortality." The only hazard to this hill was snagging her clothes on the saplings that jutted out like weeds. Not that she had seriously considered jumping. But she couldn't even pick the right place to stare down death. More derisive laughter gurgled in her throat.

She hiked back to the rocky overlook parking area. Crickets serenaded her as she sat her chilled body on her car's warm hood. Her hands still quivered with shock. Her phone buzzed in her pocket.

It was a text from Sophie. *smooth move. grounded again. next time warn me when you're going to call the house.*

Avery texted back, *next time don't use me for a cover w/o telling me, lame-o. your fault you're grounded. I've got bigger problems to worry about.*

Sophie sent back, *where are you? Jaxson is going crazy trying to find you. did you break up and not tell him?*

Avery sighed. *no. got into it with dad. don't want Jaxson to know.*

Sophie: *nice. are you ok?*

Avery: *peachy. another fun night at the Denton household. that's why I called. wanted you to talk me down.*

Sophie: *where are you? home?*

Avery: *just driving around. don't worry. I didn't jump.*

Sophie: *jump? jump where? and you better not. want to come over? spend the nite? I have to visit the nursing home as punishment tomorrow, you should go with since it's your fault.*

Avery giggled. Sophie hated the smell of old people. She texted back, *ha, ha. NO thanks. next time you'll remember to tell me to cover before I call.*

Sophie : *you sure your ok ?*
Avery: *terrific.*
Sophie: *sweet dreams, loser.*
Avery: *g'nite, hag.*

Her phone battery light blinked. It was almost dead so she turned it off. And no car charger. She dug out her pillow and blanket. Locking the doors, she leaned the driver's seat back. The hill and trees shadowed over her, hiding her. Though it was dark, and traffic this late was light, it was still unnerving to be sleeping in her car. Only a few vehicles drove by, just enough to keep her awake.

Avery got her iPod out and put it on low enough to lull her into a sleep. Pulling her pillow over her head, she dozed off.

A heavy pounding shook the car. Lights blared in from her side window. A shadow passed over.

Avery screamed.

Chapter Twenty-Five

(Truth #13: God only gives you what you can handle—with him.)

The pounding continued. "Avery! It's Jaxson. Open up."

Her heart beat out of her chest as she struggled to get her bearings. The pounding turned to slapping against her window.

"What?" She opened the door, her body buzzing from waking up so suddenly. "Seriously, who pounds on someone's window this late at night? You scared the crud out of me."

Jaxson's truck was parked in a T beside her car, the engine still running. Tire marks looked like he pulled up in a hurry and slid to a stop. "I scared you? You scared me, Avery. What are you doing out here?"

Jaxson was yelling at her? "Why are you here? And why are you yelling at me?" She tossed her iPod aside and got out of the car.

"Sophie texted me that you were out driving around. She said something about not jumping. I figured I might know where you were. Gee, guess I was right. Why are you sleeping in your car? And what was that about not jumping?" Jaxson reached out, but she stepped back.

"Sophie texted you? Since when are you friends?" Avery was going to kill her.

He stared at her. "Since you disappear without a trace and no one, I mean *no one*, knew where you were." He flung his arms out wide. "Dang it, Avery, I almost called the cops and filed a Missing Person Report. Then Sophie said 'not to worry, you didn't jump'. What do you think that does to a person?" He bent over her, hands on his hips. His lips were twisted into a frown.

Her shoulders drooped. It became difficult to breathe as a band constricted across her chest. "That's a little dramatic, don't you think?"

"I've been trying since four o'clock to call you. Why didn't you answer my calls? You obviously answered Sophie." Jaxson's taller, imposing stance shadowed her, his tone accusing.

Avery breathed in deep, cleansing breaths, easing the tightness from her chest, and walked away from him. It was all too much. Whoever said God didn't give you more than you could handle was a liar.

"Avery. Tell me what's going on, please. I don't understand what's making you act like this."

Every nerve in her body was taut as anger boiled under her skin. She couldn't handle another person yelling at her.

She spun around to face him. "Acting like what? Acting guilty like you did when I went to your camper and found out you were hiding a picture of you and MaKenzie? Then, when MaKenzie shows up, you start acting all weird." She wished she could throw something, break something. "Is that what I'm acting like? Tell me, Jaxson. What am I acting like?"

He moved in front of her, not touching, but close enough that she could smell his body spray. She put a hand over her trembling lips and dropped to the ground, leaning against her back tire. Tears streamed down her face.

"I'm sorry I didn't tell you about the note." He sat two feet away from her, the truck headlights shining on his back, casting a distorted image on the gravel parkway.

A burning ball gathered in her stomach. She threw a rock across the lot into the weeds. "You know, it's not just about that stupid note or the fact you kept it from me. This," she waved her hands out in a sweeping gesture to include the car and the parking lot, "is not about you, Jaxson."

"Avery, just tell me what's going on." He dropped onto one knee, and put his hand on her chin. The plea in his voice was almost too much to bear.

Her dad's threats about her boyfriend sped through her mind. Then she remembered Jaxson's opinion about his drunken uncle and cousins from the BBQ at his house, how he thought they were "wastes of space."

She jerked her face away. "Stop it."

"Is that a different bruise than the one from this afternoon?" He sat on his haunches, almost like the day at the beach.

She shrugged. "Went for a walk in the dark and ran into a tree. Clumsy me." Her voice cracked, bitterness eating at her insides like acid.

Nothing in her life remained good, ever. How could she believe hooking up with Jaxson would be any different? "You can't fix what's wrong with my life, Jaxson. No one can. Everything in my life sucks. Everything."

"That doesn't make any sense to me," he said, his voice tight.

"It's not supposed to make sense to you. Your life is a Norman Rockwell picture." She leveled a serious glare at him. "You have this perfect little life with this perfect little family and a perfect future ahead of you. Everything you do or have is golden. My life?" She laughed and turned away from him. "My life is about as far away from that as white is from black. So I'm giving you this chance to get out while you can. Before my life runs over into yours and you end up hating me because of it." She unclasped the necklace he gave her. "Take it and leave."

He didn't move.

She pointed to his truck. "Leave!"

Jaxson's blue eyes widened. "I don't want the necklace back. I gave it to you for your birthday. It's yours," he whispered. "You can't breakup with me. I won't let you. I don't care what you think is so bad about your life. You're wrong."

Avery swiped her runny nose. "I'm not wrong, and I'm not giving you a choice." She had to get him to leave before her heart took over. Her dad's threats might be real, or they might not be. But she knew as sure as the stars in the sky tonight that her life and his didn't mix.

She just had to convince Jaxson to leave. "I was stupid for dating someone so young. Sophie was right. You're an infant." Her heart cracking in her chest, she thrust out her hand with the necklace in it.

He stood and glared at her.

Tear streaks shimmered on his cheeks. He hesitated but turned and walked to his truck. He looked at her again before he got in. She sat unmoving, waiting for him to leave. The truck revved and pealed out. Rocks flew in every direction, smacking against the outside of her car. She held her hands up to protect her face, and a rock caught the underside of her forearm. She welcomed the pain. She deserved it for what she'd said to him.

In an instant, Jaxson was gone for good. It was for the best. This way he'd never find out about her screwed up family and her dad wouldn't have anything to threaten her with again. Jaxson would get over her eventually. He'd get a normal girlfriend, and they'd have normal fights. A gasp caught in her throat at the loss of Jaxson. His friendship. His almost love.

She got in her Taurus, started it, and drove down the empty country roads. Past her house, she pulled into the abandoned house next door. Under the cover of an old barn behind the house, she parked the car where it wouldn't be seen.

Avery picked up the blanket, held it to her mouth, and screamed until she choked. Never had the nightmares in her dreams been as horrible as the ones in her real life.

***

The morning sun rained through cracks in the barn roof. Speckled sunlight glinted off of the butterfly necklace, throwing rainbow reflections across the car's interior. Avery had thrown it on the dashboard when she left Mercer's Hill. She gathered it and stuffed it into her beach bag.

Avery turned the key in the ignition far enough to check the time. 11:45. A sharp pain pricked her neck where she had slept crooked against the window. She carefully crawled out of the car, stretched, and tried to work out the kinks.

When she was a child, she would play house in their barn, making mud pies. Towels served as curtains, crayon-scribbled pictures were her decorations.

What she wouldn't give to be that innocent again.

Behind the barn, in a vacant penned area, was an old hose. She turned it on, waited for the air and rust to clear, and splashed the cold well water over her head, allowing the refreshing onslaught to wake her up. Peeling off her clothes, she quickly dipped her body under the water. The cold water numbed her, so she used a beach towel from the bottom of her bag to scrub the feeling back.

After changing into dry clothes she'd grabbed last night, she hiked through the pastures and up to the spot where her favorite tree grew. If ever she needed to feel the problems in her life were insignificant, it was now. Her footsteps crashed through the underbrush, sending birds skittering through the trees.

The last storm's winds had broken several limbs off the tree, scattering them across the area. The trunk of her tree had another large chunk of a downed oak across it. She ran her hand across the rough bark. A breeze fluttered through her damp hair like a caress.

"Aunt Penny?" Could her aunt be there with her? She wasn't sure if she believed in ghosts or not. Her ghosts were not the apparitional type.

Bees buzzed around a patch of thistles and chicory, the purple blooms standing proud among the debris. The cornfields below were almost eight feet tall already. She shook her head in disbelief. How could things change so quickly without her noticing?

Thoughts of the past month and a half swirled through her mind. Her mother's leaving. Losing her job and the rejection she had experienced with it. Her father. Jaxson.

A butterfly fluttered and landed on her hand. Its bright blue wings pumped back and forth, as if waiting for her to do something. Four other blue-and-white butterflies flew by, sending the one on her hand darting into the air. They chased each other above the wildflowers. Avery thought of the necklace and how it had represented hope.

Elaine's face popped in her head. *"In this old world things happen that just don't make sense. Wrong, hurtful things. It's just a fact. Some people make themselves feel big by making others feel small. Their day will come. But don't you ever let them win by your feeling less than what you are or changing who you are. Ever."*

Jaxson had said similar things to her. The trouble was she didn't know what was true anymore. And after last night's conversation with her dad, she wasn't even sure he was her father. What she did know was that she was a lost soul in a broken life.

Tears stung her eyes. "God. I know I haven't talked to you much since Aunt Penny died. But, I don't know if I can handle anymore. Aunt Penny always said if you ask you will receive. I'm not strong enough to do this on my own, God. Please. You've got to help me."

The sun's warmth enveloped her in a hug.

Avery hung her head and cried.

Chapter Twenty-Six

(Lie #13: You can only count on yourself in life.)

A very shored up her strength on Monday, turning the handle to Precious Moments Studios. Her stomach churned, knowing she owed Elaine an explanation for being AWOL Saturday evening.

Elaine sat at her desk when Avery walked in, attention focused on her computer screen.

"Hey," Avery stated, testing the water.

"Come on in. I'm just going over some shots from a wedding yesterday. Have a seat. It'll only be a couple of minutes."

Avery sat on a plush couch on the opposite wall and looked around the room. Every photo on display was amazing. She hadn't noticed how beautiful they were before.

"Okay. Well, darlin', you missed out on the best part of the fair." Elaine handed her an envelope. "Wow. You look like you've seen better days." She motioned to Avery's bruised face hidden underneath a ton of makeup. "Wanna talk about it?"

Avery took the envelope, shaking her head at the question. "I'm sorry I missed out Saturday. Something came up and I had to leave."

The photographer held up her hand. "You didn't have to be there to win. But, promise me something. Next time you go off on your own, tell someone where you're going. That boyfriend of yours like to drove me crazy about you." Elaine laughed and waved her hands in the air. "I had to talk him out of callin' the cops."

Avery gave a half-hearted smile. *Great, everyone'll know I was gone.* "Ha, yeah. So I heard."

Elaine leveled her with a serious look. "So, how is your dad?"

Avery's head whipped up.

"Now, don't look so surprised. There are no secrets in small towns. The only thing that travels faster than gossip is the speed of light, and sometimes I wonder if gossip's faster."

Avery's face flushed, and she looked away. No secrets in small towns? She knew that wasn't true. But, there was obviously no keeping secrets from Elaine.

"Hey. It's okay. I don't judge. I knew about your dad before you called and wanted your senior pictures done. I know what people have been saying about your mom and Phillip Thomas." She grinned, a mischievous glint in her eyes. "Bartenders, hairstylists, and photographers. People tend to feel free to express themselves to people like us without hesitation. No filters."

She returned to her desk chair. "The thing about me you need to know is that I don't hold those things against people like others might. Everyone deserves to stand on their own merit. Now open that envelope up, girlie."

Avery slipped her finger under the flap and ripped it open. Inside was a check, written for five hundred and twelve dollars from Precious Moments Studios to Avery. Her eyes widened as she met Elaine's look. "What's this?"

"People heard about the graffiti on your portrait and wanted to help. Some of it I used to repay what I spent on your portrait that insurance didn't cover. The rest of the money's yours." She smiled.

Avery shook her head, the words refusing to come out of her mouth.

"I made an excuse for you and thanked the crowd for their love and generosity. Then the paper took my picture. Imagine that, someone taking MY picture." Elaine cackled. "The best part of this is all those people you signed up. Not only do I have business on the horizon, but you get your senior pictures for free. Well, up to a certain amount, that is."

Avery giggled at the sound of the woman's odd laugh, still a bit stunned.

"Now, it's time for you to learn what your job responsibilities are." Elaine slapped her hands together and showed her around.

Five hours later, Avery knew her way around the studio, understood the basics about the equipment, and was getting ready to leave for the afternoon.

"I need your help tonight at the Honey Creek Recreation Center. Here's the address, be there by six thirty." Elaine handed her a slip of paper.

"Will do." Avery headed to the bank, which was on the same block as the studio, to cash the check. Luckily, she already had an account from when she started working at the Valley Market last summer when she needed gas money. She had stopped putting money in the account when her mother realized she could withdraw cash out since her name was on it as the account holder. Now with her mom gone, she could start putting money in it again safely.

It was a relief to know she could buy the tire she needed for her car now.

Valley had only one tire store, the OK Tire store owned by Sean Thomas, Phillip Thomas's older brother. Avery considered going to Council Bluffs or Omaha, but it was a waste of gas, and although she had a job with Elaine and the extra cash, she knew from experience money wouldn't last long. Sean Thomas had always treated her and her mother with respect when they came in, and she hoped he would still do the same today.

The smell of grease and exhaust choked Avery when she walked into the office of the tire shop. An old air conditioner chugged out a lukewarm breeze above a metal counter. An ashtray full of butts and ashes spilled out in front of a coffee pot. The sludge at the bottom of the pot had turned black, the sour odor of scorched coffee hung in the air.

The door jingled. Bryce, the owner's stepson, strode in. Oil stains covered his gray, striped coveralls. He smirked.

"Hmm. Must be my lucky day." He wiped his hands off on a dirty rag. Having graduated two years ago, he had already gotten his mechanic's certification and worked for his stepfather in the shop. His cockiness and self-importance reminded her of MaKenzie, his cousin, although they weren't blood related.

"I need a tire." Avery handed him a slip of paper she had written the brand and size on.

He held the paper, his gaze scanning her from head to toe. "Just a tire? Sure you couldn't use an alignment or possibly a rotation? What do you say?" He gestured his fingers in a suggestive manner.

She fetched the cut-out coupon from her back pocket. "Just the tire. I have your coupon from the newspaper for it."

"That's expired." He spat on the ground.

"No it's not." She held it up at eye level.

His face darkened. "We have the right to refuse service to certain people."

"Look, Bryce. I don't want any trouble. I just need to buy a tire." Avery despised his arrogance.

Chew juice darkened his smile. "Ah. We're clean out."

She turned around, arms outstretched at the racks of tires that lined the far walls of the building. "I can see that. Is your dad around?"

His face turned red. "You need to leave, Denton. We don't have any tires for you."

The door jingled again, and Bryce's demeanor shifted. A frowning Sean Thomas walked in, holding some invoices. "Bryce, we're missing a couple of the boxes you checked in this weekend." He glanced up. "Oh, hi, Avery. Have you been helped?"

"Yeah, she's been helped." Bryce spat on the ground again. "We don't got what she needs."

"How many times do I have to ask you not to do that in here? Go get the inventory straightened out." Sean stabbed his stepson in the chest with the invoices.

Bryce dropped the sheet Avery had given him, grabbed hold of the papers and crumpled the bunch in his fists. He glared at her, his lips pinched into a frown. His footsteps echoed through the office as he stomped away.

Sean Thomas sighed. "Now, Avery. What was it you needed?" The dark hair and square jaw resembled his brother Phillip. He was not near as uptight or self-important, though.

She bent to pick up the slip of paper she had given Bryce and handed it, along with the coupon, to the mechanic. "I need a tire."

"Right over here. Do you need me to put it on for you? It's free with your coupon." He walked over to a row of tires, rolled one off, and walked back to her.

"Yeah, that would be great." Avery put her hands in her pockets, then crossed them over her chest. She hadn't considered how awkward it would be to see the brother of the man her mother ran off with.

"Normally I'd have you buy two tires so they don't wear crooked, but the tread is pretty good still. I don't think you need two. It'll only take a couple of minutes if you want a seat." He nodded toward a cracked orange vinyl chair sitting along the front window. "Keys?"

Avery would have preferred to be anywhere but there, but since it would only take a few minutes, she relented and handed him her keys. Bryce walked back and forth across the doorway in the garage, sending her dirty looks each time he passed, stopping only after his father yelled at him.

Fifteen minutes later, the ratchet noise died. Her new tire shone a beautiful black. Sean fixed the flat, and hefted the donut into the trunk. He scratched the details on a receipt.

She took it from him, confused. "You fixed the flat? I didn't ask to have that done."

The hard expression on his face softened. "I know. It's the least I can do. Life probably hasn't been easy for you lately. The money for the tire is all I need."

Avery pulled out her wallet and paid. Questions formed in her mind. Of all people Sean would have had reason to be nasty. Phillip Thomas left a mess behind when he quit his job and took off with her mom. Sean could have easily held it against her. She voiced none of this, grateful instead for his kindness. "Thank you, Mr. Thomas."

He nodded. "Next time you need any help with your car, give me a call, okay?"

Touched by the offer, she glanced up at him. "Thanks." Her throat closed off. For the second time that day people had been generous to her beyond what she ever imagined. She wiped the moisture from her eyes as she got in her Taurus and headed home.

Her tears dried up, however, when she noticed her dad coming out of the gas station. In his hands he held a long brown bag. There was no doubt it was a fifth of whiskey. She prayed silently he wouldn't notice her car.

Chapter Twenty-Seven

(Truth #14: Confession is good for the soul.)

The Rec Center in Honey Creek was almost empty when Avery drove up to meet Elaine. She wished she would have asked her boss more questions that morning about what kind of photo session they were doing, but she'd been too blown away after receiving the money. Elaine was already inside the building waiting for Avery when she walked in.

Coffee and cookies were set up in the foyer. The building was newly constructed. The bright colors of the walls and clean, fresh carpet totally were different from what she expected.

"Right in here." Elaine walked into the central room where chairs were set up in a circle. Ten kids, all looking about twelve or older, sat talking and laughing. An adult man and woman sat together at the back of the room, Styrofoam cups in hand.

The man looked to be in his late twenties. He wore a nice shirt, slacks, and dress shoes. His brown hair was combed back in a conservative, nerdy style. He stood and greeted them.

"Avery, this is Ryan West. He's a friend of mine. Ryan, this is Avery Denton, my new assistant."

Ryan shook Avery's hand. Avery looked around the circle, waiting to be told what to do. A boy about her age raised his hand in a wave and smiled at her. His black hair curled at the ends, framing his muscular neck. He looked familiar, and then it hit her: he was the football player from the Street Dance.

She half-smiled back, self-conscious because of the mediocre makeup job covering her bruises. She ran a hand through her hair, moving it over her ear to cover her cheek in a hopefully discreet way.

"Avery, I brought you here tonight because Ryan leads an Alateen group. It's a support group for kids of alcoholics." Elaine held her hand up. "I know I didn't ask you before I did this, but I didn't think you would come if I did. All I ask is that you stay tonight and see what it's all about. I promise they won't bite, right Ryan?"

The man chuckled. "No, we don't bite. That would be the Vampire's Anonymous, group." He laughed at his own joke. "You don't have to say anything if you don't want. Just sit and listen. Maybe you'll hear something that sounds familiar to you, something you didn't think anyone else goes through. It could help you remember you're not alone."

Emotions swirled in Avery. It was a pretty low blow to trick her into coming here. She turned toward Elaine, not caring that she didn't hide her anger over being tricked.

"Look, darlin', if you want to have a job with me, you're going to have to at least try this. We can talk after this meeting is over, okay?"

The curly-haired boy stepped up beside them. "Hey, remember me? I met you at the Street Dance. That was an epic fight, by the way. You want to come sit over here by us?" He was shorter than she remembered, but broad as if he lifted weights all the time. He smelled of soap and body spray, and his dark brown eyes bore a neutral, friendly look.

"Avery—meet Keaton. Keaton, this is Avery. We only use first names here. And thank you, Keaton, for inviting Avery over." Ryan glanced at his watch. "Let's get this show started."

Elaine touched her shoulder. "I'll be right over here." She pointed to a chair by the door. Avery searched the room. It was the only exit.

"It's not as bad as it seems. Besides, we get cookies," Keaton leaned over and whispered.

Avery reluctantly followed him to the circle, sitting between him and a younger girl who said her name was Gabby. The adults led the discussion. They talked about the importance of understanding what alcoholism is, why it wasn't the child's fault, and then asked the group to share something good or bad from their week.

The younger kids went first, mostly talking about genial things such as their mom or dad taking them to the pool or to the zoo. As they got older, the sharing grew a bit darker. One of the boys shared how his mother came home after drinking all night, crawling across the room crying and calling his name, waking him up. He talked about falling asleep during the day because he was so tired, which would get him in trouble at summer school.

When they got around to the teenagers, Keaton stood up for his turn. He gave a sad smile and started, "I picked my mom up off the floor in the bathroom last night. When I put her in bed, she called me all kinds of names and swore at me. I never know if she's going to be sober when I get home. Every time I hear the smallest noise I worry she's fallen or gotten hurt. This is my senior year in high school, and I can't wait for the day I walk out and leave it all behind."

Hot tears gathered in Avery's eyes. She blinked them back so no one would see. The counselors talked with Keaton, but her thoughts drowned out the words. It was the first time she had heard anyone talk about dysfunctional families in such blatant terms.

No one said anything nasty, no one called anyone names, and no one judged anyone else.

"Avery? Would you like to share anything? You can say anything and it'll stay here," Ryan said.

Tears dripped down her face, and she swiped them away, careful not to smudge the makeup too badly. "I always felt so alone. Like I was the only one."

They all murmured, encouraging her.

"My dad was sent to the ER the other night after he got into a fight in a bar. When we got home he got mad and said some really awful stuff." Avery glanced at Keaton, whose expression remained the same. There was no judgment in his eyes or frown on his lips. She choked on a sob. "I just want a normal life. I want my mom not to be gone. But I don't want her back and drunk like she has been for a long time. I want my old mom back. And my dad not to be so angry. I just want the pain to end."

The boy who shared about his mother waking him up handed her some tissues. He patted her hand and smiled sweetly at her.

Gabby stood up next, sharing her week.

Keaton reached over and squeezed Avery's hand. She smiled back at him while mopping up her face.

The meeting ended with the adults praying over them. A weight lifted off of Avery's heart. The constant, dull ache wasn't gone completely, but it had eased. She took a big breath. For the first time in a long time her chest wasn't tight with the heavy burden of stress.

Elaine grabbed her in a hug. "I know how hard that was. I'm glad you were able to share. How do you feel?"

"Besides the fact I'm a mess? I actually feel pretty good. It's kind of freeing, like something I didn't know was weighing me down is gone. Does that make any sense?" She hugged the older woman tight.

"Yes, darlin'. That makes perfect sense."

Elaine left after talking with Ryan. Avery agreed to come again the next week and took Ryan's card in case she needed to talk before next Monday.

Keaton was leaning against the bike rack when she exited the building. "Told you it wasn't so bad. Sometimes it actually helps." He held out a sugar cookie to her. "You didn't eat your cookie."

She grabbed the cookie, snapped it in half, and handed him one of the halves. Crumbs fell on his purple and yellow

Honey Creek wrestling shirt. "You said you're a senior? You're from here, right?"

"Yep. You're from Valley, right?" He motioned for her to walk with him to the parking lot.

She studied his face. The friendliness was there along with an open interest. No judgment, ogling, or condescension. "Yeah. How do you know that?"

The few remaining cars pulled out of the Rec Center's lot, leaving only her and one other rusted-out sports car. "Yours?" She pointed.

"That would be it. Runs better than it looks. My dad's a mechanic. He's helping me restore it." Keaton smacked the top of the car. "It's a 1970 Firebird."

Avery knew nothing about cars, but she didn't want to seem rude. "Nice."

"Not into cars, are you?" He crossed his arms. A dimple graced one of his cheeks.

"No, not really." She smiled in apology. "You didn't answer me. How do you know where I'm from?"

"Like I said, I saw you first at the Street Dance. Then I saw your portrait at the fair. Your name and school were on the label. It was a nice picture." He bumped her shoulder.

"Thanks."

"Hey, I'm starving. Football practice was a killer today. I didn't get a chance to eat before I came. Want to go grab something? We can swap dysfunctional stories. It'll be fun." He held the door open for her.

Avery realized she was hungry. There had been no time to go home and change before coming to the Rec Center. "Okay, but I'm driving myself. Lead the way."

They drove to the Lounge across from the city park where the Fourth of July carnival had been. Avery sat with her back toward the window so the memories of her Fourth of July with Jaxson wouldn't overwhelm her. The waitress stopped by and took their order, and they chatted about school until their food came.

Minutes later, Keaton's red tray sat empty of food, having devoured his burger and fries in record time. He snatched a fry from her basket. "So, I'll cut to the chase. You got a boyfriend? That guy I saw you with, maybe?" Keaton's brown eyes sparkled.

A piece of burger caught in her throat and she coughed. She took a drink to clear it away. "Why?"

"You're a senior. I'm a senior." He waved his hands from one to the other. "We both have crazy parents. We've got a lot in common." Keaton sat back in his chair, arms behind his head, his t-shirt taut across his muscles. "This could be the start of something amazing."

"That's a terrible pickup line. And I'm kind of in a relationship," Avery hedged.

"Either you are or you aren't. There's really no middle ground for dating."

"I did have a boyfriend. We got into a fight after the fair, the night my dad was in the ER." She picked at her hamburger bun.

"Oh." He drew the word out.

She scrunched up her nose. "What, oh?"

"He doesn't know about your family, does he? Or, he does and he thinks your life has too much drama, and he kicked you to the side." Keaton pointed a ketchup-laden fry at her.

"Quit eating my food." She slapped his hand. "No, he doesn't know, nor do I want him to." She paused, her throat tightening. "He's—his life is the opposite of mine. And he's perfect. I broke it off. It's for the best." She stared at the table.

"You know, your dad's drinking and your mom's leaving isn't your fault. None of it is. You're just left trying to hold all the pieces of your life together. Besides, if he was so *perfect*, he could handle the truth. Anybody worthy of loving wouldn't let you go." Keaton's eyes were almost black in the café's light. So different from Jaxson's gorgeous blue eyes. Just as entrancing.

"He tried. I'm pretty stubborn when I want to be." She quirked her eyebrow.

"I like stubborn women." Keaton grinned before changing the subject to school and college. He doodled on napkins, and they talked until the café closed at ten. He walked her out to her car and handed her a napkin. "Here's my number. You can call me if you need to talk. Let me know if you want me to go knock some sense into that boyfriend of yours."

"I broke up with him, remember?" Having her burdens lifted left her feeling lighter than she had been in a long time. In an act of impulse, she hugged Keaton. It was like he was the first person that could understand her fully, without reservation. "Thanks for tonight."

A squeal of tires at the stop sign behind them drew her attention. A blue Chevy truck peeled away and sped off out of sight. A woman she'd met during the Fourth of July parade stood beside her car parked on the other side of the street. Jaxson's aunt. She stood, frowning as she stared at Avery.

Chapter Twenty-Eight

(Lie #14: The early bird catches the worm.)

School started on a Wednesday, two weeks after she'd watched Jaxson peel out. The heat of summer still topped over the hundred-degree mark, and classes were scheduled for only half a day. Construction of new air-conditioning units on top of the high school building—which were scheduled to be done before school started but weren't—created a zoo-like atmosphere throughout the building and parking lot.

"Why couldn't they finish this during the summer break?" Sophie whined into her locker next to Avery's.

"I know. Parking today was a nightmare." Avery had picked Sophie up since she was still grounded and refused to ride the bus or walk the dozen blocks across town.

"Have you talked to Jaxson yet?" Sophie glued a compact sized mirror on the metal door. "Remind me to get a bigger mirror."

Avery shook her head. "He won't answer any of my calls. If you woke up fifteen minutes sooner, you wouldn't have to apply your makeup here." She'd told Sophie about Keaton. A cloud of hairspray hit her in the face. "Geez, Sophie." She waved her hand to dispel the fog.

"Oops, sorry." She fluffed her hair and put the can on the top shelf. "Anyway, I think Jaxson's overreacting. Especially after that kiss with the princess at the fair. You'd think he would understand." Sophie snapped her locker closed.

"I have two words for you: girl's bathroom. It's an amazing thing. They have sinks and these gigantic, reflective square things." Avery tapped her finger to her temple. "What are they called again? Oh, yeah. Mirrors." She closed her locker as well.

Although they had received the Superintendent's letter stating everything was perfectly safe, they worked their way through a maze of dangling electric lines and ladders. Orange safety triangles, similar to the ones on the driver's ed course they'd had to navigate, lined the halls.

"Maybe you should give this Keaton a chance. I saw his picture in the paper for the Honey Creek football team. Oh, that curly hair." Sophie bumped Avery with her hip. "I could spend all day running my fingers through it. And, wow. What a body."

"Who's got a wow body?" Katie stuck her head between them. Her skin almost sparkled with perkiness. Somehow she always managed to smell like sunshine.

"This guy who's crushing on Avery," Sophie teased.

Katie looked stricken.

Avery glowered at her friend, wishing she had some duct tape to stop the leak in Sophie's mouth. "Nobody's crushing on anyone."

"Well, if you're not going to give it a shot, throw him my way." The hallway forked out ahead of them. Lights above them flickered as an electrician adjusted something in the ceiling.

MaKenzie walked around the corner, her skirt swaying with every step. She bowed her perfect brunette head at them. "Tweedle Dee, Tweedle Dumb, Tweedle Dumber." Lauren and Asia followed after her, giggling like hyenas.

Katie's jaw dropped, her eyes wide. "Did she just call us names?"

Sophie snorted. "Not like the names I call her."

The bell rang, and they hurried off in different directions.

***

The week flew by faster than Avery could blink. Because of the construction and the differences in classes, Avery had yet to catch sight of Jaxson. She strolled down the underclassmen's hallway half a dozen times but always came up empty. It was almost a relief, though, as she had no idea what she would say to him when she did see him.

She spent the weekend helping Elaine with a senior shoot and a wedding, which kept her busy enough to avoid thinking. But, everything from cows grazing in the pastures to denim-blue skies, reminded her of Jaxson. The ache of missing him grew to a gaping hole that sucked out all goodness and light around her. She shook her head at the thoughts, reminding herself he was better off without her. If she said it enough, she might start believing it.

Most seniors had short days, scheduling college credit classes in the afternoons at Community College in nearby Council Bluffs. She had written off going to college last year when she realized she'd need her parent's help to get in. But with Elaine's urgings, and a newfound interest in photography, Avery had decided to sign up. She skimmed under the deadline, paying for two classes each semester so her basic entrance classes would be finished before she even started college the next year.

Sophie agreed to sign up with her, converting her grounding into what she referred to as "community service." Her mom allowed her to go to school functions and extracurricular activities if she took the college courses and maintained at least a C in each class.

"I hate Mondays," Sophie repeated for the twentieth time that morning.

"I am well aware of your aversion to mornings, Monday mornings in particular." Avery knew she sounded crabby, but she had an aversion to Sophie on Monday mornings. They split for their first class, heading down different hallways. "Don't forget: we have English Comp class at Community College this afternoon. I'm leaving the parking lot at 11:30 sharp." She spoke to Sophie's retreating back.

"Hey, what are you doing tonight?" Katie sidled up beside Avery, her face glowing.

She hesitated. Mondays were Alateen nights. And though Keaton wasn't going to be there due to football practice running later now, she still wanted to go for the support. The only person—other than Keaton and Elaine—who knew she was going to Alateen was Sophie, and Avery wanted to keep it that way. "I might have to help Elaine," she lied. "Why?"

Katie put her hand to her mouth and whispered, "Jaxson's coming over. I thought maybe if you wanted to talk, it would be a good time to catch him."

Avery put her hand against her mouth. "Katie, this isn't a library. You don't have to whisper."

Her friend continued on in a regular voice. "He's going to spend the night. You could just happen to stop by, and then you guys can get back together." Katie's smile filled her face as she bounced and clapped her hands.

Avery studied her friend. The dark blue eyes, the freckles across her nose, the puppy dog-like anticipation. If Katie had a tail, she'd be wagging it. Avery wished she could be so positive and hopeful. "Or it could turn ugly and your mom would ban me from your house forever."

"Don't be silly. She only bans people for a month at a time." Katie continued jabbering while they walked to Government class.

Out of the corner of her eye, she spied a tall blond. She glanced sideways. Her heart stopped at the sight of him. His hair was cut shorter; no doubt his mother made him cut it for school. He looked up and their eyes met. She felt her face heat up in a deep blush. Brushing her hair over her face to hide it, she walked faster down the hall and into the bathroom.

"Avery, what are you doing?" Katie's appalled voice followed her into the room.

"Jaxson. I just saw Jaxson." Avery breathed as if she'd just run a marathon. She turned on the cold water and splashed her face.

"The bell's going to ring." Katie fanned Avery with a notebook.

Avery wiped her face, glad she hadn't worn much makeup today, now that the bruises were gone. *Breathe, just breathe.* Once her pulse died down and her breathing steadied, she spoke. "Okay. He's probably gone. Let's go."

Jaxson stood waiting for them outside of the bathroom. Avery's heart dropped to the floor. Katie bounced off, mumbling something Avery couldn't hear over the sound of her own heartbeat.

"Hey." Jaxson's blond hair still fell over his eyebrow, although it wasn't in his eyes now. Her fingers itched to move it away.

"Hey." Her mouth became dry. She clasped her notebooks tight to her chest.

He stuck his thumbs through the loops of his jeans. "Can we get together and talk tonight?"

Avery's eyes widened. It was Alateen night. But she'd miss it for a chance to talk with Jaxson. "Yeah, sure. What time?"

"After practice at eight. At Michael's house?" Jaxson's expression gave nothing away.

She scanned his face for any sign of emotion but saw none. Realizing he waited for her to answer, she shook her head. "Yeah. Sure."

The bell rang. Jaxson turned and strode in the opposite direction. He didn't look back.

Chapter Twenty-Nine

(Truth #15: Everyone has secrets.)

Avery and Sophie walked together into English Comp at Community College. The room engulfed them. It was larger than any of Valley's rooms, except for the gym.

Someone whistled, and they turned to see who it was. Keaton waved, beckoning them.

Avery spoke through clenched teeth. "Do not make me regret telling you about him."

Sophie growled. "Oooo. I likey!" Sophie stuck her chest out and used her 'runway walk' as they walked toward Keaton. It would have been hot. Except Sophie was pigeon-toed. And she wasn't willowy or tall.

Avery smacked her friend in the arm. "You look like that old cat of yours that would stick its hind end up when she rubbed my leg."

Sophie pawed the air with her hand just as they stepped up to Keaton. "Meow."

"Hey!" Keaton hugged Avery tight. "Who's your feline friend?"

"This is Sophie Morris. Sophie, this is Keaton Miller." Avery looked him over, trying to be objective. He was quite hunk-a-licious—in a sports stud kind of way. His neck and chest were thick and his waist narrow. Tight jeans showed off the strength in his legs, and the t-shirt he wore only enhanced his muscles.

She mentally compared him to Jaxson. Keaton had curly, dark hair. Jaxson had straight, blond hair. Keaton's brown eyes were adorable like a puppy dog's. Jaxson's were so blue you could lose yourself in them. Keaton was buff where Jaxson was tall and sinewy strong. *What was she doing?* She shook the thoughts away.

"Hello, Keaton." Sophie sang her greeting, dragging the words out meaningfully, and held out her hand, which he shook.

Avery motioned to her friend's chin. "I think you have some drool right there." She grinned.

"Very funny." Sophie gave her an annoyed look.

Keaton touched his thumb to her chin. "I can wipe that off."

Sophie smiled back at him.

Avery glanced at the ceiling, praying for patience. Katie walked in the room and squealed.

"Hold on to your ear sockets, Keaton." Sophie cringed and stepped back.

Katie bounded into Avery, knocking her backward with her hug. "Oh my gosh! We're in the same class."

"Kay, dearest. You knew we had the same classes last week when we got our updated schedules." Avery put her hands on Katie's bouncing shoulders. They'd driven separately because Katie had a senior cheerleading meeting.

"I know! Isn't this great?" Katie grabbed her arms, almost tipping Avery over as she bopped around.

"Ahem," Keaton interrupted them.

Avery took a deep breath. "Katie Carter, this is Keaton Miller. Keaton, this is Katie."

Katie smiled widely at the curly haired boy. Her eyes twinkled in interest. "Hi. How do you guys know each other?"

Avery hurried to explain. "I met him through the studio. Precious Moments, that is. Elaine introduced us."

Keaton raised his eyebrows at her. Sophie stifled a laugh. She shot them both a withering glance.

Katie's eyes remained on Keaton. "Nice to meet you. So, are you a model?" She flipped her hair over her shoulder.

Avery smacked Katie's arm to get her attention. Snapping out of it, Katie pulled Avery aside. "Michael said that Jaxson told him you guys are going to get together to talk tonight?"

Avery nodded her head and was swept up into a massive hug again. "Oh my gosh. I'm so excited. You're getting back together!"

Keaton gave her an inquisitive look. "You and Mr. Perfect together again? My congratulations. Or is it condolences? I always get those mixed up. I'll just send flowers." He looked toward the door where MaKenzie and two of her friends walked in. "Well, hello gorgeousness."

Avery pinched his arm.

"What?" Keaton rubbed the sore spot.

"If it isn't Queeny and her new Prin-sluts," Sophie snarled. "I'm thinking getting grounded sounds much better than spending another minute with them." She crossed her arms, glowering at MaKenzie and the two girls. Avery recognized them as seniors from other schools in the area. All of them were from wealthier families in the county.

"I'm your ride. Besides, someone needs to be here in case I need bail money." Avery sat down next to Sophie, ignoring MaKenzie and her entourage.

Keaton sat next to Avery, balancing his arm on the back of her chair. "I'd be your bail buddy any day. But, do you have her number?" He grinned.

"I got her number all right," Avery mumbled.

Katie flopped down next to Keaton.

The teacher entered the room and called the class to order. Time dragged on after the initial five-minute lecture and instructions to read the first million pages of their textbook. As a bonus, the class ended with the professor giving them homework.

"Who gets homework on their first day of classes? This stinks," Keaton complained as he walked to his car.

"Nice wheels," Sophie exclaimed, running her hand over the faded red sports car.

"Wanna go for a ride? I could drive you home. I have time before practice." Keaton beamed. He bumped Avery in the arm. "Finally. Someone who gets me."

"Uh, yeah!" Sophie was in the passenger seat before Avery could blink.

Avery laughed. "Never seen you move so fast, Sophie."

Sophie ran her hand across the dash. "You've never seen me in a Firebird."

"You guys behave." Avery pointed at them.

Sophie stuck her head out the window. "Or what?"

"I tell your mom and she takes you out of your college classes." Avery yelled over the revving engine.

"Promises, promises," Sophie squealed as Keaton took off.

"How did you get a guy like him to sit with you losers?" MaKenzie's voice drifted over Avery's shoulder. She sashayed across the parking lot. Several guys in the area turned and watched her.

Avery cursed her luck under her breath. She turned to face her nemesis. "What's it to you?"

"Nothing. Just wondered if that's who you dropped Jaxson for." MaKenzie flipped her hair over her shoulder. "Then I saw Sophie leave with him and remembered you couldn't possibly get anyone so hot. Unless you're putting out."

Katie's eyes grew large and her face bloomed red. She puckered her lips. "Avery didn't cheat on Jaxson. She's just friends with Keaton. Something you wouldn't understand. For your information, Avery and Jaxson are getting back together. S—so stick that in your ear."

The insult was a simple one, but coming from Katie it was a scathing remark. Avery put her hand on Katie's shoulder. It was unusual for her to be angry about anything.

Although she was hopeful about Jaxson, she didn't want to discuss it in front of MaKenzie, of all people. "Kay, it's fine. I can handle this."

MaKenzie flipped out her cell phone. A red light flashed above the camera lens. "How precious. Sweet virginal Katie is angry. This makes such a great video, don't you think? Would mommy dearest flunk you out of her celibacy class? Maybe she'll ground you from the cheerleading squad."

Katie's cheeks reddened like Michael's normally did when he got mad. "You take that back."

MaKenzie ignored Katie and turned toward Avery. "You know you're not good enough for Jaxson, right? People like you? Girls who end up with multiple baby-daddies, living off welfare their whole life. It's a shame, really."

Avery recalled similar words coming out of MaKenzie's mother's mouth before the Fourth of July parade. Adding that insult to the fact she put Katie down, Avery's vision darkened. "You're the worst kind of hag." Avery grabbed for the phone in MaKenzie's hand, but the other girl was faster.

"Uh, uh, uh. One press of a button and purity girl's rudeness is all over the internet. What would Katie's dear mother say?" She wiggled the phone in her hands, an evil smile on her face. She flipped her long brown hair over her shoulder.

Avery wanted to rip the extensions out of her hair, one by one until she screamed for mercy, then make her eat them strand by highlighted strand. "You know, I may not be good enough for Jaxson, but at least I didn't beg him to go out with me and get turned down flat. You're just jealous that I had what you could never have. Love that isn't bought or begged for. You're a petty, vindictive, sad excuse for a person, and I feel sorry for you."

MaKenzie glared at her. "What did you just say?"

"She called you a petty, vindictive…"

MaKenzie cut Katie off. "Not that, Tweedle Dumber, the other part." She stepped toward Avery, her bright red lips curled in a snarl.

"The part where you tried to go out with Jaxson, and he'd have nothing to do with your high and mighty, sorry self? That part? Or was it the part where he turned you down flat?

Flat like a pancake." Avery flattened an invisible pancake in her hands and then motioned to her chest.

"Who told you that?" MaKenzie's voice pitched high, her face reddened.

"Ha! Everyone except the boys you haven't dated knows about the flat chest part. I've seen you in the locker room. You use padded bras to get that kind of alpine line." Avery moved toward the other girl, her hands clenched at her sides to keep from slapping her.

"You're such a loser. I'd watch my back if I were you." MaKenzie flung her phone in her purse and flounced off to her green car parked across the lot.

Avery shook, liquid boiling in her veins, as she watched the other girl get in her car and leave. A hand on her shoulder made her jump.

"Did she actually ask Jaxson out, and he turned her down?" The light was back in Katie's eyes.

"According to Jaxson's cousin, Trisha, she did. Remember, they used to be friends? I'm pretty sure she'd know." Avery dug out her keys.

"She was pretty mad. I can't believe you told her off like that. She deserved it though. Celibacy class. As if. It's a purity class. Like she'd know what that was." Katie giggled then turned somber. "You don't think she was serious about us watching our backs?"

Avery's stomach flipped. What wouldn't she do? "You mean worse like someone spray painting my portrait at the fair? Yeah, I think she's serious." She put her arm around her friend. "I'm proud of you. You stood up to her. Did you wear your big girl panties today or something?"

Katie pushed at her, embarrassment coloring her cheeks. "I get mad."

Avery hugged her tight. "No, you don't, and I love that about you. Don't you worry about the big bad wolf. She can huff and puff all she wants, but she's only full of hot air."

Katie smiled at her like a child whose parent scared away the boogie man. Her world was back to good. Avery would make sure MaKenzie wouldn't change that.

***

Avery slathered a yogurt mask over her face and body. The organic recipe was a cheap one she and Katie had tried a couple of years ago when puberty hit. Katie, though, never needed to use it then or now, having been born with fairy glitter in her blood. Avery hoped to gain some confidence from it before seeing Jaxson that evening.

She soaked in the tub, shaved, and loofahed until her body was pink. Her hair was curled and she'd done the best she could with her makeup, only smudging her mascara twice and having to completely start over that second time. By six o'clock, she decided she'd done all she could to prepare.

Walking past the table, she fingered the portrait Elaine had given her the last time she'd worked. Her boss had framed it with some old wood from one of her props she didn't use anymore.

She studied her picture, marveling at how incredible the circumstances were that gave her the rainbow. Aunt Penny used to tell her rainbows were promises that were never broken.

On the back porch Avery found a nail and a hammer and, with clumsy hands, managed to get the nail in the wall without bending it over too much. Light from the windows made the picture shine. Avery pressed one hand to the glass.

"Please, God. Let this promise of a better life remain unbroken."

On impulse, she pulled out her cell phone and dialed her mother's phone. It went automatically to voice mail. Avery pressed the end button. Disappointment stung her eyes.

At 6:45 she entered her room, and searched for something to wear. She'd already worn her new clothes for senior pictures to school, and there was nothing clean. Again. If only she had time to wash something. She trudged down to her mother's room, kicking herself for not keeping up with the laundry.

Avery hadn't been in the room since the day she found the yearbooks in her mother's closet. She could do it. Deep breath. She swung the door open. She expected to see the yearbooks on the bed first thing, but they were gone.

She rushed over to the bed, running her hands over the mess on top. Not there. A cloud of dust flew up from the dust ruffle between the box spring and the floor. Underneath the bed, three boxes and an old jewelry box lay hidden. She brought them all out, looking through the boxes, but finding nothing interesting, so she put them aside. The jewelry box was locked.

The skeleton key! Avery ran back upstairs, got the key, and returned.

It fit.

Old tarnished necklaces with stars and hearts tangled in a heap on top of the velvet inside. A few dated earrings and rings were in the top drawer. Slipping it out, Avery found that the inside of the box overflowed with folded-up letters and notes.

A frayed red string held the letters together. It looked as if someone had read the letters over and over because the pages were worn and yellowed. She untied them.

Opening the first letter, she skipped to the signature to see whose letters her mother had kept for so long. It wasn't her father's handwriting. Or should she call him Greg now? The handwriting matched the paragraph in the yearbook, sweeping and effeminate. Sweat broke out along her hairline. She flipped the sheets back and began to read.

Dineen,

I was sorry to get your letter after you returned home, too late to talk to you face to face. I'm engaged to be married. We're already having our own family. There's no room for anyone else in my life right now. I'm sorry. I will help you in whatever way I can. But please, for both our sakes, find someone and move on. I wish you nothing but the best.

Yours Truly.

Avery's heart ached for her mom. It was obviously a break up letter. Why would her mom keep it for years, though? Had she been in love before and never had the feelings returned? It would explain the stoic letters from her dad—to an extent.

Avery's hands itched to tear the letter into tiny little pieces. Beneath the letters was a larger envelope with a baby's footprint on it. Her birth certificate?

She'd had to have it to get her driver's license, but it was different than this one. This one was the original certificate the hospitals give out.

Avery pulled it out. It was from the hospital in Grand Island, Nebraska. It listed the time and day she was born. The doctor's name was indecipherable in the center of the thick certificate. Below the doctor's name were lines for mother and father's names. Her mother's signature filled her line, but there was no father's signature.

Her dad hadn't signed the original birth certificate? He must've been telling the truth. But, who was her father, then? Why had her mother never told her? Heat rushed from her scalp down her body, and pooled in her gut. Why did she not know any of this?

The phone rang, breaking her train of thought. She hurried over to it, thinking it could be Jaxson since her cell phone was plugged in her room, charging.

She slipped on some clothes near the door and smacked her leg into the doorframe. Clutching the throbbing shin with her hand, she stumbled over to the phone.

The caller ID on the phone lit up with a familiar number, but it wasn't Jaxson's.

It was her mother's.

Chapter Thirty

(Lie #15: A Band-aid will hurt less when pulled off quickly.)

She stood, frozen, and let the phone ring, and ring, and ring. Voicemail kicked in, just like it had for her in five moments of weakness when she'd dialed her mom's cell. Her mother had never answered her calls. She never returned those calls, either. Was she just so busy having fun with Phillip Thomas she couldn't be bothered to check on her one and only daughter?

No, Avery wasn't answering that call.

Avery's leg thrummed, a goose egg forming under her sweating hand. She looked at the clock on the DVD player. It was time to leave, and she hadn't gotten dressed yet. She entered her mother's room, stuffed the letters and jewelry back into the box, and shoved everything under the bed.

There was no light on the phone indicating a message as she dashed upstairs, scorning her mother's clothes. She changed into a simple shirt and jeans from her room that were fairly smell-free, and slipped the butterfly necklace on at the last minute for luck.

Back down in the living room, she picked the phone up and dialed voicemail to be sure. No messages. If her mother did call, why didn't she leave a message? Had it been a fluke? An accidental dial?

Avery hurried as fast as she could. The bright orange haze of the setting sun guided her way down the rock road. Each day it came earlier and earlier. The harvest wouldn't be long now, and winter's cold hand would soon slap them with snow.

Summer was over. Avery fought off the wave of sadness creeping into her heart. She wished she could go back and relive summer. Do things differently. Everything except for Jaxson. A falling star wish for lasting happiness.

But Avery knew wishing on stars was for the naïve and pure of heart. And she was neither.

Jaxson's blue truck was in the Carter's driveway when Avery pulled up. It wasn't just the heat making her sweat when she got out of her Taurus and walked to the front deck.

Jaxson stepped out of the attached garage. "Hey. Follow me."

Avery let him pass by her and followed him under the stairs where the lawn mower and garden hoses were. His abrupt manner was disconcerting, making butterflies morph into angry bees in her stomach.

He turned toward her, his face grim. A chorus of crickets sang all around them, their noisy clicking joined the loud ringing in Avery's ears. His blond hair was still damp from the showers. She could smell the scent of his soap. A flare of familiar desire shot through her, and she clenched her hands together to keep from touching him.

Avery's nerves after reading the note and her mother's phone call were already taut. She shuffled her feet, crossing her arms against an invisible chill. "Jaxson, what is it? You wanted to meet me, remember?"

He blew out a breath. "I know. Look, this summer was amazing. It seems like I waited forever to tell you how I felt. It was almost like a dream come true." His smile was sad. "But somewhere along the way it just wasn't what I thought it would be. You know? I guess in my head things played out differently somehow. I just wanted to make it official because you said you didn't want to not be friends. That way there's no hard feelings."

Her heart skipped a beat. She touched the necklace, hoping she'd heard him wrong. "Make what official?"

He eyed her hands on the necklace, a crease forming between his eyes. "That we're through. You and me. I thought that's what you wanted on Mercer's Hill. You told me I was an infant and to leave you alone. What am I supposed to take from that, Avery, except that you want to break up?" Jaxson's voice rose in frustration.

Avery threw her hands in the air, trying to keep her voice down. "I don't know what I want. Okay? I miss you. But things are so complicated right now. There's just so much stuff going on."

"Why? What's going on? I know your mom's gone. But she was gone before we even started dating. The Fourth of July was so great. Things just seemed to go downhill from there." He ran a hand through his hair. "If I'm your boyfriend, Avery, why can't you tell me what's going on that's so complicated?" His lips twisted into a frown.

She couldn't form the words. If he was embarrassed by one small argument his uncle had at his house, what would he think of her family? The only person she knew would understand and not judge her dysfunction was Keaton. As much as she liked Keaton, she didn't have feelings for him like she did Jaxson. She loved Jaxson.

Everything seemed to slow down. She *loved* him? Avery put her hands over her ears and closed her eyes, shutting out all the noise. Except the noise was coming from inside her.

Jaxson touched her wrist. "Avery, what can't you tell me that you can tell that other guy? The one I saw you with in Honey Creek. Are you dating him now?"

She looked him directly in the eye. "I'm not dating Keaton. He's just a friend." Could she tell him? What would he think of her if he knew the truth about her life? He'd probably run screaming in the opposite direction.

"Then what's so complicated?" He stepped closer, his thumbs in his belt loops. Shadows from the deck above them made it impossible to see his face. Jaxson's beautiful blue eyes that she would gladly drown in.

She could just make up a lie. Something small, so she could smooth things over with him, as if everything in her life wasn't messed up beyond belief. It would be so easy to just pretend. She'd become good at hiding the truth with lie upon lie. So many lies. But lies hurt. She couldn't do that to Jaxson.

"Keaton gets me on a different level. I'm sorry, I never meant to hurt you." She dug the toe of her shoe into the ground, kicking a pebble into the dark grass. "You wanted it official? Well, it's official. We're done. No hard feelings." Her chest tightened as she spoke, threatening to choke her.

Without waiting for him to answer, she ran to her car, backed out of the driveway and left. Snot ran down her nose and tears washed down her cheeks. A deer jumped out of the ditch, and Avery swerved to the side of the road. Her car slid sideways to a stop. Her heart pounded in her chest. Clouds of rock dust swirled around the car as her emotions churned a storm in her heart. Head on the steering wheel, she cried until she could cry no more.

***

"How're you doing?" Keaton whispered during their college English class a week later. Their professor had been replaced mid-term with another one who liked to sleep after giving out the day's syllabus. They sat around tables, Katie bent over her notebook, scribbling. Sophie was asleep with her head on her arms.

"Fine, why?"

Keaton had been more than attentive since she and Jaxson had "officially" broken up. Avery waffled between feeling like she was a horrible person for using Keaton to get over her broken heart and being grateful for his support. She'd almost agreed to date him, and she knew deep down he was waiting for her to give in and say yes. But she just couldn't.

"I saw your car in the parking lot. Nice graffiti job. Who'd you make mad this time?"

"What are you talking about?"

"Your car." He raised his eyebrows. "It has spray paint all over it."

She stared at him, sure her mouth hung open wide enough for a pig to crawl in.

Keaton frowned. "You didn't know?"

"No, I didn't know." Just like her portrait at the fair. Understanding dawned on her, and she swiveled to look behind her where MaKenzie sat with her cronies.

MaKenzie glanced up, caught Avery looking at her, and smiled like an over-enthusiastic toothpaste whitening salesman.

Avery's hand itched to slap the grin off of her face. "MaKenzie is such a hag!"

Katie turned in her chair, solemnly holding up a flyer showing the Valley Homecoming H.S. King and Queen Candidates. "Speaking of MaKenzie, we have to get you a dress for the dance, Avery. You can't not go to the dance. You're a senior for crying in the rain." Katie was pitted against MaKenzie for queen, and since Valley boasted queens who were cheerleaders, it made sense one of them would win.

Avery's heart twisted at the photo of Jaxson, who was up for king of the sophomore class. The school body would vote next Wednesday at the Spirit Rally. The votes would then be announced Friday night during their Homecoming's halftime. It was a huge spectacle with the court sitting in fancy cars, grade by grade, smiling and waving at everyone. If Jaxson won, who would be sitting next to him? She shook the thought off.

"I don't have to go to the dance. Right, Sophie?" Avery flicked her friend's ear to get her attention.

"I'm going with Brody." Sophie poked her head out from the shelter of her arms and looked Avery in the eye.

Avery's mouth dropped open.

"Oh, yeah. By the way," she held up her hand. "We're back together." On her middle finger was a ring with a teensy-weensy diamond speck in the center.

"Shut up! Are you guys married?" Katie squealed.

"It's a promise ring. It's like your purity rings, only I don't have to be pure to wear mine." Sophie chuckled. "I got it this weekend. I didn't call or tell you because I knew you'd be a downer about it. Brody's up for an overseas tour in March. I think he'll ask me to marry him over the holidays." Sophie polished the ring on her shirt.

Heat flickered in Avery's gut. It caught fire and spread through her body in a blazing flash. "A promise ring? He gave you a promise ring? Since when did you lose your mind and take Soldier Boy back?" She thought Sophie had dodged the bullet named Brody Hunt. Obviously he was sneakier than she gave him credit for, and that was saying something.

"I know you don't like Brody, but you've got him all wrong, Avery. He was so sweet this weekend, even coming over to meet my mom." Sophie held her hand out to adjust the band, trying unsuccessfully to get the minuscule diamond chip to glint in the light. It was probably a fake gumball machine ring that would turn green when wet. "This is my last semester with you guys at good old Community College. I won't need the classes now."

Throwing her hands up in the air, Avery yelled, "What? Why? He's a jerk, Sophie. How do you not see it?"

Several people glared at her. She lowered her voice but only a fraction. "He was the one who kissed me and lied about it. He assaulted me at the Chute. He's a giant nub." Now that she was on a roll, Avery didn't care about people giving her dirty looks; they weren't really studying anyway. She *did* care about Sophie getting hurt by that jerk Brody again.

"You had it mixed up from the beginning, Avery, just admit it. You don't like him because you get left out when we're together." Sophie's hands motioned over her shapely body. "Never fear, there's more than enough of me to go around."

Avery held her hand out to block the image from her mind. "Ew. Gross. And I'm not jealous of the time you spend with him." She slapped her hand on the table. "I. Don't. Trust. Him. He's a user loser."

A crease formed between Sophie's eyes for a fraction of a second before her face became an infuriating blank one. "I'm done with this topic. It's locked and thrown away. Next topic. Homecoming. Yes, you have to go, Avery. Brody and I are going to be there so you have to come, too. You need to find a date. And a dress. Not necessarily in that order." Sophie crumpled a piece of notebook paper into a ball and threw it at her, hitting Avery in the forehead. Keaton laughed.

"I don't want to go with anyone to the dance. I don't want to see MaKenzie, Jaxson, or anyone else on the royal court." She put a hand on Katie's arm. "Sorry, Katie. I don't mean you. I just—" She hesitated, holding back the panic and pain. "I can't do it." Avery clasped the table tight, thumping her head down against the wood hard enough to sting.

"Breathe, Avery. You really need to see a doctor about that." Sophie raised a hand to pat her on the head.

Avery dodged her friend's hand and glared sideways at her.

"Hey ladies, I have the perfect solution to your problem." Keaton kicked his feet up on the table.

Avery raised her head after the silence went on too long. Katie and Sophie sat smiling, though unspeaking, as if everyone were in on a big secret except for her. She finally broke the quiet. "Ok, spit it out, what's the solution?"

"Take me."

She glared at him like he was crazy. "Take you. As my date?" His brain must be with Sophie's—somewhere in the land of ridiculousness.

Keaton scowled at her. "Yeah, as your date. Geez, Avery. I don't have an STD."

Avery narrowed her eyes. She only wanted to go to the dance with Jaxson, but that wasn't going to happen now.

"Don't you see? It's the perfect solution. If Jaxson's there with someone else, you have me to deflect. And from what you've said about MaKenzie, bringing me will drive her crazy. Besides, I'd get to crash your homecoming after my team beats yours to a pulp during the game. Win-Win-Win."

Avery glanced at Sophie, they shared a look, and together they took one of Keaton's feet that was propped on top the table and flipped Keaton out of his chair onto the floor.

Avery laughed at the surprise on Keaton's face. "As if. Our Warriors will tear your Panthers up and make them beg for mercy."

Several annoyed people turned and shushed them. Their sub teacher only bobbed his head, snorting his way back into a deep slumber. His phone alarm went off, signaling the end of class torture, and everyone rose to leave. Keaton rubbed his arm where he fell on the floor. "Good luck with that, ladies. Have you seen your starting line this year?"

Avery frowned. Jaxson was on first string. "Touch Jaxson and I'll personally take you out." She smacked him in the chest as they gathered their books and headed out of the classroom.

Keaton put his arm around her shoulder. "So that's a 'yes'? Please, please, please?" Keaton turned his dark-brown puppy dog eyes on her.

"Ugh, I'm going to regret saying this." She pinched the space between her eyebrows, fighting the headache coming on. "Fine. I'll take you to the Homecoming Dance, but no contact of any kind with MaKenzie. Period." She stabbed him in the nose with her finger.

Keaton caught her arm and spun her against him in an awkward dance move as they made their way out of the building. "You won't regret it, I promise."

She watched him as he put on his seatbelt and drove off. He was everything a girl could want in a boyfriend and more. He was funny, good looking, charming. But he wasn't Jaxson. A dull ache centered itself over her heart. She had to get over him. Maybe Keaton was the way to do it.

"Now we just have to get the dress." Sophie stole the keys out of Avery's hand. "My turn to drive."

Chapter Thirty-One

(Truth #16: It's the clothes that make the person.)

"Pull over. I think I'm going to hurl," Avery yelled from the backseat.

"That hasn't worked for the past three miles. Now pipe down. You're going dress shopping and that's final," Sophie yelled back while swerving into the Interstate's middle lane. Beside her Katie squealed with delight.

Her stomach lurched once again. "I'm serious. Slow down or I'm aiming at you!" Avery hoped no cops were close by. Though she'd went through two washes and used a special expensive industrial cleaner to get the paint off her car—a huge waste of her money, the outline of nasty words could be seen in the light of day. It wouldn't be hard for a cop or a camera to ID them. "You're paying any tickets we get!"

"We only have an hour and a half before Katie has to leave for cheerleading." Sophie steered the car in a hard right onto the off ramp of West Dodge Road. Midtown Mall stretched out to their left. Avery flew into the back of Katie's seat. Sophie met her furious glance in the rearview mirror. "Sorry. Red light."

Sophie took off again, jerking Avery around. Avery rubbed her forehead where it smacked the window, despite the seatbelt. "You are NEVER allowed to drive my car ever again. Never. Ever."

They zipped through the parking area, and screeched into a spot. Avery's hand clenched the door handle as she got out.

"Look! Tire marks." Katie pointed at the cement.

Avery snatched the keys away from Sophie. "It's bad enough that I have paint all over my car, you have to draw attention to us by screeching into a parking spot. Add tires to the list of things you'll owe me in your lifetime."

"Just loosening up the gears. Vehicles break down when they're not exercised right." Sophie quipped as she strode into the mall.

Katie bounded past Avery and into the aisle of the mall. "I've never heard that. Is that true?" Stores lined both sides of the mall. Music from a video store drifted through the conditioned air.

"That's the biggest load of boloney I've heard in a long time." Avery hurried to catch up. Who told you that?"

"Brody."

Strong perfumes wafting from a candle kiosk assaulted Avery's nose.

"That figures. No, it's not true, Katie."

"Yes, it is. If you don't blow the gaskets out once in a while, they get corroded." Sophie yanked the other two girls into Frenzy, a gothic store.

Three stores later, Avery stood in the dressing room eyeing the tenth dress of the day: a slinky green one with holes in the side.

"Asparagus? Sophie, you have to be kidding me! This is the same color of that zombie outfit I wore the last time we went trick-or-treating. Like three years ago!"

Sophie laughed. "I couldn't help myself, I had to. Remember? You ate all that chocolate and threw up in the Whitmore's bushes?"

Mrs. Whitmore had been their junior high band teacher. "Yeah, Mrs. W couldn't find my flute for a month." Avery hung the dress up without trying it on.

"Quitting band was the first smart thing you ever did." Sophie laughed. "Mrs. W. was so mad." Sophie's voice was muffled as she flipped through a rack of gowns not far from the dressing area.

She remembered that Halloween, the one before Aunt Penny died. It had been the best, and her mom had helped make the zombie costume. Tears stung behind her eyelids as Avery leaned back on the dressing room bench. It would be so nice to have her mom there, shopping with her.

"Here, try this one." A gorgeous cloud of silver and aquamarine sailed over the locked door.

Avery swiped the wetness from her eyes so she could see clearly. With a deep breath, she slipped on the A-line, mid-length dress. She zipped it and turned to check her reflection in the mirror. The door of the changing room rattled, halting her inspection.

"C'mon Avery. We don't have much time left. Let's see it," Sophie called out.

Katie gasped when she stepped out of the closet-sized room. "Oh, Avery."

Avery chanced a look at her friend's shocked face. "That bad?"

"No, that good. You must get that dress. And wear it every day from this point forward. It's amazing!" Katie's quiet awe rose into a shriek. She fingered the iridescent material on the skirt. "It's beautiful."

Avery turned toward Sophie. "Well?"

"We have ourselves a winner. Now, let's go before Cinderella here turns into a cheerleader." Sophie pointed to Katie and together they ushered Avery back into the dressing room.

Avery glanced back at herself in the mirror before taking the dress off. A sunburst of silver sequins rested over a sea of blue. She swung her hips back and forth, loving the swish of the silky fabric with the tulle underskirt. Silver sequins on the neckline and straps winked in the light, moving down into a starburst which ended at the waist. There the color of blue morphed into a lighter shade until it reached the hem. A slight snag on the back of the dress caught her eye.

She changed and handed the dress over to Sophie. "You dragged me here, now work your magic. There's a snag in the back. See how much you can work it down."

Avery waited while Sophie haggled with the salesclerk. It had taken a call to a floor manager, but she'd managed to get thirty percent off the price. "Now I don't owe you for tires."

"Yeah, no. It's a good start, though." Avery pulled out her money.

"Homecoming is going to be so awesome!" Katie hugged Avery as she paid for the dress. "I can't wait."

"This weekend we go shopping for shoes and accessories," Sophie announced as they walked out of the mall.

"I can't. I'm babysitting," Katie whined.

Avery groaned. "I'm driving this time."

***

The unmistakable rumble of tailpipes interrupted Avery's peaceful Saturday morning breakfast. She rushed to the kitchen window, hoping she was mistaken about the sound. Frowning, she saw Brody with his tricked-out truck. The devil himself helped Sophie down from the passenger side.

She has got to be off her meds. Avery fumed. She hurried to get her purse and leave before anyone could come in and see the state of the dining room. Her father's car sat beside the barn, the only sign of him being home each day, besides the keys in the bowl on the table by the front door.

The morning sunlight shone high in the cloudless sky. Avery loped down the deck's walkway toward the two lovebirds.

"It's too nice of a day for a practical joke, Sophie. I thought it was just you and me going shopping." Brody returned her glare with an innocent smile.

"He offered to take us to Kansas City for some real shopping. It'll be fun. You got a photo of the dress so we can match colors easier, right?" Sophie snuggled against her much taller boyfriend.

"I'm seriously going to vomit. And I don't want to go that far. That's two and a half hours away. By the time we get there, go shopping, and get back, it will take all day." Avery's voice twisted into a whine, but she didn't care. "And why Kansas City?"

Brody spoke up. "It's the best place to go according to my mom, who's a fashion diva. She works at the flower shop and knows these things."

"What do flowers and Homecoming fashion have to do with each other?"

"Oh, c'mon. You don't have to work today, right? It'll be fun." Brody fluttered his eyes at her and held his hands over his head like a halo.

Yeah, right.

"Please, Avery. This will give you and Brody a chance to get to know each other better. I promise after today you'll change your mind about him." Sophie grabbed Avery's hand. "Besides, we need to show up Miss Queeny-Pants MaKenzie. You can't deny you wouldn't give your left kidney for that opportunity."

Behind Sophie's back, Brody crossed his heart and held up his hands in surrender. Avery narrowed her eyes but received only a sincere look back. She didn't want Sophie to be with Brody, but if she didn't go, it seemed like a win for him. And she refused to let him win. "Fine. But I swear, Brody, one move out of line, and you're toast."

"You won't regret it." He opened the passenger door for Sophie to sit in the middle. Avery sat against the passenger door. With a rev of the engine, they were on their way to Kansas City.

Avery held onto the armrest, staring out the window.

"And of course you'll be my maid of honor. I'll let you pick out the dress." Sophie yammered on and on about Brody and their future plans.

She peeked at Brody out of the corner of her eye. He paid no attention to Sophie's grand plans for their future. His attention was on the satellite radio channels. His hand smacking the dash broke Avery's bored trance. "What guy in his right mind owns a sweet ride like that and lets his girlfriend drive it?"

They passed an old Ford truck with monster truck tires and a mountainous lift kit on it. Sexist cartoons dotted the tinted back window. A blond girl, hair flipping in the wind of the open window, glanced over and smiled at Brody as they passed.

Sophie's expression was thunderous. "Yo, Brody. Eyes on the road."

"Looking at the ride, babe. Just looking at the ride." Brody said, quirking the corner of his mouth.

Sophie sat rigid beside her. Brody went back to fiddling with the radio while Avery stared out of the window until they reached the outskirts of Kansas City.

The Country Club Plaza had sidewalks decorated with statues and artwork and had street entertainers on almost every corner. They walked from one store to another, some of which Avery had never heard of before.

Avery followed Sophie and Brody from store to store, wishing she had just stayed home instead. At every store they visited, Sophie got more and more irritated at something Brody did. Avery found a pair of silver heels on sale that matched her dress, so she decided the trip hadn't been a total failure. Yet.

Sophie waited in line at Flare, an overpriced, high end store, holding a pair of blood-red stilettos. "Look, Avery. Aren't they amazing? Wait 'til they see me in these at Homecoming!"

"Yeah. I can't wait to see you walk in them." *Or try to walk in them.* Avery stared around the store. Even the socks were too expensive for her here. It's a wonder they didn't charge to breathe the heavily-scented air. "Where's Brody?"

"He had to go to the bathroom," Sophie answered, her attention on her cell phone.

Avery realized she needed to go, too. The sign on the cashier desk said *No public restrooms.* "Where are the bathrooms?"

Sophie pointed toward the entrance. "Cashier said to the right and behind the Gourmet Chocolate store. I'll meet you there."

The scent of expensive perfume hit Avery before she saw her. Sidled up beside horse-toothed Brody was MaKenzie. She gazed up at him and flung her hair over her shoulder as they laughed about something. Avery hung back, hugging the corner of the chocolate shop, trying to eavesdrop without getting caught.

"Hey! Are you done already?"

Avery jumped. Although she would love to get Brody out of Sophie's life, she didn't want it to blow up like this. Avery placed her hand on Sophie's arm. "Toilet's broken. Let's go see if we can find another one."

"But I've got to wait for Brody. Look, Avery, I get that you don't like—"

MaKenzie's flirty giggle mingled with Brody's sickening laughter. Sophie pushed past Avery before she could catch her friend.

Sophie's face reddened as she took in the sight. "What the—?"

Avery grabbed for her arm again. "Let's just go. She's so not worth it."

"Well, if it isn't Tweedle Dee and Tweedle Dumb." MaKenzie's grin showed she knew exactly whom she was flirting with.

"Hey, babe! Guess who I just met? Someone from your school."

He can't be that stupid. Can he? Either that or he was such an expert at lying and hiding his actions that it came to him easy as breathing.

"Yeah. She's from my school. From the hag section. She's first chair."

MaKenzie screwed her face up and stuck her tongue out at Sophie. "You're so lame."

Sophie moved to attack, but Avery caught her. "You think so, huh? You're the freaking lame one, talking to MY fiancé."

"Your fiancé? Are you sure?" Makenzie blinked faux innocent eyes toward them. "Then he must be trash."

"Hey!" Brody towered over the brunette. "I'm not trash."

"If you're dating her you must be. Sorry. Wasting my time." She waved her manicured hands at them. "See you in school, losers."

Brody looked like a puppy that had just gotten scolded for the first time.

"What was that?" Sophie demanded now that MaKenzie was gone.

"What was what, babe?" he snorted. "That girl? She said she saw us together and knew you. She was asking questions. All I was doing was being polite and answering them."

"Bull."

"Bull? What's bull?" Brody's expression twisted into a snide grimace.

"You talking with her." Sophie took a step toward her boyfriend. "You weren't just talking." She took another angry step. "You were leaning down with your face barely an inch from hers." She was standing in front of Brody now, her head almost reaching his shoulders, a finger poked into his chest. "You were coming on to her."

"That's bull. I wasn't doing anything wrong."

"You're unbelievable!"

Avery looked around them. The crowd walking from store to store closest to them was starting to stare. "Uh, guys."

"You're such a baby. Every time we go somewhere you yell about me flirting with other girls. It's all bull." Spit flew out of Brody's mouth.

"Ha! *That's* baloney, and you know it. You've been flirting with girls all day. Even that hick girl in the truck on the way down here. And you expect me to put up with it. You're delusional."

"You're being ridiculous. I've done nothing wrong. I brought you and your stupid friend down here just because you wanted something special for homecoming."

Sophie clenched her hands. Avery put her hand on her shoulder. There were too many witnesses in case she hauled off and smacked him. "Let's go, Sophie. Let's go get something to eat and cool off. Then you can talk about this rationally."

"I'm not being irrational about anything." Sophie lifted herself up onto her tiptoes. "We're done. Through."

"Yeah?" Brody glared at her.

"Yeah! We're so over," Sophie yelled.

Dread passed over Avery. "Uh, Soph—"

"Fine." A bright smile covered Brody's face. "Good luck getting a ride back home. Babe." Brody whipped around and left Sophie standing open-mouthed.

Avery slapped a hand to her forehead, and rubbed at a headache threatening to bloom.

"He didn't just leave us! Tell me he didn't just leave us." Sophie squeaked.

"Nice move." MaKenzie stepped out from the other side of the walkway. "See you if you manage to get home."

Chapter Thirty-Two

(Truth #17: A friend in need is a friend indeed.)

"Don't forget our deal," Keaton said to Avery, his eyes crinkling up at the corners. His dark hair curled under his ball cap. "I'll think of something for you too, Sophie."

A full moon beamed down upon the Missouri countryside as Keaton drove Avery and Sophie home. The seat was slick on Avery's backside. The scent of leather cleaner and new car air freshener filled the enclosed space.

After a half an hour of bickering with Sophie about her and Brody's fight, Avery realized she was just as mad at herself for agreeing to come along on this road trip as she was with Sophie for picking the fight with her nub boyfriend. Though she was happy Brody was out of the picture, anger over being stuck hours away in Kansas City was stronger. They came to the conclusion there was no one else but Keaton they could call that would travel that far. So they'd enlisted him, who just happened to have a free Saturday and was only too eager to come and get them—for a price: Avery would go out on a date with him. And give him a kiss.

"It's a long way home. Am I going to have to talk to myself? I'm interesting, but do you really want to hear me go on for the next two and a half hours about the grand being that is me?" He turned and grinned at Avery.

"Thank you for coming to get us. I don't know how else we would've gotten home," Avery said over her shoulder, more to Sophie than to him. "At least not without someone's head rolling."

"I'm sorry. I'm sorry a million times. I'm sorry. How many times do I have to apologize for Brody being a ginormous nub?" Sophie yelled and bumped Avery's seat.

"As many times as it takes to get it through your head he's a loser!" Avery yelled back.

"Hey, hey, hey! Don't be hating on my baby." He rubbed Avery's seat. "Now, girls, are you going to let the nub-faced loser get in the middle of your friendship?" Keaton asked, one half of his mouth turned up in a grin.

"Yes!" both girls screamed at the same time.

"All righty then. Can someone tell me what made the guy up and leave you three hours away with no way to get home? There has to be a good reason." Keaton's driving was as bad as Sophie's. He took a curve too fast, throwing Avery into his arm.

"Keaton!" Avery righted herself before giving him a dirty look, catching the glint in his eye and the smirk on his face. The jerk was using the fact her seatbelt didn't work to his advantage.

"This stupid car isn't as comfortable in the back seat," Sophie whined.

"Good. You don't deserve to be comfortable."

"Do I need to pull over and make you both walk?" Keaton threatened, laughing and swerving to the side for emphasis, tossing Avery back against him.

"Not funny, Keaton. And get your seatbelts fixed, would ya!" Avery glared at him. She was grateful to him for coming to their rescue, but she wasn't the one who got into a fight with Brody. She was cursed with MaKenzie's presence every time something bad happened in her life.

"Mom's going to kill me. It'll be after ten o'clock by the time we get home." Her phone chirped. "Great. Speak of the devil."

"It *is* funny since I'm not you guys." Keaton flicked Avery's nose. She grabbed his finger and bent it back. "Ow. Ow. Mommy."

"Shhhh," Sophie's hissed. "I told you. I'm Homecoming shopping with Avery. We're going to get something to eat now and then come home."

Sophie's mom's voice carried through the silent vehicle, raising an octave at the end.

"Here," Sophie gave the cell to Avery. "Tell her we went shopping and will be home after we get something to eat."

Lips pursed, Avery grabbed the phone, covering the speaker. "You didn't tell her we went to Kansas City, did you?"

"No. She'd never let me go, you know that. Just tell her." Sophie pushed the phone closer.

"Fine." She took her hand away from the speaker. "Hello, Mrs. Morris. Yes, we had a great day of shopping together. We're trying to decide where to eat, and then we'll be home."

"You girls should've told me, I would've come with you and bought you supper. Make sure you bring everything over so we can have a modeling session, okay?"

"Will do, Mrs. Morris. See you soon." She handed the phone back to Sophie, who finished up the call.

"Geez. Can't I get a break?" Sophie flopped against the seat, crinkling the bags on the seat next to her.

"So, why—"

"MaKenzie," Avery spat.

Keaton laughed. "What?"

Sophie shifted in her seat. "MaKenzie showed up and found Brody. We saw them flirting in a back alley. She's such a hag! First with Jaxson and now with Brody." Sophie sighed.

Avery ignored Keaton's sideways stare. "Well, she is kinda hot."

Before she knew what she was doing, Avery slugged him. "Ow!"

"You deserve that." Avery slid closer to her window. "It wasn't just MaKenzie, anyway. Brody flirts with anything that has two legs and breasts."

"I see it. I'm not stupid." Sophie's voice thickened.

"Then why do you do it? Why do you girls let guys treat you horribly and keep coming back?" Keaton rubbed his arm where Avery had hit him. The questions he asked held more emotion than they should have.

"I don't know. I guess because nobody else even looks at me. He's the only one who has ever been this interested in me."

Avery wanted to refute her friend's comment, but as she thought over it, Sophie was right. As much as she hated to admit it, most guys wanted the beautiful, confident girls like MaKenzie, and they passed over others like Sophie because they weren't the model-looking type. Guys like Brody zeroed in on the girls who were too eager to be in a relationship.

"Look, Avery, I'm sorry. Maybe you were right about him, and I just didn't want to see it. He's so sweet all the rest of the time." Sophie laughed. "At least he didn't take all the stuff he bought me. Bonus."

"If there's one thing I've learned from my mom's dating, it's that guys will say and do anything to get you. Once they have you, it's a different story." Keaton glanced at Sophie in the rearview mirror. The blinking highway lights flickered across his eyes.

Avery studied Keaton's profile as he drove. The dash lights glowed off of his dark curls, making him look younger than he was. Or maybe he just seemed younger because of the comments he made, she could see that lifestyle and his mother's drinking was screwing up Keaton's life. Just like her parents were screwing up hers.

"You realize you just insulted your own gender." Sophie moved again, crinkling the bags as she tried to get comfortable. "Remind me next time to call dibs on shotgun."

The vulnerable look Keaton had was instantly replaced with a smirk. "Nah, I'm the exception to the rules. Want to test me?" He put his hand on Avery's, his eyebrows raised in question.

She stiffened briefly then turned to stare back out at the darkened landscape. "I don't know, Keaton. I just broke up for good with Jaxson. I'm not sure I'm ready." The shadows along the roadside chased the car as it sped along the interstate back to Iowa, the light of the moon brightening their ghost-like appearance. Keaton squeezed her hand and let go. She thought she heard him say, "I'll wait," but she couldn't bring herself to ask him to repeat it.

"Got any friends that would be willing to go out with me?" Sophie asked him. "Or a nice, hot older brother?"

Keaton laughed. "Nope."

Two hours later Keaton dropped Sophie off at her house. Avery went in and listened while Mrs. Morris chatted about "Sophie's Brody" the whole time.

Avery raised her eyebrows at Sophie behind Mrs. Morris's back, to which her friend frowned, nodding at them to leave.

Keaton pulled into Avery's driveway fifteen minutes later. Trees rustled with the autumn wind, sending trembling shadows across the house's dark exterior. He shut the ignition off and turned toward her.

"I know today was a rotten day for you, but it was kind of cool for me." He rubbed her arm with the back of his fingers. "I got to be a shining knight and come rescue you."

"Keaton—"

He leaned his head back on the headrest and groaned. "Don't say it, Avery. I know you're hung up on Mr. Perfect. I'll still be here when you realize he's not so perfect, you know. Nobody is." He sat up and stared at her hands before looking up in her eyes. "We're so similar, you and me. All I ask is that you keep an open mind. Whatever happens, we'll still be friends. No matter what." He put his forehead against hers, and she leaned against him.

A light flickered on in the house. Her heart sank.

"Want me to come in and help diffuse the situation?" Keaton stared at the house, creasing his brows.

Her breath caught in her chest. She remembered her dad's threats about boys. "No. That's probably not a good idea."

"You sure?" He didn't sound convinced.

Avery reached over and squeezed his forearm. The moment was so quiet, so intimate. Goose bumps flickered across her arms.

The light went back off. They both sat and waited for a few long minutes. "Thanks for everything tonight, Keaton. I'll owe you forever."

Keaton leaned over and hugged her. "Be careful, okay? I know what can happen with an angry drunk."

He was close enough for her to smell the mint on his breath. Close enough to kiss. Avery's heart twisted painfully when she looked into his dark eyes, instead of the bright blue ones she adored.

She went to kiss his cheek, and he turned at the last minute. Heat flared in her gut long enough to make her lose conscious thought. When her sense returned, the kiss was over. Keaton kissed her forehead. "Thanks for the payment. You'd better get in before your dad really does wake up."

Her head spun. She just kissed someone else besides Jaxson. Guilt and remorse battled with the hormones telling her it was a really good kiss. Really, really, good. She cleared her throat. "Thanks for saving us."

He chuckled, the warmth of his voice gave her the strength she needed to get out of the car and go inside. "Give me a sign if the coast is clear, and then I'll go."

Avery tiptoed to the back door and opened it. She leaned over the side of the house and waved at Keaton, signaling she was safe. When he pulled away, she walked through the laundry room to get to the kitchen.

Glass shards and food lay scattered across the vinyl floor and counters. She stopped, trying to figure out what happened. Had someone broken in? Did her dad have some sort of alcohol-fueled melt down?

Nothing seemed to be taken. Items were smashed or splattered with ketchup and mustard. The tangy acrid smell of the condiments made her already-knotted stomach churn.

She stepped over the biggest pieces, guided only by the bright moonlight shining in the windows and green digital lights from various appliances. Each footstep crunched against the hard floor, and she was glad she wore her tennis shoes instead of flip-flops.

In the dining room she found more plaster from the ceiling lying all over the floor. The phone lay in pieces on the table, and she could see inside the bathroom through a hole punched in the door

Meltdown it was. Avery thanked God for having missed out on whatever caused her father to go berserk. Being in Kansas City all day had been a blessing.

The stairway door hung from the frame when she opened it; only the bottom hinge held it to the wall. Her father's telltale snores resonated through his open bedroom door. He was still alive. She was torn—should she go check on him to make sure he wasn't bleeding to death, or should she get the heck out of there?

Ryan West, her Alateen counselor, had told them to keep safe first. Never enter a situation when an addict was out of control, thinking you could handle it. *Never wake a sleeping bear.* Her nerve endings flared into overdrive when she saw the door to her mother's room laying on the couch, clothing strewn about, and items smashed and littered across the living room. Her senior photo she had just hung up was slashed, the knife still sticking out of the canvas.

Emptiness gathered like a big ball in her chest. She grabbed her phone and dialed Sophie. "Hey, can I take you up on that sleepover?"

Chapter Thirty-Three

(Lie #16: Blood is thicker than water.)

"I can't believe your father got so mad at you for staying out late." Mrs. Morris doted on her the next day. She touched Avery's hand. "You sure it didn't have anything to do with that cute football player who drove you home?"

"No, Mrs. Morris. Dad was having a bad day or something. I just knew if I stayed there, it would get worse." Avery couldn't look her in the eyes when she spoke. "Without Mom home now—" She couldn't help the tears that burned her eyes, praying the woman would drop the subject, even if it was underhanded to use the situation with her mom that way. If anyone knew the truth of her situation . . .

Mrs. Morris's hand flew to her mouth. "Of course, I'm so sorry, my dear." She hugged Avery tight. Her voice brightened. "I know. We'll do that spa day. Remember, we were going to do that before? I'll go get the hot wax."

Avery nodded, her assent sending the woman into a flurry of activity. She ran to the bathroom, leaving Sophie and Avery alone.

"Are you going to try to go home and get your stuff?" Sophie asked when she was sure her mother couldn't hear. She pointed to the short shorts tied with a string around Avery's waist and oversized shirt she let Avery borrow. "You're not going to fit in anything I have. Do you have any cash left to buy something new?"

"Nope. Not since school started and my hours have been cut down. I'm pretty broke. I have some money for gas and food, but not enough to buy a new outfit. I suppose I could wear my same clothes again on Monday," Avery whispered.

"I don't think that'll fly with the parental unit." Sophie nodded toward where her mother had gone to get the hot wax for their hands. "How bad was it?"

Avery cringed. "It's never been that bad before. Something had to have happened. Maybe I can drive by this afternoon and see if he's home. If he's not, I'll grab a bunch of stuff. Do you think your mom'll let me stay for a few days if I come back with another sob story? I don't want to lie, but it looks like a tornado paid a visit and stayed awhile."

"Do you want me to come along?"

Avery shook her head. "No. I'll be fine as long as he's not home. I'll make it super quick."

"You going to call that Alateen dude? Maybe they can help."

"If I tell them, they'll contact the county." She shrugged and her heart raced thinking about it. She just needed to buy some time until she graduated. But even that was months away. She had to play it cool.

"I don't have any relatives to take me in. I'd be put in foster care." Avery dug her hands into her tangled hair. "I'm NOT going to foster care."

"Okay, okay. But be careful." Sophie squeezed her arm.

Mrs. Morris returned, smiling and chatting about facials and nail polish. Sophie and Avery exchanged glances before laughing.

By one o'clock that afternoon, Avery had been buffed and waxed all she could handle. She'd made an excuse about going home to try to make up with her dad. No one was home when she pulled into the driveway.

The front door swung open to an unbelievable mess. What darkness hid the night before was plain in the light of day. Everything glass or breakable had been shattered. The refrigerator was unplugged and the door open, its shelves sat lopsided and the glass vegetable tray cracked.

Her breathing came out in labored gasps as she tried to gather her wits. She hurried upstairs, stopping by the closet in the office to grab two old suitcases. Her room remained untouched. Handfuls of clothes went in the suitcases. She shoved her computer, iPod, phone charger—all the essentials from her room—into the second case. Shoes, a jacket, and the stuffed cat Sophie won for her went in next.

It took three trips to ensure she got everything she needed, she even grabbed her bedding, pillows, and a couple of towels in case she needed to spend the night at the RV site and use their showers.

Her heart and mind warred about what she should do. If she asked Ryan, her Alateen sponsor, he would tell her to call the authorities, or he might call them himself if he suspected anything. But, if she called the authorities and they couldn't get a hold of her mom . . .

"This is my senior year," her wail echoed over the chaos. She sniffed away the tears. "I won't be taken away. I can't tell anyone."

She took one last look around and slipped into her mother's room. She ran her hand underneath the dust cover but couldn't locate the jewelry box. She found it inside the closet, below a gash in the wall, broken into pieces.

A cracking noise from outside made her jump. Her heart raced, and she struggled to catch her breath. She laughed when she saw it was only a squirrel jumping from limb to limb on the tree outside of her mom's room.

She waited for a few minutes, but there was only silence. She held her head up as she walked to her car and turned to look back at the farmhouse. The grass came up to her knees; the lawn hadn't been mowed once this year.

There's nothing left here for me now. Avery grabbed her stabbed photo and clutched it to her chest as she walked out. She threw the knife into the weeds under the deck. She didn't look back as she got in her car and drove away.

***

It had taken some finesse, but she managed to convince Mrs. Morris to let her stay at their house for the week of Homecoming. Sophie's closet was jam-packed, so Avery's dress hung in Mrs. Morris's closet.

Mrs. Morris's screams kept her from oversleeping the next morning. Overnight, someone had placed the Valley Latrine in the center of the Morris' front lawn. A sign taped to the lid read, "Traveling Toilet. Removal cost $20. Proceeds go to Homecoming." Phone number and website information for the student council was printed in small print at the bottom of the sheet.

Sophie giggled, drawing her mother's ire.

"You tell that idiot student council to get that filthy piece of ceramic out of my yard. Or else!"

"You know the drill, Mom. Pay the twenty bucks and it's gone."

"I know the drill. Every year for the past five years I've known the drill. It just gets funnier and funnier." Mrs. Morris shoved her purse onto her shoulder and left, mumbling about stupid Homecoming traditions.

Avery giggled. "It's the only reason I like living in the country. Too much trouble for the football guys to drive the 'Homecoming Throne' out that far and then go pick it up again."

"Those decorations better be awesome. Not like last year's lame crepe paper designs." Sophie pushed her way past Avery to take a picture of the toilet as they left.

At school, Avery slammed open her locker door. A photo fluttered to the ground. She picked it up to find a grainy, blown-up picture of her and Jaxson from the beach the day after she found out about her mother's affair. Jaxson's hand was on her back, rubbing in the suntan lotion. His back was to the picture, but her face was turned up to him. The expression on her face had been marked over with a permanent marker. The words TRAILER TRASH ruined the beauty of one of the best moments in her life. Just like her senior picture at the fair. Just like the photo her father stabbed.

The two-minute bell rang. Avery stuck the picture in her purse, choosing not to show Sophie. She glanced around, but nobody was watching. Everyone was intent on getting to class. Was it MaKenzie or someone else? Well, the joke was on them. Avery had bigger problems than stupid messages on photos.

Later that day after English comp at Community College, she and Sophie raided Keaton's trunk for the items they bought in Kansas City.

"Where's Miss Perky Pants?" Keaton joked.

"Katie texted me saying she was sick. Sore throat or something. Good thing, or we'd have to explain to her why we have a bunch of bags in your car." Avery packed the last bag into her trunk. It was crammed full now.

Keaton eyed the contents and leaned against the side of her car. "How'd it go with your dad after I left?"

Avery frowned, slamming the trunk harder than it needed to be. She gave him a sour look. Sophie pounded on the passenger side window showing her displeasure. Brody had texted her apologizing, and she was busy chewing him out via instant message.

"That good, huh?" He took a packet of gum from his pocket and offered her a piece. "So, wanna talk about it?"

She took a piece and chewed it for a second before answering. "I don't know. Something went down when we were gone. The place was trashed. I'm staying with Sophie until I can figure out what to do."

His face was full of concern. "How bad was it?"

Her hands froze. "Bad. Really bad. I can't stay there. But I don't want to report it and end up one county over in foster care." She flopped against the door beside Keaton, staring unseeing into the distance.

"Yeah. I get that. But do you think living out of your car is the best solution?"

"I don't know, Keaton. I just don't have a lot of options at the moment."

A flock of geese flew over the parking lot, honking. MaKenzie walked across the blacktop, ignoring them. She wore a checkered shirt, jeans, boots, and a pink cowboy hat for Monday's Western Dress Up Day for Homecoming Week. Keaton wolf whistled at her, drawing a snide remark from MaKenzie.

"Keep that up and you're not going to Homecoming with me." Avery leaned her head on his muscular shoulder.

Keaton slipped his arm around her back and leaned his head against the top of hers. "You don't have any family?" His voice held a note of hope.

"Nope. My mom's parents are dead. Greg was a foster child. My aunt was my mother's only close relative, and she died two years ago." Avery watched the clouds float by. "It's so peaceful here right now."

"We could run away. Get a place together. You could get a job, support me while I work on the roadster. We'd get matching GED's. Pop out a couple of rug rats." Keaton laughed as she pushed him away. "It was just a thought."

"I never told you I found my original birth certificate. It didn't list a father." Avery looked down at her tennis shoes. "After what my dad said that night I brought him home from the ER, maybe he's not my dad. What if everything those snotty, rich women said was true? What if my mom got pregnant in high school and I'm a bastard child?"

"What if you're really an alien placed here as a decoy?" Keaton moved over her, tickling her sides. "Take me to your leader."

"Stop, stop." She bumped him with her hip. "I just wonder what else in my life has been a lie." She glanced at MaKenzie putting on lipstick in her car. "Why is it that life isn't fair?"

Keaton forced her chin up so she had to look at him. Tears stung behind her eyes.

"Hey. Nobody said life was going to be fair. But I promise you're going to make it through this. We're going to make it through." He took one of her hands in his. "We will have the best life ever because we know what it's like to have life suck so bad you can't stand it. It only gets better from here. Okay?" He wiped the tears falling down her cheeks away with his thumb and kissed her forehead. She clasped his wrists.

"Thanks," she whispered and pressed her head against his chest.

His laugh rumbled in her ear. For a moment, she felt safe and hopeful. Until she saw MaKenzie hanging out her car window, phone in hand, taking pictures of them.

Avery stiffened. "That little—" She removed herself from Keaton's hold and ran toward the green car. MaKenzie started it and sped off, laughing and waving the phone at them as she left.

Sophie ran over and stood next to Avery. "This. Means. War."

Chapter Thirty-Four

(Truth #18: There are no dress rehearsals for life.)

Avery rolled up the last background screen, packing it with the dozen other screens Elaine used in her studio. Hay bales, which had sat in one corner of the setup, had been used as a trampoline by three cousins from a multi-generational family shoot. Straw was scattered from one end of the studio to another. She swept up the carnage with a broom and dustpan.

"Whew! Glad that one's done. I adore children, but boy can they be a handful." Elaine lined the chairs and props against the far wall and turned toward Avery. "It's late, darlin'. Why don't you go ahead? I'll clean this tomorrow."

"Don't have to tell me twice." Avery propped up the broom and headed into the lobby. She glanced at her portrait on the wall and smiled. It may not have hung on her wall at home, but Precious Moments had started to feel like home to her.

"You wouldn't believe how many people ask me if I can get that rainbow in their picture now. They must think it's a green screen background or something!" Elaine laughed. "So are you going to be able to go to Homecoming this weekend?"

Avery glanced at Elaine. "Yeah, why?"

Elaine hesitated. She leaned against the corner of her large wooden desk, crossed her arms, and leveled a serious look at Avery. "My sources say your dad's drinking has spiraled out of control." Again she hesitated. "Is everything all right at home?"

Avery didn't know how to answer without lying. "I've been staying with friends." She shrugged. "I haven't seen much of Greg lately."

If Elaine thought using her dad's name was odd, she didn't show it. "Has your mom tried to contact you at all?"

Avery shifted around. "No." She didn't really consider that lying since her mom didn't leave a message when she called a couple weeks ago. If she had wanted to get a message to Avery, she could have very easily in that moment.

But she hadn't.

Elaine studied her for what seemed like an eternity. "Well, you just let me know if you ever need anywhere to go. You can always stay with me." She pushed herself off the desk and turned to settle into her leather chair. "At least until we can figure something else out."

Avery's eyes widened. *Figure what else out?* Surely she didn't mean DHS. "Yeah. Sure. I'll keep that in mind." She hurried to collect her purse and rushed outside to her car.

The streetlight above shone a cone-shaped spotlight upon her windshield, highlighting a piece of paper stuck under her wiper. It was a photo of her and Keaton from the parking lot that afternoon. Their heads were bowed together, Keaton's arm around her. Across the center was the word LOVERS.

She stuck that photo in her purse beside the first photo of her and Jaxson. She'd love nothing better than to get even with MaKenzie. Her mind wandered as she drove down the interstate.

Red and blue lights flashed on the other side of the highway. An ambulance, a fire truck, and two police cars lined the side of the road. Traffic on the interstate braked as Avery drove by the accident. A semi passed her on the left, and the rumble as it shifted gears drowned out the siren's blare, allowing her only a glimpse of a vehicle flipped over in the ditch.

Avery gripped the steering wheel tight as the people in front of her slowed to almost a stop to gawk. She relaxed her tense fingers from gripping the wheel as she drove down the off ramp and headed toward the Carters' house.

Butterflies did a frantic dance in her stomach when she pulled into the driveway. A familiar blue truck sat in the driveway behind the Carters' vehicles. Mr. Carter's tractor took up the open space between the driveway and the fence surrounding the pasture, leaving her no options but to park next to Jaxson's truck.

Mrs. Carter welcomed her. "Thanks for coming over tonight to help Katie catch up on her homework, Avery. The boys are downstairs in the family room. Why don't you girls go upstairs to her bedroom and hang out until Jaxson goes home?"

Avery nodded in agreement. However, she realized her backpack with everything she needed was still in the trunk. She ran to get it before Jaxson could come out and see her. The stuff in the trunk had shifted around, probably from having to slow down so quickly on the interstate. The once-neat piles and suitcases were strewn about, the backpack strap just visible beneath the heap toward the back of the trunk. She put down her purse and crawled over everything to get to the strap.

Footsteps crunched on the driveway behind her. She yanked hard on the strap, but it wouldn't budge. Again she pulled without success.

"Living out of your car now? Should we get you one of those grocery carts to pull around your stuff, and a box for you to sleep in?" Jaxson's teasing voice came from the right side of her trunk.

She *thunked* her head against the inside of the hood. "Ow." Her hair snagged in the trunk clasp. Just like the backpack, her hair wouldn't come loose.

Great. Not only was she embarrassingly stuck in her car, Jaxson had guessed correctly about her living out of her car.

"Here, let me help." Jaxson's adept fingers made short work of freeing her.

"Thanks." She rubbed the sore spot on her scalp.

"Sure. What are you doing here?"

"Spending the night." The backpack rested halfway out from beneath one of her suitcases. She grabbed it and knocked over her purse, which sat on top of the heap.

"So, what's with all the stuff in your car?" Arms crossed, he stood taller than she remembered.

Avery avoided looking into his eyes. She hugged her bag to her chest. The close proximity to Jaxson, the weight of his body spray mingling with the clean smell of soap, caused her mind to malfunction. Her thoughts jumbled into an incoherent mess. Running a hand through her tangled hair, she tried to recall what she had been doing.

"Are you okay? You look a little dazed." Jaxson caressed her upper arm just beneath the short sleeve.

"I'm fine." She shrugged off his hand. "I can't think straight when you do that." She dropped the pack on top of the clutter. "I'm sorry, that came out way meaner than I meant it to."

Jaxson's eyes narrowed at something. "What's that?"

Avery's hands turned cold. It was the photo of her and Keaton in the parking lot. She crumpled it and pushed it back into her purse. *Geez, can I ever catch a break?*

"Can you move your car over a little so I can back out?" His voice was strangled and his words clipped.

"Sure." Avery watched him as he got into his truck and slammed the door. She backed up and re-parked half in the grass, giving him room to leave. Her lungs constricted as her heart broke into jagged little pieces all over again.

***

Avery's eyes had dark rings under them the next morning.

All the cheerleaders were wearing football uniforms for Team Spirit Day. Michael's old jersey from the previous year fit tight on Katie. Avery chose a green t-shirt with a random number on it, hoping to fit in.

"You should've come with me to buy Jaxson's jersey at the auction this weekend." Katie bounced beside Avery in the bathroom. Every year, as per Valley tradition similar to the traveling toilet, the school auctioned off the practice jerseys or old uniforms of the players to raise money.

Avery frowned into the mirror at Katie. She had avoided the auction, knowing she would see Jaxson there, and possibly witnessing the purchaser of his jersey. She prayed one of his family bought it.

"As long as it's not MaKenzie wearing it, I'm good." Avery thought about the hurt on Jaxson's face when he left last night. Pain pierced her chest. "Besides, I can't wear it. We broke up."

"Girls! You're going to be late!" Mrs. Carter called through the door.

At school, students and teachers alike were dressed up for the day. A Warrior mascot strutted down the hallways, high-fiving students and pumping his arms.

"Traitor!" Sophie—dressed in a gray shirt, black jeans and strappy heels—grumbled as Avery approached. Their school colors were green and yellow, and everyone except Sophie and possibly one of the dead-head stoner hicks wore school colors.

"I told you yesterday to wear something green. Even if it was that awful venom-colored shirt you like." Avery opened her locker. Another picture was stuck in the vent on the locker door. Holding the door back so Sophie didn't see, she plucked it out of the metal and looked at it. It was the photo from the Fair with Jaxson and MaKenzie as the King and Queen. The caption, *Who's laughing now*, darkened her mood even more.

"Earth to Avery." Sophie snapped her fingers.

Startled, she glanced up. "What?" Avery held the photo, picture side in, against the locker door.

"I asked why you look so tired. Don't you have an eight o'clock bedtime at Katie's?" Sophie's gaze fell on the slats of her locker. "What is that?"

"Nothing." Avery tried to put it in her purse, but Sophie snatched the picture out of her hand.

Sophie blew out a breath. "Where did you get this?"

Avery put her books in her bag and slung it over her shoulder, trying to waste time.

"Avery, where did you get this picture?"

"In my locker. Just like the other ones." Avery said, knowing Sophie would not rest until she got all the information.

Sophie's back straightened. "What other ones? Tell me or I'm going to Principal Field about a certain hag's harassment of you on school grounds. You and Princess Picture-Taker will get to chat with him about what's going on. Then they'll call your *parents* to come in and talk about the situation."

"Fine, whatever." Avery pulled the out the other two photos.

Sophie grabbed both of them, holding up the picture of her and Jaxson. "That would be sweet except for the terrible handwriting." She switched to the one with Keaton. "What about this one? When'd you get it?"

"It was on my car last night after work."

Sophie raised an eyebrow.

"When I went over to Katie's, Jaxson was there. He saw it when it fell out of my bag."

"What'd he say?" Sophie hid the pictures against her chest when Lauren Hughes, one of MaKenzie's avid followers, walked by. Every inch of her poured into a pair of football pants—no pads needed.

Avery drew in a quick breath. "Jaxson asked me to move my car so he could leave. Then he left." She shrugged. "The thing is, I don't know why she's doing it. Jaxson and I aren't dating anymore. You'd think she'd back off."

"The reasons don't matter. This is war. Casualties are to be expected." Sophie pointed at her before spinning around and huffing down the hall.

Just what she needed: Sophie going all ninja-commando-crazy. A weight settled on Avery's shoulders as she headed to her first class of the day.

Halfway through class, the overhead speaker crackled.

"Mrs. Conway, Avery Denton's presence is needed in the office." Their school secretary, Mrs. Novak, sounded annoyed as usual.

I'm going to kill you, Sophie! Avery walked around the outside of the room, but she could still feel every eye on her back.

In the office, Avery saw MaKenzie enter into a small meeting room. The jersey she wore just happened to be number forty-eight. Jaxson's freshman jersey. She clenched her fists to keep from reaching out and shaking the first person who walked by her. Not only was MaKenzie rubbing her and Jaxson's break up in her face, but it was also her fault Avery got called to the Principal's office.

She walked up to Mrs. Novak, wishing she had sunglasses. The secretary had dyed her hair a bright red, and wore a robin's egg blue suit with a neon pink blouse under it. The scent of oversweet perfume clouded the desk area, offending her nose as much as the outfit offended her eyes.

"You just called me out of class?"

"Have a seat. I'll let Principal Field know you're here." The secretary eyed her as she lifted the phone, covering the mouthpiece and whispering into it.

Avery flopped into the hard plastic chair against the wall.

The office intercom buzzed. "Send Ms. Denton back."

The secretary directed her toward the room MaKenzie had just entered. Avery stomped down the cheaply carpeted hallway.

She stood at the closed wooden door; the blinds on the windows of the meeting room shut tight, concealing what lay beyond the wall. Determination made her square her shoulders. She'd done nothing wrong. However, proof of MaKenzie's taunting lay within the confines of her purse. With a tug of the door handle, Avery entered the room and stopped dead in her tracks.

Four people sat around the rectangular table, with MaKenzie standing against the far wall, arms crossed and face as red as Michael's when he blushed. At the table sat Principal Field, Phillip Thomas, a serious looking man she didn't recognize, and the last person she expected to see.

Her mother stood, smile hesitant. "Hello, Avery."

Chapter Thirty-Five

(Lie #17: It's never as bad as you imagine it is.)

All Avery could do was stare. Three months had passed since the day she left. For weeks she had missed her mom, wishing she would call or come home—make everything right again. Now that she was there, all of Avery's emotions jumbled up in a ball, clouding her thoughts.

She cocked her head to the side. "What are YOU doing here?"

MaKenzie muffled a giggle. Everyone turned to look at her. She coughed and turned away from the attention.

Avery turned back and studied her mom. She'd lost weight since she'd been gone. Although puffy, her mom's eyes were no longer bloodshot but a clear, sparkling green. Her skin didn't have the pallor it had before, and her hair was shinier. The butterflies in Avery's stomach caught fire, leaving sizzling trails as they circled around. Having an affair looked great on her mother.

"Sweetheart, we can talk details later. We have some other business to attend to first. Then we can have some personal time to sort this all out."

Avery lifted a hand to her aching chest. "Details? That's what you call showing up in my principal's office three months after leaving? No calls, no contact, nothing? Just *details*?"

Principal Field broke in. "Avery, I understand this is difficult for you. Please sit down and let's discuss this as rational adults." His hands motioned with his words, like they always did when he talked. The gray hair along his balding head spiked up as if he had run his fingers through it. His suit was a much cheaper version of the sleek one Phillip Thomas wore.

MaKenzie snorted. "Rational adults? Maybe you're a rational adult," her voice dripped with acid, "but you can count me out of sitting down and talking rationally to anyone in this room. Where's my mother?"

The unidentified man held up his hand. "Miss Thomas, I'm Chris Pryor, your father's attorney. We are here to discuss an issue that concerns you but does not concern your mother. She has reluctantly given us permission to speak to you today." He flipped through a file and handed her a legal document.

MaKenzie's eyes flicked over the page. Her mouth hung open, then she snapped it shut. "I don't care what my mother signed. I'm not going to be a part of this little soirée." She moved behind the chairs heading for the second door at the back of the room.

"Sit down, MaKenzie. Now!" Phillip Thomas stood and pointed to a chair on the other side of him. His deep voice boomed across the room.

MaKenzie spun around and faced her father, stamping her feet on the ground. Tears glittered in her eyes. "Why should I listen to you? You quit your job, created a huge scandal, and left Mom and me. As far as I'm concerned, you're not my father."

"Our relationship is not the point of this meeting. *You* are not the point of this meeting." He pulled out an empty chair. The quiet intensity of his words was scarier than his booming voice. "However, to save time and to make things easier, you will stay. And if you do not sit down, I will take everything away from you, including your car. Do you understand me?"

Avery stared at the other girl, almost feeling sorry for her. Almost, but not quite. Avery waited, wide-eyed, wondering how far MaKenzie would take her tantrum.

Phillip turned and sent a piercing look at Avery. "And as for you, you will respect everyone in this room and take your seat. Is that understood?"

Avery stiffened as if cold water had been thrown at her. "Who do you think you are?" She swung a look at her mother, whose trembling hands clutched an insulated coffee cup.

The same ominous feeling she'd had when her father told her about her mother leaving poured over her. She shivered.

Phillip began. "As a matter of fact—"

The attorney held out his arm. "Please, ladies. This will not take long once we sit down and get to business."

MaKenzie clicked her tongue and flounced over to a different chair than the one her father pointed to. Avery could imagine steam coming out of the girl's ears as she crossed her legs and *thunked* her arms on the table. Avery slowly put one foot in front of the other, pulled the chair back, and sat carefully down on the opposite side of the table.

The attorney cleared his throat. "Thank you for your cooperation." He pulled out several files and flipped through them before handing one to the principal to look over. "Due to a tragic, fatal accident involving Mr. Greg Denton last night, custody of Ms. Avery Denton has been transferred."

Avery gripped the arms of the chair. Her head swam. Tragic? Fatal? "Wait, what?" She stammered. Pity and shock played across MaKenzie's face, disappearing the second Avery scowled at her.

Her mother answered, "Honey. I'm sorry to have to tell you this way—"

"Avery, the man you knew as your father died in a car accident last night."

"Phillip! You said I would be able to tell her." Her mother's mouth dropped, then her cheeks flushed bright red, and finally her face seemed to crumple in on itself.

"Dineen, this is not the time to sugarcoat the truth." His glance at Avery was direct, but not entirely unkind. It still gave her chills. "You've been doing that all of Avery's life. It's time to get the truth out."

Disbelief widened her mother's eyes. "I wasn't going to sugarcoat anything. You didn't even give me a chance to get the words out."

Avery stood up, sending the wheeled chair spinning behind her. "Tell me WHAT?" Her screams drew everyone's attention.

"I'm your father. Your biological father."

Avery's mother dropped her head into her hands. MaKenzie showed no surprise, just annoyance for having to be there. Principal Field, though, sputtered like a drowning man.

The lawyer stood up. "Order. Please. Look, Ms. Denton, Mr. Thomas and Mrs. Denton have asked me to come here to serve as their legal representative. With the death of Greg Denton, a petition has been filed and granted by the judge this morning stating that Phillip Thomas is indeed your biological father."

"Mom?" Avery's voice shook.

Her mother didn't look at her, but she nodded her head. "I'm sorry Avery. I never wanted you to find out this way."

The attorney continued. "Because of Mrs. Dineen Denton's stay in an alcohol rehabilitation center, she was found unsuitable for sole custody of Avery Denton. Until she is declared fit to be granted custody of Avery Denton, Mr. Thomas will become sole guardian for Avery—a custody that will expire when she turns eighteen."

Although the lawyer kept a running conversation with Principal Field, handing him files and papers as they conversed, Avery heard nothing else. The blood rushed to her ears, and her hands turned cold from the blood loss. Phillip remained quiet, his eyes fixed on Avery. Her mother stared at the table, her fingers still gripped tightly around her cup.

"Rehab?" Avery's voice came out in a strangled whisper.

"What?" The attorney's gaze darted back and forth trying to figure out what he missed.

She glared at her mom. "Rehab? That's where you went?"

Her mom's mouth thinned, and a hardness glinted from her eyes. "Yes. I'm sorry. Didn't Greg explain anything to you?" She glanced at Phillip. "You told me Greg was supposed to explain everything."

"Greg was encouraged several times to tell Avery what was going on since rumors of our supposed affair spread," Phillip said. "That way she would at least know those hateful speculations were false.

"Your mother came to me desperate to get clean. I found a center for her and took her there myself to make sure she didn't change her mind." Phillip neatened a stack of papers on the table before him. "During this time, I had a previous engagement I could not get out of and had to be out of town for an undetermined amount of time. With your mother incapacitated, she felt it was in your best interest to stay with Greg until she could return, and I agreed."

He took a breath before continuing. "Although he wasn't supposed to tell you about me, Greg was supposed to let you know about your mom so you wouldn't feel as if you had been abandoned.

The principal shot up out of his chair, papers in hand. "I'll just go make copies of these and let you talk." In his haste, he walked into the door before he managed to open it. His face turned bright red as he finally shuffled out.

Phillip, ignoring the principal's clumsy departure, turned toward MaKenzie. "You, on the other hand, knew I left your mother before any of this happened. Her behavior and yours have been inexcusable, hurtful, and damaging. Since you've been more than eager to get yourself involved in Avery's life, I thought it best you should be here when the truth came out. That way you could no longer pull any more antics. We're going to have a long talk later."

Thoughts and emotions spun in Avery's mind until she was dizzy. A tremble started from her toes and made a slow progression until it hit her scalp. Phillip was her real father? How could that be? It didn't make any sense. "How long? How long have you known I was your daughter?"

"Since you moved here," MaKenzie snapped. "My mother told me. Only I wasn't allowed to talk about it, though. Was I, *Dad*?"

Phillip slapped the table in front of him, making Avery jump. "That's enough. Not one more word."

The principal returned with the legal papers. "Here you go. That's all the school needs. Now do we need to bring in Mrs. Dooley, the guidance counselor?"

"That won't be necessary. I have a family therapist already." Phillip stood and buttoned his jacket.

"Yes. Okay. Ms. Denton and Ms. Thomas are free to go then." The principal's arms were spread wide, ushering them toward the door.

The lawyer took the papers back from him, filing them neatly into his bag. "Principal Field, we'd like to request Avery and MaKenzie leave for the rest of the morning. Is there anyone that can contact Community College to let them know they will be gone for today due to a family situation?"

MaKenzie exploded. "Voting for Homecoming Queen is this afternoon! I can't leave."

"You can and you will," Mr. Thomas stated.

"Not a problem. I'll take care of excusing them myself." Again, the principal waved them toward the door. Sweat beaded along his balding brow.

"Let's go, girls." Phillip stated walking toward the door and held it open for them.

MaKenzie's body was rigid as she hustled out of the room. Avery followed at a slower pace, her head still twisting.

Class was out when they walked into the hallway. Everyone's eyes were on them as they walked out of the school, the three adults following them. MaKenzie's chin jutted upward as a couple of freshman girls put their hands up to their mouths. They pointed and whispered as she walked by.

There would be no hiding the information now, especially with Mrs Novak as the school's gossip guru. Everyone would know by the end of the day that the man she called dad was dead and Phillip was her biological father. Chills spread through her, and she shivered. Her dad—correction: Greg— was dead. She tried to remember happy memories with him but came up blank. She remembered he hadn't wanted to move to Valley. Her parents had argued about it before and after the move.

But his death still stung.

It hit her then: she and MaKenzie were half-sisters. Could life get any worse?

Avery caught sight of MaKenzie's little green car first. In the front seat sat the Valley Latrine, its bowl overflowing with toilet paper. The tissue had been wrapped in messy streamers around the vehicle, the ends still clung to their gray-brown rolls a few feet away. A picture of MaKenzie, wearing her Harrison County Fair Queen sash, standing beside a heifer was blown up to poster size and taped to the windshield. The words HEIFER QUEEN were written across the poster in red paint. Sophie must've skipped class again. Avery wanted to hug her and punch her all at the same time.

MaKenzie looked up from her purse and stumbled to a stop on the blacktop parking lot.

Avery bit her tongue to keep from smiling at Sophie's handiwork, but her footsteps faltered when she glanced up to see the graffiti written across her own windshield. The word LOSER was written numerous times in different colors, leaving barely an inch of glass untouched. Both of the back tires were flat. She spun back around, sending MaKenzie a disgust-filled stare. Makenzie returned her stare with a glare of her own.

Phillip strode over to the green car and tore off the photo from the window. He crumpled it up, pointing to Avery's Taurus as he spoke. "I don't know what is going on here, but this," he shook the crumpled paper at them, "stops now. MaKenzie, in my truck. Avery, go with your mother. We'll get your cars later."

Chapter Thirty-Six

(Truth #19: The truth will set you free.)

Avery's mother drove behind Phillip Thomas's extended cab truck with its flashy rims and chrome detail work. They headed south toward the farm, riding in her mother's Honda Civic.

"Where are we going?" Avery slumped in the passenger seat, staring out the window.

"I need to get some stuff from the house. We'll stop by there first. Then I can explain what's been going on so you can understand why I did what I did." They pulled onto the country road that wound out to their house.

Avery grew more uneasy the closer they got to the house. The truck in front of them kicked dust into the air. She stayed silent, her heart stuttering, knowing what shape the house was in. Should she say something? Anger toward her mother and shock about Phillip overruled common sense. Nobody found it necessary to tell her anything. Let them figure it out for themselves once they got there.

Her mother seemed to be deep in thought. They pulled into the driveway behind Phillip, who got out and waited while her mother got her keys out of her purse and headed across the deck. She looked over her shoulder at Avery. "You coming?"

Avery shook her head. There was no way she was going in with her mother, even if the house wasn't trashed. "You first."

Her mother unlocked the door and swung it open. She stood in the doorway, transfixed. "What happened?"

Avery glared at her mother. "I guess my temporary guardian had a few temper tantrums while you were gone."

Her mother stepped inside the house, feet crunching on the glass that covered every inch of the floor. Phillip followed her mother. Curiosity finally spurred Avery into action, and she stepped in to watch from the doorway.

Hot, stuffy air filled the space. Without the air conditioner turned on, the house was hotter inside than the weather was outside. Gnats circled piles of spoiled food on the counters and in the open refrigerator.

Avery followed her mother to her room; the door still balanced on the couch. Her mother stood mesmerized at the broken pieces of her life. All of the boxes full of her belongings had been smashed, torn, or broken. The bedding had been slashed with something sharp, probably the same knife Avery tossed under the deck, leaving it in tatters. The window facing the backyard was cracked.

Phillip put his arms around her mother's shoulders. "They're just things, Dineen. They can be replaced."

Her mother dropped to the floor, her shoulders shaking.

Phillip cursed under his breath. "Things, Dineen. They're just things. If you want to stay sober, you need to focus on the future now. Not this. Not the past."

Avery backed out of the room, uncomfortable watching Phillip comfort her mom.

She headed back outside to escape the heavy odor of the house and sat on the old metal lawn chair. A squirrel ran across the yard and up the silver elm tree, chittering as it went.

Avery marveled at how the world kept going despite her life coming to an abrupt halt.

Her mother came out of the house, holding a small box full of her belongings. Her eyes were red and swollen, her cheeks splotchy and pale. "Avery, honey, I'm so sorry for leaving you to deal with Greg. I honestly didn't know he'd come unhinged like this. Did he hurt you?"

"Does it matter to you if he did?" Avery turned her head away from her mother.

"Of course it matters. I never wanted you to get hurt." Choking on her tears, her mother bent in front of Avery and set the box on the wooden slats of the deck beside her.

"Then why did you leave without telling me anything? I come home from work one day and find out my whole world has just been turned over and you're," Avery sobbed, "you're just gone. Who does that to their kid?"

"I'm sorry. I wish I could go back and do things differently. We trusted Greg to tell you what was going on. There'd never been anything to indicate he'd go crazy." She sighed. "He was always so jealous." She stopped and took a deep breath. "Greg was my first boyfriend, you know. At least until he went to college and broke up with me. I got a little wild, drinking, and messing around. My parents couldn't handle me, so they sent me to live here with my Aunt Penny my senior year."

"Why'd I never know this?" Avery stared out at the trees in their pasture.

"Aunt Penny had just been diagnosed with skin cancer when I came to live with her. I helped her with things like doing housework and taking her to chemotherapy. She helped me get past my reckless tendencies. When I moved here, I met Phillip. But I fell for his brother, Sean. He was married, but told me he would leave his wife for me." She closed her eyes as if replaying the memories in her mind.

"But that all ended after Sean's wife found out about us. I kind of lost it. Phillip and I ended up at the same party that night. We were both drunk." She shrugged as if it was apparent what happened next. "I got pregnant." A tear slipped down her cheek. "I was scared and horrified at what I'd done. Somehow Monica, Phillip's girlfriend, found out." Her mother twisted her fingers together in her lap.

Avery stiffened. She was a bastard. No wonder Monica had said what she had at the parade. Avery gazed across the fields that surrounded them. "What'd you do?"

"Monica gave me money to leave and never look back. I took everything I owned, left Aunt Penny a note, and drove. Just drove." She stopped, thinking. "I ended back up near Grand Island when my car broke down." She laughed bitterly. "Greg helped me get my life together. I owed him."

Mom grabbed Avery's hand in her cold one. "Look, Avery, I was in a bad place when I went to recovery. I honestly thought I was making the right decisions for you. I'm sorry you got caught up in the fallout."

"Dad—*Greg* told me you and Phillip were having an affair. That you were getting a divorce. He said he should throw me out because I was useless just like you." Avery swiped at the tears on her cheeks, searching her mother's eyes for the answers she needed. "Why didn't you call me?"

"Oh, Avery. He shouldn't have said that." She tried to hug Avery, but Avery held her at arm's length. "I tried to call you. I snuck a call once, but right at the end I got caught. They took my privileges away. It was another month before I was allowed to use the phone, unless it was for emergencies." Her mom looked out toward the barn. "I should have never trusted anyone else to your care. But I wasn't much of a mother to you in the end, anyway." Her shoulders slumped. "I'm so sorry, Avery."

Avery should have felt bad for her mother, but there had been too many secrets. "What about Phillip, Mom?" Phillip shut the door and came to stand behind her mother, a sleek contrast from the worn deck rail.

"I didn't know about you until years later. I overheard my wife talking to another woman about what she had done to Dineen. So I went looking for you both." His gaze on her mother was full of emotion. "Your mother refused to acknowledge me. We battled for a while in the courts, but finally came to an agreement. She would move back to Valley so I could be near you as you grew up. You wouldn't be told of me until you were eighteen." He smiled, but pain glittered in his green eyes.

Avery always thought she had her mom's green eyes, but seeing them up close, she realized her eyes and her eyebrows came from Phillip. She frowned. Aunt Penny had been right. She did look more like her dad.

"How'd MaKenzie know, then?"

"When you and your mother moved back, Monica was furious. She discouraged MaKenzie from being friends with you. Monica had a bad habit of talking about things when MaKenzie was around. I'm not sure when she figured it out, but it's been about a year now." He glanced out toward his truck where MaKenzie sat impatiently waiting.

"About the time she started coming in the store and harassing me." Bitterness rolled off Avery's words. "How did you get together with Greg, then?"

"Your Grandma Vicky and I had a falling out over my involvement with a married man and ending up pregnant. I couldn't call her for help. When Greg offered to help me, I accepted. He was ready to get married." She shrugged. "And since Greg and I dated in high school, it was easy, convenient. But he was always resentful that you weren't his. It wasn't bad at first, but after Phillip found us, it got worse and worse." Her face flushed, tears sparkled in her eyes. "I should've done things differently. I've made so many mistakes."

Phillip put his hand on her mother's shoulder. "We've all made mistakes, Dineen. None of us are perfect. You couldn't know what was going to happen."

"I should've. Greg's drinking had been getting out of control since Aunt Penny died. Then mine did as well. Greg was never violent, but he had a temper. He was never happy. I was never happy." She shook her head. "It all became a vicious cycle, and I wasn't strong enough to get out."

She took Avery's hand in hers. "I hit rock bottom a couple of months ago when you told me you hated me and if I fell off the face of the planet you wouldn't care. When you left, the house was so quiet." Her mother sniffed. "I couldn't take it. I figured you were better off without me. I just wanted to die. So I called Phillip. He found a rehabilitation center and had his lawyer notify Greg I was leaving."

Phillip continued when her mother choked up. "After much discussion, Greg agreed to be your guardian until your mother and I could return. We never dreamed he would do this." He motioned toward the house. "We would never have left you here if either of us thought anything like this would happen."

Avery thought back on the last three months and everything that happened. Hot bile burned in the bottom of her gut, racing up to her throat. "Why couldn't you just tell me in person before you left? It would have been easier to know the truth than to listen to everyone talk. I lost my job. Cindy Herman canceled my senior pictures. MaKenzie harassed me the whole time. Greg was completely off the rails." She rose and stomped down the stairs, wading through the knee-high grass toward the barn.

Her mother followed after her. "We should've. We should've done things differently. Not telling you about Phillip made sense when you were little. We thought it was too confusing, especially with MaKenzie involved. Then one lie led to another, and before I knew it, I was in too deep."

Knee-high lies.

She put her arms around Avery's shoulders, hugging her from behind. "And if I had to face you before I went to rehab, I don't know if I could've done it. You were always such a good girl, helping me and Aunt Penny whenever we needed you. Never complaining about anything. Taking care of yourself after Penny died, when I couldn't do it. I wanted to get sober, for me and for you. I told myself when I was in a better place, I'd tell you. Then I could fix everything. I shouldn't have waited to fix it. Mothers aren't perfect. Like Phillip said, no one is."

Avery hung her head, her eyes closed. "You know the worst part?"

"No. What?"

"I'm related to MaKenzie."

Her mother let out a pained laugh.

Phillip got off his cell phone and walked over to Avery and her mother. "I have a crew coming by to clean up the house and take care of the yard." The businessman was back, all softness gone.

"When will that get done?" Avery's mother left her side to face him.

"It'll probably take a week. You'll have to stay at one of the motels in town until it's finished. The house is pretty much trashed. There're also all the details to take care of for Greg's funeral. You're going to have your hands full with that alone."

He turned toward Avery. "I have a rental house with an extra bedroom. Get your things together. You'll be staying with me until further notice."

Chapter Thirty-Seven

(Lie #18: Blest are the ties that bind.)

"What do you mean, staying with you?" Panic edged into Avery's voice.

"Listen, Avery. We have a big bucket of mess to clean up, and not everything is going to get settled today, or tomorrow. It's going to take time to get things figured out." His banker-like stare burned into her. "I'm going to ask one thing of you: give us a chance to work through this with you. Your mom's fresh from rehab and she's walked into a very stressful situation. She's not ready to take responsibility for you. She may not be ready to be responsible for herself yet. I'm sure you want your mom to be successful with her sobriety."

Although she could sense the truth in his words, the thought of him, MaKenzie's dad, bossing her around sat like thorns in her skin. Besides, she'd been taking care of herself just fine. She didn't need him to take over. "Don't talk to me like I'm a child. I'm seventeen. Besides, I don't know you. I hate MaKenzie. I'm not staying with you."

Avery glanced at her mother, who stared at her feet, hidden beneath the jungle of grass.

Phillip rolled up his sleeves against the heat of the day. "I realize you don't know me. But you're never going to, either, if we don't start somewhere. And as for MaKenzie, I'll handle her. You won't have to worry about her antics again. I promise."

"Look, Mr. Thomas—"

"Let's start with Phillip. I know this is awkward, Avery. But it really is the best for now. You'll be free to see your friends, live a normal life. Give me a chance. Please." Phillip's smile was charming.

"Normal life. That's rich. Nothing about this is normal."

Phillip laid his hand on her shoulder. "It can be, given time. I have the room all ready. You obviously can't stay here."

She stood stiff beneath his hold. "I have friends."

"Avery, please. He's not a bad guy." Her mom carefully pried Avery's crossed arms away from her chest. "Do it for me. When things settle down, we can change the arrangement. You really don't have any other choice."

Except run away. And wouldn't that make MaKenzie happy? "Fine. But I'm not promising to just let everything go and be all sweet and loving to her." Avery pointed to the truck.

Her mother squeezed her hand, drawing her away from Phillip and out toward the pasture. "It's not that we're saying you should be best friends with MaKenzie. That will probably never happen. But look at it from her eyes. Her mother never said anything good about you or me. Probably never will. She's been filled with hate from the day you got here. Wouldn't you grow to resent you, too?"

Avery pursed her lips. She did not want to feel bad for MaKenzie "Heifer Queen" Thomas. No matter what, Avery would never have treated anyone as awfully as MaKenzie had. It also didn't explain why Phillip swung in at the last minute to be the Good Samaritan father, like an absentee superhero after the world had gone up in flames.

No, she wasn't about to just let everything MaKenzie did wash under the proverbial bridge. "That still doesn't excuse her for writing stuff all over my portrait or humiliating me. She got me fired, Mom. Just because of some bank thing where her gold card wouldn't go through. She knew it wasn't my fault, yet she got me fired anyway. And that's just the tip of the iceberg. I'm not feeling the love for the girl. Ever."

"I'm sorry she did that. Can't you feel the slightest bit sorry for someone who has to sink that low to try to feel better about herself?" Her mom pushed a strand of hair behind Avery's ear. Gently, her mom tipped Avery's face up to look at her. "Things are going to be different now, I promise. Can you find it in your heart to try and give Phillip a chance? You never got to see it, but he has always wanted you. Please say you'll give this new life a chance? Give me a second chance at being the sober mother I want to be?" Her mother looked younger than she remembered.

Avery wiped at her wet face. She wanted to believe her mom. The last three months had been too much for her to handle. "I don't know. I'm still mad at you."

Her mom nodded in agreement. "That's fair. I get that. I've done things so wrong. Promise me you'll learn from my mistakes. That you will live a life that's not filled with regrets and lies."

Avery studied her mom's clear eyes, so unlike what they had been the past few years. Her anger thawed, if only slightly. "I'll try. So what was rehab like?"

Her mother made a face and laughed. "No TV, no belts, lights out at nine, and session upon session of counseling either one-on-one or group therapy. So much fun, let me tell you."

They walked back over to Phillip. Avery ignored MaKenzie's snarling face in the truck window.

"Avery, if you need anything, now's the time to get it. I doubt we'll be back until I get the house fixed up for your mom."

"All of my stuff is in the trunk of my car."

Phillip's eyebrows rose. "Why?"

Avery shrugged. "I've been avoiding Greg by staying at Sophie's and Katie's houses. Only Sophie knows about Greg's drinking and messing the house up. But I didn't tell her exactly how bad it was either. Please tell me no one will find out."

Phillip glanced at MaKenzie. "Nobody will know. You have my word. And this living out of your car ends today. MaKenzie and I have some things to discuss. Go with your mom to get your car. I'll call and meet you at the house later."

Fifteen minutes later, her mom drove into the high school lot and parked next to Avery's Taurus. The OK Tire truck pulled up beside her car, and Sean Thomas stepped out. Avery watched him, wondering if Sean had been nice to her simply because of his past with her mom. It was too weird to

consider them being her age. *And cheating on Sean's wife.*
Bryce, Sean's step-son's actions made sense now. It wasn't just
because of MaKenzie that he'd been rude. He was still
disgusting, though.

In no time, Sean had Avery's tires fixed. He'd brought a
bottle of industrial window cleaner, and while he fixed the
tires, Avery cleaned up the graffiti on the windows.
MaKenzie's car, however, remained decorated. Luckily school
was still in session, and the only ones who would've seen
anything would've been the seniors leaving early.

Her mother thanked Sean for his help. "Honey, I'm going
to go book the motel room at the Hillside Inn for tonight.
Phillip will give you a call later. You said your stuff is in the
trunk of your car?"

Avery nodded. "Everything except what's at Sophie's
house."

"Call me. We'll get together later and talk more. I have my
cell phone back now. I promise to answer it this time." Her
mother got in her car. The smile she gave the mechanic was
shy, her face turning a nice shade of pink. "So nice to see you
again, Sean."

Shaking her head, Avery dug in her purse for her keys.
Instead, she felt the wadded up photograph. No matter if she
were related to MaKenzie or not, she would vote for someone
who deserved Homecoming Queen much more than
MaKenzie did. She turned and headed into the school to fill
out the ballot.

The secretary's eyes widened when Avery walked into the
office. "Can I help you, Ms. Denton?"

"Yeah. I'd like a Homecoming ballot please." She headed to the corner of the office where there was a chair and filled the sheet out. A couple of junior girls walked in the office, laughing. They stopped giggling as soon as they saw her. Avery held their stares until they left. She folded the sheet so no one could see whom she voted for and placed it in the box on the counter.

She spun around to leave and stepped into someone. "Oh, sorry. I didn't see . . ."

Jaxson's arms steadied her. "Hey. What are you doing here this time of day?"

The principal stepped out of his room. "Ms. Denton, er Thomas, er Denton." He stuttered over Avery's last name, unsure of which to use. "Mr. Stewart." He turned past Jaxson and rushed out the office door.

Jaxson's blue eyes sparkled with humor. "That was awkward. How'd he get you and MaKenzie mixed up?"

Avery's laugh was stilted. "Yeah. Right."

Jaxson raised his eyebrows, but he didn't say anything about it. "Well, see you later."

Her stomach twisted. All that her mother told her about keeping secrets and having regrets spurred her on. If nothing else Jaxson deserved to know the truth. Her heart hammered in her chest. "Um, Jaxson, I . . . I need to talk with you. Can we get together sometime tonight?"

"Look, Avery—"

"I promise it won't be like last time. I'm not expecting anything from you; I just want to talk. Please?" She knew she probably looked like a mess, face red and blotchy from crying.

He held her gaze for what seemed like forever. "Fine. Practice ends early tonight, how about 6:30? Where do you want to meet?"

Avery's heart beckoned her to the first place she felt something for Jaxson. "Willow Park."

***

A fingernail moon grinned in the sky above Willow Park as a familiar blue Chevy crunched over the gravel road. Avery sat on the hood of her car, waiting while Jaxson parked next to her Taurus. Her heart raced in her chest at the sight of his long body coming toward her. She sat on her hands, the heat from the motor warming her chilled limbs.

"Hey." He sighed. His hair was wet, the lamplight above them made his blond head glow like a halo.

Her smile halted as she took in his grim face. "Hey."

He sat on the hood beside her. "I heard about your dad's accident at practice. I'm really sorry. Is that why you wanted to talk to me?"

She inhaled a deep breath and let it out. "Thank you. Yeah. That, and, before you hear it somewhere else, my mom is back in town."

Jaxson lowered his head to study his hands. "Really must suck, huh? Getting your mom back when you lose your dad."

She fought the tears stinging behind her eyes. "Yeah. Well, actually, he's not my dad." She let out a bitter laugh. "Kind of got dropped on me like a bomb today in school. Long story short, Phillip Thomas is my biological father. MaKenzie and I are half-sisters. How ironic is that?"

Jaxson's mouth dropped open, and his eyes were like blue Frisbees. "Are you serious?" His hand raised and then lowered as if he was going to touch her but changed his mind.

She shook her head. "Serious as a heart attack."

"So MaKenzie knows?"

"Yeah. She's known for a while. I'm guessing it's why she's always been such a hag toward me." She briefly filled him in on what happened with her mom, Sean, Phillip, and Greg. She put her head down, focusing on her hands in her lap. She ended with her mother's stay in rehab and MaKenzie and her mother Monica's attempts to make it look like she and Phillip were having an affair. "It sounds so horrible when you put it into words."

"Wow. So you and MaKenzie? Half-sisters. Huh." He laughed. "Bet that'll make for some fun holiday get-togethers."

She looked up into his sparkling blue eyes and chuckled, despite her heavy heart. "Hadn't thought that far ahead. Thanks for giving me something to look forward to."

Jaxson ran his hands across his jeans. "Any time."

Avery shifted, facing him. "Mom and I had a long talk today. She told me if she hadn't kept so many secrets, her life would've been so different. The one thing she said that stuck with me was that after she began hiding things, life became so complicated it was impossible to go back and make things right. Knee-high lies."

"What?"

"She was caught in lies that were knee-high and she couldn't get out of them. So she kept lying because it was easier than telling the truth." Avery tried to memorize his handsome face, knowing he would never want to talk with her again after she finished apologizing to him. "She told me not to make the same mistakes, only I have. I lied to you the same way and covered up everything that was going on, for whatever reason." She waved her hand. There were so many reasons. Where could she begin?

Jaxson placed his warm hand on her shaking one. She slid it out of his grasp and hugged herself.

"So here's the honest truth." She explained about her dad the night she went AWOL at the fair.

She took a breath. "When you showed up on Mercer's Hill, I couldn't tell you what happened. Not after your comments at the BBQ this summer about your uncle and cousins. I was too afraid to say anything. I thought with everything else people said about me, the truth about how bad Greg's drinking was would just make everything worse." More tears burned behind her eyes. "I didn't want you to think of me as a waste of space or a loser."

He took her hand again, holding it tight so she couldn't pull away. "Avery. *None* of that is your fault. I wouldn't have thought any less of you. If anything, it means you're stronger for making it through that without going crazy yourself." He hesitated for a moment. "I'm sorry about what I said about my family. For the record, you are nothing like them. You're not a loser or waste of space."

Avery nodded, unable to speak for a few seconds. "There's more. Elaine took me to an Alateen meeting the week after I disappeared. She knew about Greg and his problem and introduced me to a bunch of kids that had a lot of the same experiences. I finally felt like there were people that understood what I was going through. I wasn't alone any more. It's where I met Keaton, the guy you saw me with."

Jaxson tensed. He pulled his hand away and stood so fast the car wobbled. His face was red and angry. "I thought you said this wasn't going to be like the last meeting, Avery. I should have known this would come back around to him."

Avery's heart dropped to her stomach.

Chapter Thirty-Eight

(Lie #19: You can't go home again.)

Avery slid off the hood. She put her hand on Jaxson's arm. "It's not about him. I was just trying to explain how we became friends." Jaxson spun away from her, but she followed him, determined to make him see. "His mother is an alcoholic, too. When you saw us hugging that first time it was because he understood what I'd been going through. That's all. There's nothing going on between us."

"What about the picture, Avery?" His voice rose. "Explain that to me."

Frustration burned in her. If only MaKenzie had kept her nose in her own business. "It's a long story."

He faced her, his thumbs through his belt loops. "We've got all night. I think I deserve to know."

"You do deserve to know. But it *is* a long story. It started that night at the fair when I found that photo of you in the trailer. Trisha said MaKenzie had tried to get you to date her. I'm sure she was the one who ruined my portrait. After seeing her come in your trailer, it really ticked me off. And after the fight with my dad, Greg, I just didn't feel like talking to you or anyone."

He flung his hands out. "Really, Avery. I was scared to death something happened to you. You never just go off like that."

"I know. I'm sorry. I was wrong to do that and wrong for not answering your calls." Avery realized she sounded like her mother. Maybe they had made the same mistakes, but she refused to keep making them. With a sigh she continued, "Sophie knows about my life, so I called her. My phone died right after our call."

"That doesn't explain the part about the jumping or the mark on your face. What else aren't you telling me?" Jaxson turned toward her, frowning.

A cloud passed over the moon, casting a shadow over them.

Avery rubbed the side of her face where Greg struck her, recalling that night. She wished now she could go back and have a do-over. Things with Jaxson could have been different if she'd only known about her mom and Phillip, if they had told her the truth years ago. "Greg slapped me for talking back. I didn't feel like I had anywhere I could go."

She kicked a rock, sending it skittering across the parking lot. It landed with a *bloop* into the lake. "I was upset. I wasn't thinking straight. I drove around until I found myself on Mercer's Hill. You'd mentioned how you went there when things get crazy in your life. I felt close to you there, even though I didn't feel like I could talk to you."

She dropped her hands. "I wasn't going to jump. It's like I was faced with this opportunity to go one way or the other. I didn't want to die. I just wanted to see if I was strong enough to say, 'No, that's not my choice. I'm better than that.'"

He sat back on the car. "Why didn't you tell me? I would've helped you, Avery. That's what friends do. It's what boyfriends do."

Avery rubbed her face and took a deep breath. This was so hard to do after the fact. "Greg knew about you and used our relationship to threaten me." She grabbed his arm and turned him to look at her. "He could have—would have—hurt you. I wouldn't let that happen." Avery took a deep breath. Her stomach jumped into knots. "Jaxson, you live this terrific, perfect life—nothing like mine. How could you understand?" Although she finally confessed to him how she really felt about their lives being so different, she wasn't sad. She felt weirdly freed. She knew in that moment she would do anything for her blue-eyed cowboy.

"My life isn't perfect. I'm not perfect. Do I act that superior to people?" The question was low and quiet, as if he really thought it was true.

"No, you don't. That's the point, Jaxson. You have these great parents, a wonderful life, and you're such a terrific guy that it's intimidating. When you've lived such a crappy life as mine, it's hard for people like me to look at people like you and measure up." She swiped at her runny nose.

Jaxson's face reddened. "Is that why you're with that other guy? Because both of your lives are so screwed up, you *understand* each other?"

She cringed. "It's not like that. I'm not with Keaton. He's just a friend. That's all." When he didn't look convinced, she sighed. "Remember at fair when you told me that you knew you loved me when I stood up for you to Billy Hammer on the bus that day? That there was never anyone else but me after that for you? No matter what the picture looked like, Jaxson, it was just MaKenzie's stupid attempt at making me feel bad after I broke up with you."

Avery walked over to the fence beside the beach and stared at the spot she had sat the day after she found out about her mother. Pain and happiness warred in her heart. "Since that day you stopped by to make me feel better, there's never been anyone else but you. Not Keaton, not anyone. He doesn't measure up to you. How could he? I don't love him like I love you." The dam of emotions she'd held onto broke. Hands up to her face, she began to sob.

Jaxson's arms enveloped her. She clasped his shirt tight in her hands and clung to him. It was like coming home again. His shirt was soaked beneath her face when she gained control again.

"I'm sorry. You probably think all I do is cry." She stepped back and wiped her face with her hand.

Jaxson took his shirt off and handed it to her. "Here, use this. It can't get much worse than it already is." He chuckled.

She used it to mop her face off. The clean scent sent goose bumps down her arms. "Keaton rescued us after Sophie's nub boyfriend left us in Kansas City." She twisted the shirt in her fingers. "When I got home that night, it looked like an angry, vindictive tornado went through the house. Keaton's support helped keep me sane." She clenched her hands tighter. After all of her lies, would he believe her now when she poured her heart out on the sand? He grabbed the scrunched up fabric from her hands. "Easy there, tiger. I like this shirt. So, you're going to Homecoming with Keaton?"

Avery knew she was sunk now. She should never have agreed to go with Keaton. "Keaton offered to go with me so I wouldn't have to go alone." She looked up at his face, trying to gauge his reaction.

"So, it's not a real date? He wouldn't mind if you didn't take him? Like if you went with someone else, maybe?" He brushed his hand across her cheek.

Her heart soared into her throat. Ignoring the guilt that dropping Keaton like a hot pancake gave her, she dared a look up at him. "Seriously? After everything that's happened?"

His blue eyes shone down into hers. A small smile quirked the corners of his mouth. "My feelings for you never changed. Yes, I got angry and jealous about that other guy. Can you blame me?"

Avery shook her head. Between the princess that kissed him at the fair and MaKenzie's crush on him, she knew only too well what jealousy felt like.

His eyebrows furrowed. "But I don't ever want to see another picture of you and him like that, okay?"

She chewed her lip. "Do you promise you don't like MaKenzie?"

He laughed. "Not even close."

Butterflies danced on the inside of her stomach when he lowered his head to hers. His kiss was as sweet as the first time on Mercer's Hill. She wound her arms around his back, looping her hands together and holding him close.

***

Avery swished her dress around her, modeling it for her mother in the motel room before the Homecoming dance. Together they curled her hair and put her makeup on, just like real mothers and daughters did.

"Jaxson is going to trip over his tongue when he sees you. What'd Keaton say when you called him?" Her mother fussed over a strand of her chestnut hair that wasn't curling quite the way she wanted it to. With a snap of the butterfly hair clip, she had it in place.

"He said he understood, but it really sounded like he was disappointed. I feel so bad about everything. He's a good guy. I think he likes me, I just—"

"I know. It's different with Jaxson, huh?" Her mother walked over to get the perfume off of the plain dresser beside the full-sized motel bed.

"Yeah. It is. I don't know how to explain it." Avery's face heated. It had been so long since she'd been able to have conversations like this with her mom.

"You don't have to explain anything to me. I was young and in love once or twice, you know." She handed Avery the jar.

After spraying on her perfume, Avery fluffed her curls, amazed at the beauty that reflected back at her in the mirror. She adjusted the necklace, Jaxson's butterfly necklace, watching it glitter around her neck.

"Talk about Jaxson tripping. I hope I don't trip with these shoes." Avery ran her hand over the silver sequins and down the blue, silky material. She was so glad Sophie and Katie made her go shopping that day, which felt almost like a lifetime ago. So much had happened since. A knock on the door made her turn around, the skirt flourishing as she moved.

"That's your father."

Phillip had texted her saying he would be over to take a picture with her so he could have one of them together. Avery wondered if she would ever start thinking about him as her father. She still had trouble getting her mind around the fact Greg was dead and that she and MaKenzie were related.

Phillip walked in, his casual shirt and slacks a contrast from the suits he normally wore. It took away some of the severity about him. She liked it.

Her mother stood back, smiling. "Isn't she stunning in that dress?"

"She looks amazing." Pride shone in Phillip's eyes. He reached into his pocket and took out an envelope, handing it to Avery. "This is for you, just in case you need anything."

Avery opened the envelope. Inside was a debit card with her name on it. Her mouth hung open when she glanced back up at Phillip.

"Phillip!" Her mother exclaimed. "I don't think it's such a good idea to give a teenager a credit card."

"Don't worry, Dineen. It's a debit card with a limit of three hundred dollars. It's money that is rightfully hers, and not enough to do any real damage. Just enough to buy her a few things she may need for her new room; some clothes maybe, or gas for her car."

Avery held the card with the tips of her fingers as if it might burn her. An image of MaKenzie's gold card tapping on the check-writing stand flit through her mind. "I don't—"

"No arguments. You're going to need it. Now I'm sure you don't want to be late for your date." Phillip closed her hand over the card. The expression on his face, though kind, was firm.

Her mother snapped a few pictures of her and Phillip. Then Phillip returned the favor for her mother.

"So, how're you getting to the dance? Is Jaxson picking you up?" Phillip asked her.

"No, I told him I would meet him there. It was going to take him a while to shower and change after the game." Avery picked up her purse and dropped her keys, phone, and the debit card inside it.

Phillip grinned. "Well then, your chariot awaits. I'll take you so Jaxson can bring you home."

Avery couldn't hide the surprise on her face. "What about MaKenzie?"

"She's already there, her mother helped her get ready."

Avery had to admit that was better than driving to the dance herself. But it was weird having a parent who was so interested in doing things for her. "Okay. Thank you."

Phillip drove her across town to the high school in silence. The parking lot was filling up. Girls in colorful dresses and slicked-up boys littered the pavement. He pulled along the sidewalk so she could get out. "Have fun. Don't forget your curfew."

"What curfew?" she teased him. He and her mother had put it into immediate effect when they realized Avery was dating Jaxson. No more spur of the moment drives into the country for them unless it was before midnight. It didn't matter to Avery as long as she and Jaxson were together. That's all that counted.

The dark look Phillip gave her made her grin.

"Midnight. Yes, I know." She opened the door to get out, pleased to find Jaxson standing there, ready to help her down from the truck.

Phillip waved. "Have fun. But not too much fun."

The humor in his voice startled Avery. Jaxson chuckled. She stared at Phillip's truck until it turned out of sight, emotions warring within her. "I don't know if I'll get used to that."

"Hey." Jaxson hugged her close. "It's a good thing. It means he cares."

Avery shook her thoughts away. This was their night.

Nothing was going to ruin it now.

Jaxson took her hand and twirled her in a circle; the silver-and-blue dress sparkled underneath the street lights outside of the school. He caught her close and kissed her. "You look stunning."

Her cheeks hurt from smiling so much. "You're pretty stunning yourself, handsome."

A hand slapped Jaxson on the back. "Sorry to interrupt you two lovebirds." It was Keaton.

Chapter Thirty-Nine

(Truth #20: Wishes Do Come True.)

Shocked, Avery waited to see how Jaxson would react. Confusion at seeing Keaton dressed up ready for the dance made her speechless for a second.

Sophie teetered over in her stilettos and put her arm through Keaton's. "Oh, forgot to tell you. I invited Keaton to come as *my* date."

Jaxson held out his hand to Keaton, who grasped it in return. "Glad to see you're taking this so well." He nodded at Avery.

"Yeah, well, we all want what's best for Avery, don't we?" Keaton's tone was friendly enough, but Avery didn't miss the glimmer in his eye when he looked at her. "Besides, how could I turn Sophie down? Someone needs to keep an eye on her."

Sophie snorted and pulled on Keaton's arm. "Come on, big guy. We've got some dancing to do." The cherry red dress Brody had bought her fit like a glove, but she hung on Keaton's arm in order to walk in her prized shoes. Avery noticed that he didn't seem to mind a bit.

"That went well, considering," Avery said when the others were gone.

Jaxson put his arm around her, escorting her into the gym. "Yeah, maybe."

A squeal split the night air. Katie rushed over to Avery and grabbed her in a tight hug. "Oh my gosh! You look so beautiful." Katie wore a baby doll pink dress with a high neckline. The ballerina style dress looked fabulous on her. Wisps of strawberry blonde hair fluttered around the intricate knot piled on top of her head.

"So do you." Avery grinned and looked around. "Where's your date?" With all the craziness of the last couple of days, she hadn't asked Katie who she was going with.

"Shane's meeting me here since he had to clean up after the big win tonight." Katie's blue eyes twinkled.

"Shane Pratt?" Avery gawked. "He's your date? Does your mother know?" She put her hands on her hips and stared at her naïve friend.

Katie giggled. "Shhh. I had to pay Michael off not to tell her." She waved her fingers goodbye. "Gotta go. Oh, hey. I almost forgot. I want pictures of us together later. Okay? Don't forget." She pirouetted away and was gone.

"I'm. Going. To. Murderize. Him!" Avery fumed. Who did Shane Pratt think he was asking the biggest virgin in their class out? "This had better not be some notch on his belt loop."

Jaxson hugged her to his side. "He has notches on his belt loop?"

She pushed his arm. "You know what I mean. Everyone knows he's a player."

"I'm sure it's nothing. Besides, Michael's parents wouldn't let them actually date."

Avery's advice to Katie about learning to lie slowly so she could keep her dating life a secret from her parents came back to mind. If she wasn't wearing a dress right now, she'd kick herself.

Jaxson steered her to the gym, which was decorated with stars and streamers. It was as though they stepped into the Milky Way. The walls sparkled in shades of silver and deep blue in an unending ocean of glimmering waves. The only light came from the dots of clear Christmas lights poking out from behind the sheets of decorative paper on the walls. More sheets of silver and blue paper—with stars glued on them—covered the floor.

Avery stared open-mouthed at everything. "Wow, they did an amazing job this year."

"How touching. Too sweet for words really. You two match." Avery stiffened as though MaKenzie had just dropped ice down her back. Her newly discovered sister wore a bright green dress that showed off her tanned cleavage. Her skirt was short and the back dipped low. If poison had a color, she was wearing it.

"Nice dress, MaKenzie. Shows off everything but the dimple on your—"

Jaxson bumped her arm. "Let's play nice, please. This is supposed to be a drama-free night." Jaxson sent her a pointed look. "Remember, Avery?"

Avery frowned. "Fine. You look lovely, sister dear." She was going to choke on the sugar-covered words.

"Aren't you so . . . cute? So, if we're playing nice, does that mean I can have a dance with Jaxson here? Hmm?" Her false eyelashes fluttered above a maliciously innocent smile.

So that's how we're gonna play nice? Avery took a step toward the girl.

Jaxson put his arm around her shoulders and smiled at MaKenzie. "All of my dances will be with my girlfriend. But thanks for asking."

MaKenzie crossed her arms over her chest. "How precious. You're exclusive now. What did poor Keaton think?" She turned her head toward Sophie and Keaton. "Ah, I see. Your second boyfriend dropped you for your best friend. Do you swap often?"

Avery fumed. "Don't you have your own date to worry about? No? Aww, poor baby. No one advertising for a date?"

"As if." MaKenzie strode off, head held high.

Sophie walked over, holding onto Keaton. "Did you see that dress MaKenzie has on? I'll bet she bought it at Hookers R Us."

Keaton snickered.

Jaxson smiled. "Okay, guys. We have much better things to worry about tonight than who is wearing what dress."

Sophie and Avery exchanged looks. "Oh, no we don't," they said at the same time.

Katie shuffled across the floor, half-sliding-half-running on the slick paper strung across the floor. "Picture time.

C'mon, let's go." She grabbed Sophie and Avery's hands and began slip-sliding them across the floor to the photo booth.

"Elaine!" Avery screamed. "You're the photographer?"

"Of course I am, darlin'. Wouldn't want anyone but me taking your picture, now would you?" Elaine winked at her. She squatted, holding a mega-lens camera in her hands, readying for the next couple in line.

"No. I'm so glad it's you." She bent and whispered, "I'm here with Jaxson. We made up. Keaton's here too, with a friend of mine."

She whispered back, "I figured that out when I saw the payment slips with the names on them." In a louder voice she added, "now are you girls ready? Go stand over there, and you can pose any way you like." She took a couple of pictures and motioned for their dates. "Guys next."

Jaxson, Keaton, and Shane stepped up behind the girls. Avery smiled despite having Keaton on her left and Shane on her right. When the pictures were finished, they split into pairs for couples' pictures.

Massive sets of speakers were set up on either side of the stage, and flashing lights swirled across the gym. Music blared out at them as dozens of students filled the room. Avery spotted Trisha, looking sleek in a glittering black dress, standing with her boyfriend, Landon, and brother Davis.

"Hey, Jaxson. Hey, Avery," Davis greeted them. "You guys back together again, huh?"

Avery squelched the unease that swept over her at the sight of him. He was Jaxson's cousin, after all. "Hey, Davis. Yeah. We're back together." She worked to keep her voice calm.

"Cool. You know, I never got to dance with you at the street dance. Maybe you can save me one tonight?" His eager expression was like sandpaper to her nerves.

"Sorry, cuz. All her dances are taken tonight. There's a bunch of girls over there, though, who didn't bring dates." Jaxson moved behind her, placing his arms around her waist in a protective stance. He pointed toward a wall where a dozen underclassman girls stood, whispering and giggling.

"Yeah. Sure." Davis turned and left, disappointment clear on his face.

"Whew! Thanks. I know he's your cousin and all, but, wow. He just doesn't give up." Avery tilted her head to look at him.

Jaxson grinned. "He's okay. Mom says he reminds her of a puppy. All paws, slobbering tongue, and wagging tail."

The music stopped, and Principal Field grabbed the microphone. The Homecoming Court had been announced during half time. Katie won Homecoming Queen by a minority vote, less than one percent more than MaKenzie. Jaxson, of course, won Sophomore Class King. The dance floor cleared and the Court took their positions for the photo for the local newspaper.

Avery jumped at a warm hand at the base of her back. Keaton stood beside her, a wide grin on his face. "Geez. You scared me."

"I just had to say you look amazing tonight. The most beautiful girl here, hands down." His glance took her in from her toes, and stopped at her lips before traveling further up to her eyes. "Did you tell Mr. Perfect we kissed?"

"Keaton," she warned. She had planned to, but Jaxson had taken her back before she got around to explaining that part. She hadn't wanted to ruin the moment. She'd come clean on everything else. Jaxson didn't need to know, because it was never going to be an issue.

"Don't worry. I'm not here to steal you away or rat you out. But I do want you to know I'm not going anywhere. We're friends."

Before Avery could say anything back, he left. The principal announced the court dance, and she glanced back toward the dance floor.

Jaxson crooked his finger at her when a slow song began to play. A thrill raced through her veins. Spotlights fell on the Court as their partners joined them on the dance floor.

The warmth of his arms enveloped her. Avery breathed in the essence of his body spray laced with soap. Leaning her head on his chest, she closed her eyes and allowed herself to feel the rhythm of their dance. It was the most relaxed she'd been in far too long.

A camera flashed, making her open her eyes. Elaine moved among the dancers taking pictures, having finished with the majority of the group photos. She smiled and gave Avery a thumbs up.

Jaxson pulled back, his fingers grazing her chin. "You're so beautiful tonight, like a shining star. My bright and shining star. I love you, Avery Denton Thomas."

His hair fell over his eyebrow, and she brushed it back. She allowed herself to get lost in the blue depths of his gaze. "How did I ever get so lucky to have someone like you love me?" She placed her hand on his chest, over the scar above his heart. "I promise no more secrets. I'll never break your heart again." She ignored the small niggle that reminded her of Keaton's kiss.

"I'm tougher than you think. Besides, I know a good heart doctor." He took her hand in his and kissed her palm.

Fire flew through her limbs. For a second, she imagined she could see the glint of stars in his eyes.

Somehow her life was starting to come together. On one hand, it scared her because nothing good ever lasted, and on the other hand she was happier than she had ever felt before.

Jaxson pointed to the ceiling where the vents blew out air into the gymnasium. A star twirled and swung back and forth. "Make a wish," he said moments before the string broke and the star tumbled to the floor.

Avery smiled up at Jaxson. "It's already coming true."

The End

About the Author

Dawn Ford lives in a small town nestled among the Loess Hills in Western Iowa with her husband, youngest son, and a wonder beagle. Dawn's love for stories came naturally to her as a child who was lucky enough to be able to explore the Iowa pastures and countryside in search of adventure.

Dawn adores anything steampunk, is mesmerized by shiny, pretty things and fashionable shoes, and needs at least one good, strong cup of coffee to wake her up a day.

Dawn's novel, *Kingdom Come,* won the 2016 ACFW Genesis Award in the Speculative Genre. Her flash fiction stories have been featured in Splickety Publishing Group's Havok magazine.

Reach out to Dawn Ford via her website: www.dawnfordauthor.com,

Facebook: https://www.facebook.com/DawnFordAuthor/,

Twitter: https://twitter.com/dawnfordauthor,

Instagram: https://www.instagram.com/dawn_ford_author/, and

Pinterest https://www.pinterest.com/dawnfordauthor/.

She'd love to hear from you!

Acknowledgements

For my reader, I hope KHL has made you laugh, cry, or brought a little entertainment into your life. If I've done all three, I consider myself a successful author.

As a writer, I want to thank God for taking the broken parts of me, turning them into my testimony, and inspiring this story. For those of you who are or have grown up under a cloud of addiction, know you are not alone. You are worthy, valuable, and can overcome.

For my husband and family who have supported every step of my journey, you will never know how much I love you for it. You are the stars in my night's sky.

Lorna Seilstad, you took me along for a ride. Who would've known where the road would lead us? You were the first to believe I could do it, and you never wavered in your support. To Judith Miller, my mentor and friend, your quiet support has been invaluable.

Alyssa, Jenn, Kathy, Mary, and Shelly: my amazing critique partners. You have become more than just crit partners. Our sisterhood and friendship mean the world to me.

For Jeff Deitering and Brenda Anderson who tirelessly read through KHL numerous times and gave me valuable feedback—you guys rock! And to Cheryl St. John, I adore you.

To Sarah Grimm and Josh Beaumont, my editors, you both are awesome, incredible, wonderful, did I say awesome already? Thank you doesn't express it enough. To Ben Wolf, you took my hand and helped me to rise above who I was when I started at Splickety. Everyone needs a Ben Wolf in their corner.

Linda Fulkerson from Book Marketing Graphics, you are a Godsend. I owe you so much. For Jaclyn of Photos by JackiO and Madi Ogle, you pulled my dream together in the form of a picture, the cover photo. You are both a blessing to me.

And my amazing launch team, thank you for all the work you did to get news of KHL out into the public. You guys were phenomenal! Lastly, to the unnamed that have supported me through the years, you know who you are and I love you for it.

Thank you!

Thank you for reading Knee-high Lies! I hope you enjoyed Avery's story. Please take a few minutes to leave a review of this book at Amazon.com.

I would really appreciate it!

65187351R00215

Made in the USA
Lexington, KY
03 July 2017